STRANGE

The Doctor Strange of Death

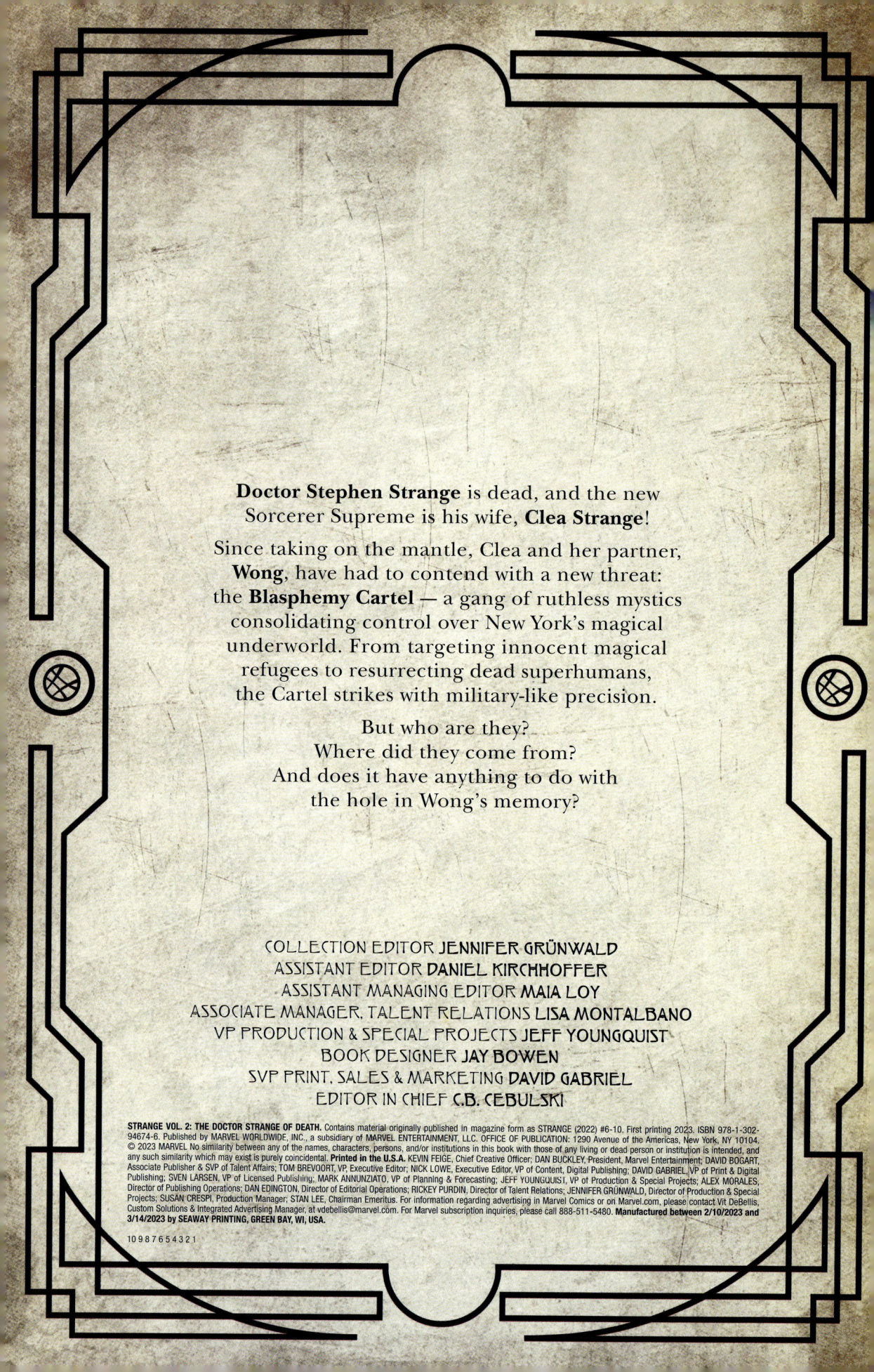

Doctor Stephen Strange is dead, and the new Sorcerer Supreme is his wife, **Clea Strange**!

Since taking on the mantle, Clea and her partner, **Wong**, have had to contend with a new threat: the **Blasphemy Cartel** — a gang of ruthless mystics consolidating control over New York's magical underworld. From targeting innocent magical refugees to resurrecting dead superhumans, the Cartel strikes with military-like precision.

But who are they?
Where did they come from?
And does it have anything to do with the hole in Wong's memory?

COLLECTION EDITOR **JENNIFER GRÜNWALD**
ASSISTANT EDITOR **DANIEL KIRCHHOFFER**
ASSISTANT MANAGING EDITOR **MAIA LOY**
ASSOCIATE MANAGER, TALENT RELATIONS **LISA MONTALBANO**
VP PRODUCTION & SPECIAL PROJECTS **JEFF YOUNGQUIST**
BOOK DESIGNER **JAY BOWEN**
SVP PRINT, SALES & MARKETING **DAVID GABRIEL**
EDITOR IN CHIEF **C.B. CEBULSKI**

STRANGE VOL. 2: THE DOCTOR STRANGE OF DEATH. Contains material originally published in magazine form as STRANGE (2022) #6-10. First printing 2023. ISBN 978-1-302-94674-6. Published by MARVEL WORLDWIDE, INC., a subsidiary of MARVEL ENTERTAINMENT, LLC. OFFICE OF PUBLICATION: 1290 Avenue of the Americas, New York, NY 10104. © 2023 MARVEL No similarity between any of the names, characters, persons, and/or institutions in this book with those of any living or dead person or institution is intended, and any such similarity which may exist is purely coincidental. **Printed in the U.S.A.** KEVIN FEIGE, Chief Creative Officer; DAN BUCKLEY, President, Marvel Entertainment; DAVID BOGART, Associate Publisher & SVP of Talent Affairs; TOM BREVOORT, VP, Executive Editor; NICK LOWE, Executive Editor, VP of Content, Digital Publishing; DAVID GABRIEL, VP of Print & Digital Publishing; SVEN LARSEN, VP of Licensed Publishing; MARK ANNUNZIATO, VP of Planning & Forecasting; JEFF YOUNGQUIST, VP of Production & Special Projects; ALEX MORALES, Director of Publishing Operations; DAN EDINGTON, Director of Editorial Operations; RICKEY PURDIN, Director of Talent Relations; JENNIFER GRÜNWALD, Director of Production & Special Projects; SUSAN CRESPI, Production Manager; STAN LEE, Chairman Emeritus. For information regarding advertising in Marvel Comics or on Marvel.com, please contact Vit DeBellis, Custom Solutions & Integrated Advertising Manager, at vdebellis@marvel.com. For Marvel subscription inquiries, please call 888-511-5480. Manufactured between 2/10/2023 and 3/14/2023 by SEAWAY PRINTING, GREEN BAY, WI, USA.

10 9 8 7 6 5 4 3 2 1

STRANGE

The Doctor Strange of Death

Jed MacKay
WRITER

#6
Lee Garbett
ARTIST

#8
Stefano Landini
ARTIST

#7, #9-10
Marcelo Ferreira
PENCILER

Marcelo Ferreira
PRESENT DAY PENCILER

Roberto Poggi
INKER

Roberto Poggi
PRESENT DAY INKER

Java Tartaglia
COLOR ARTIST

VC's Cory Petit
LETTERING

Lee Garbett
COVER ART

Kat Gregorowicz
ASSISTANT EDITOR

Darren Shan
EDITOR

DOCTOR STRANGE CREATED BY STAN LEE & STEVE DITKO

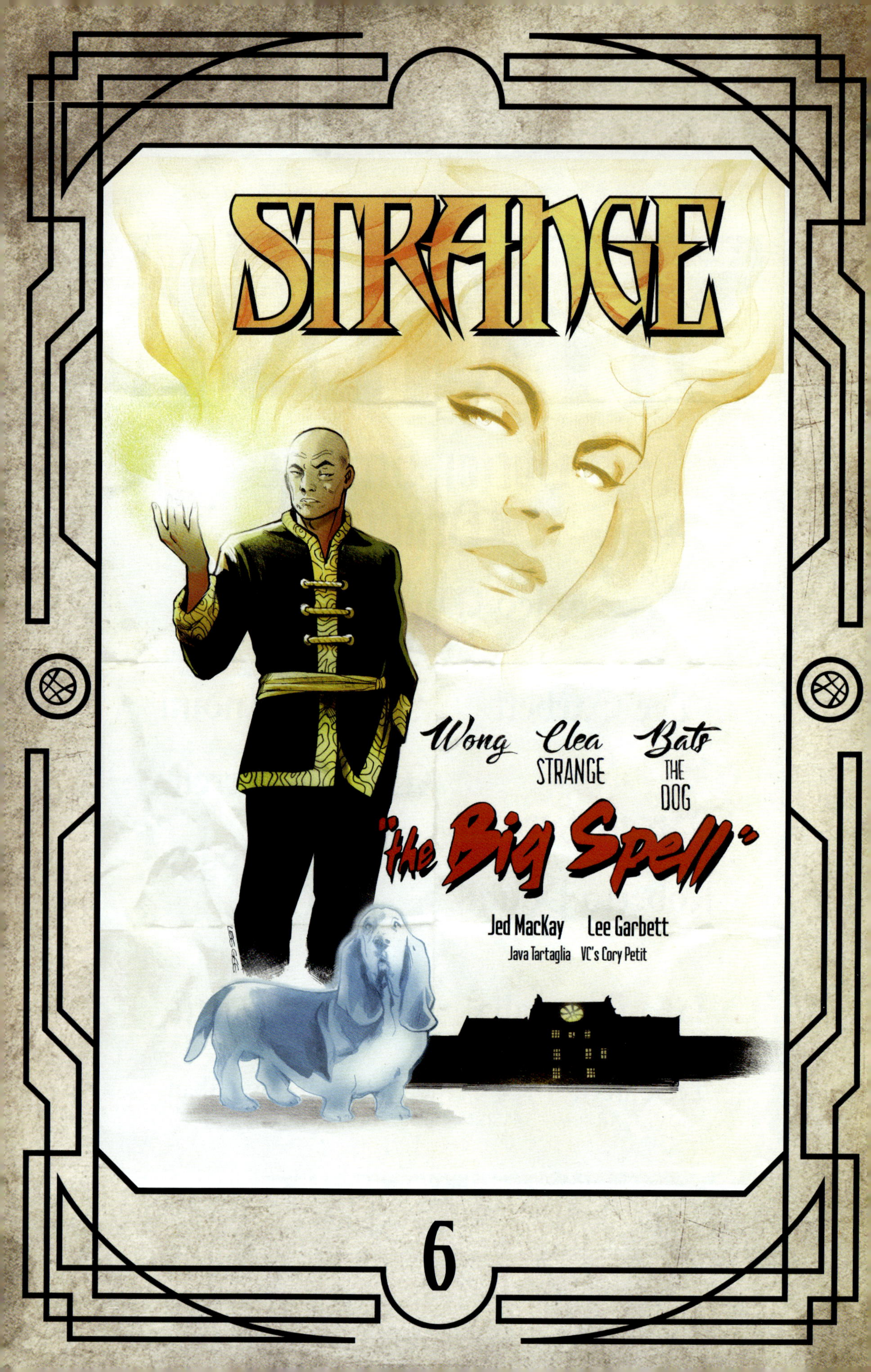
STRANGE
Wong
Clea STRANGE
Bats THE DOG
"the Big Spell"
Jed MacKay
Lee Garbett
Java Tartaglia
VC's Cory Petit
6

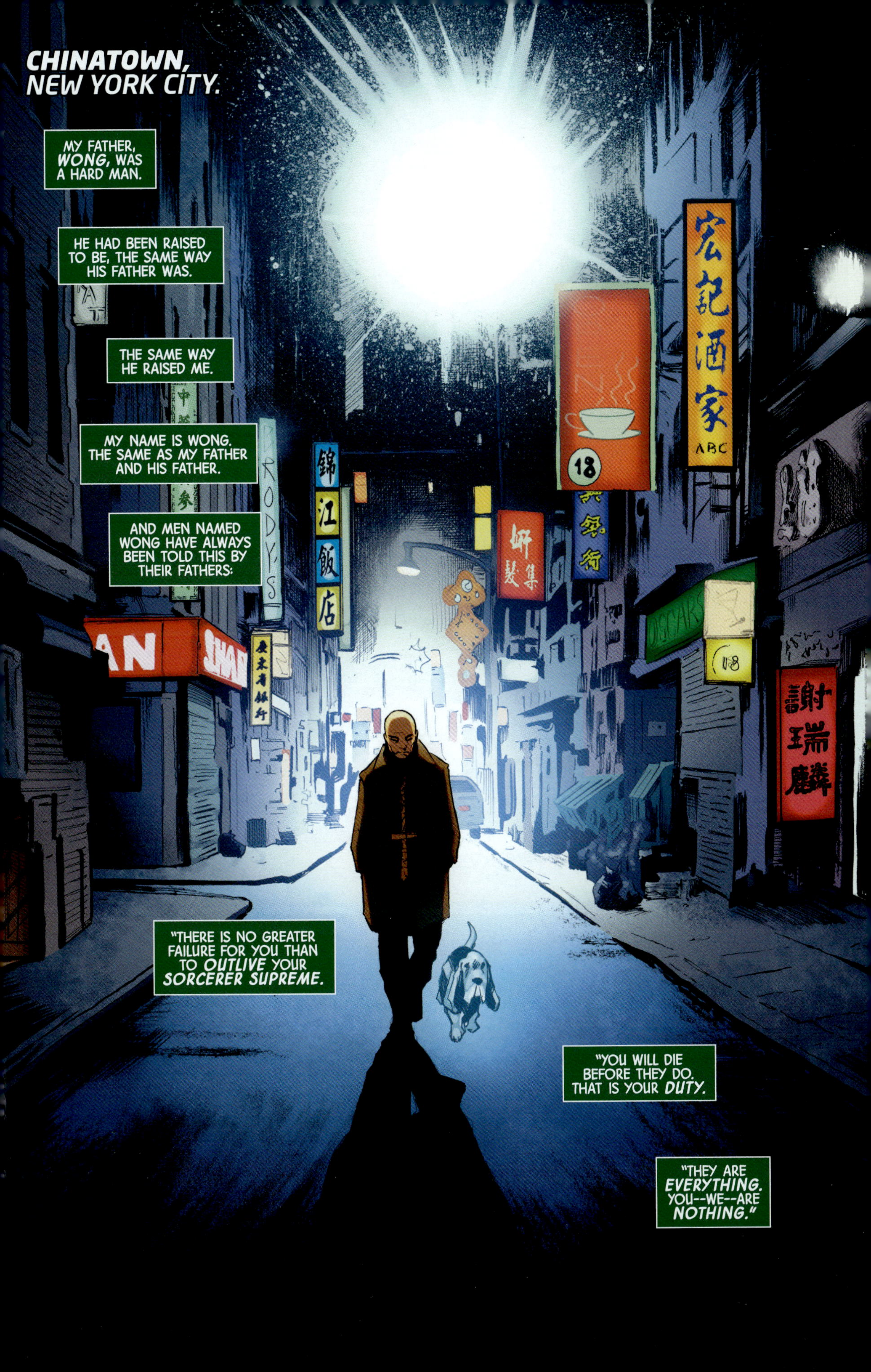
CHINATOWN, NEW YORK CITY.
MY FATHER, WONG, WAS A HARD MAN.
HE HAD BEEN RAISED TO BE, THE SAME WAY HIS FATHER WAS.
THE SAME WAY HE RAISED ME.
MY NAME IS WONG. THE SAME AS MY FATHER AND HIS FATHER.
AND MEN NAMED WONG HAVE ALWAYS BEEN TOLD THIS BY THEIR FATHERS:
"THERE IS NO GREATER FAILURE FOR YOU THAN TO OUTLIVE YOUR SORCERER SUPREME.
"YOU WILL DIE BEFORE THEY DO. THAT IS YOUR DUTY.
"THEY ARE EVERYTHING. YOU--WE--ARE NOTHING."
宏記酒家
ABC
錦江飯店
BRODY'S
謝瑞麟

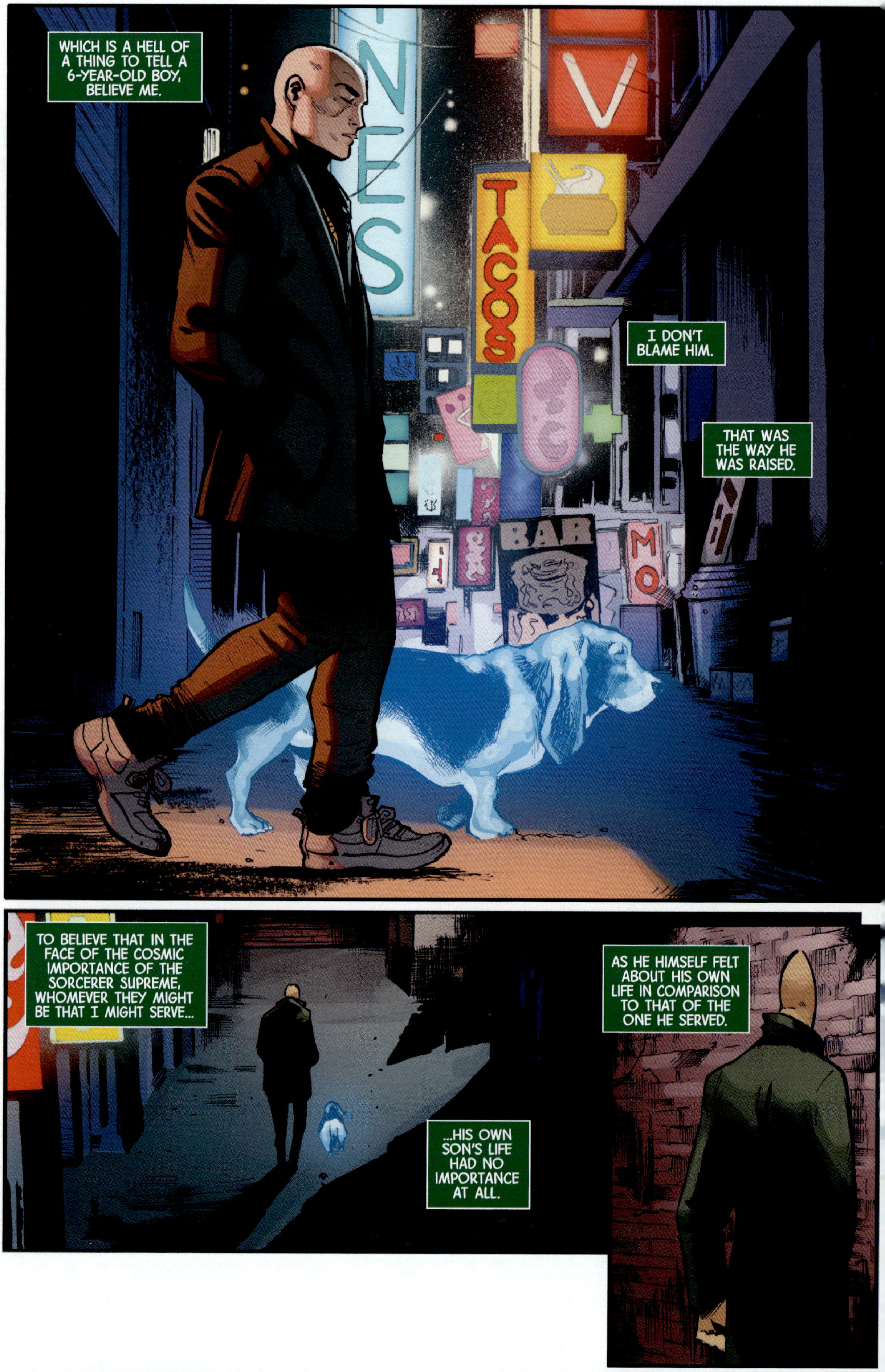

WHICH IS A HELL OF A THING TO TELL A 6-YEAR-OLD BOY, BELIEVE ME.
TACOS
BAR
MO
I DON'T BLAME HIM.
THAT WAS THE WAY HE WAS RAISED.
TO BELIEVE THAT IN THE FACE OF THE COSMIC IMPORTANCE OF THE SORCERER SUPREME, WHOMEVER THEY MIGHT BE THAT I MIGHT SERVE...
...HIS OWN SON'S LIFE HAD NO IMPORTANCE AT ALL.
AS HE HIMSELF FELT ABOUT HIS OWN LIFE IN COMPARISON TO THAT OF THE ONE HE SERVED.

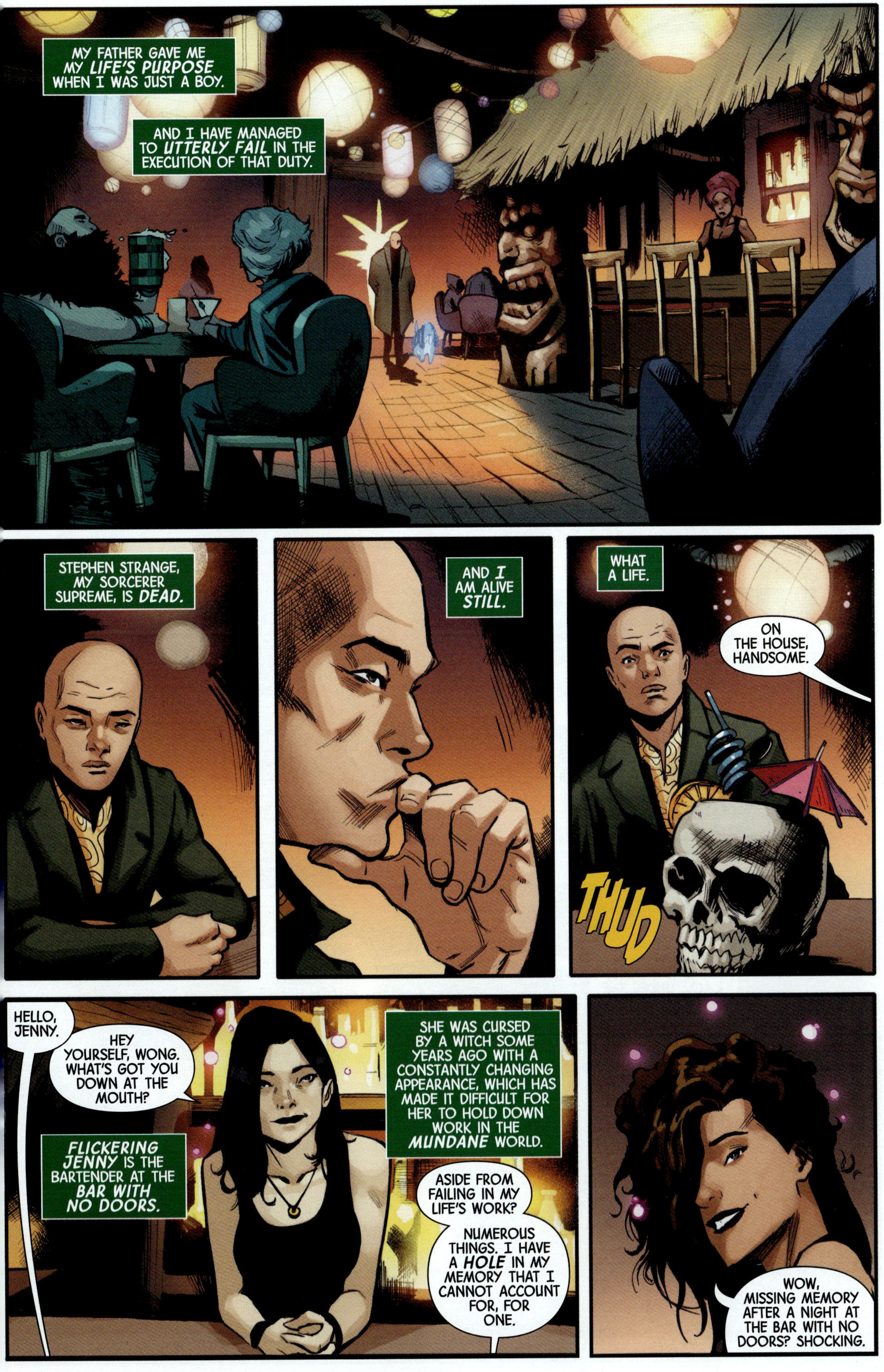
MY FATHER GAVE ME MY *LIFE'S PURPOSE* WHEN I WAS JUST A BOY.
AND I HAVE MANAGED TO *UTTERLY FAIL* IN THE EXECUTION OF THAT DUTY.
STEPHEN STRANGE, MY SORCERER SUPREME, IS *DEAD.*
AND *I* AM ALIVE *STILL.*
WHAT A LIFE.
ON THE HOUSE, HANDSOME.
THUD
HELLO, JENNY.
HEY YOURSELF, WONG. WHAT'S GOT YOU DOWN AT THE MOUTH?
FLICKERING JENNY IS THE BARTENDER AT THE *BAR WITH NO DOORS.*
SHE WAS CURSED BY A WITCH SOME YEARS AGO WITH A CONSTANTLY CHANGING APPEARANCE, WHICH HAS MADE IT DIFFICULT FOR HER TO HOLD DOWN WORK IN THE *MUNDANE* WORLD.
ASIDE FROM FAILING IN MY LIFE'S WORK?
NUMEROUS THINGS. I HAVE A *HOLE* IN MY MEMORY THAT I CANNOT ACCOUNT FOR, FOR ONE.
WOW, MISSING MEMORY AFTER A NIGHT AT THE BAR WITH NO DOORS? SHOCKING.

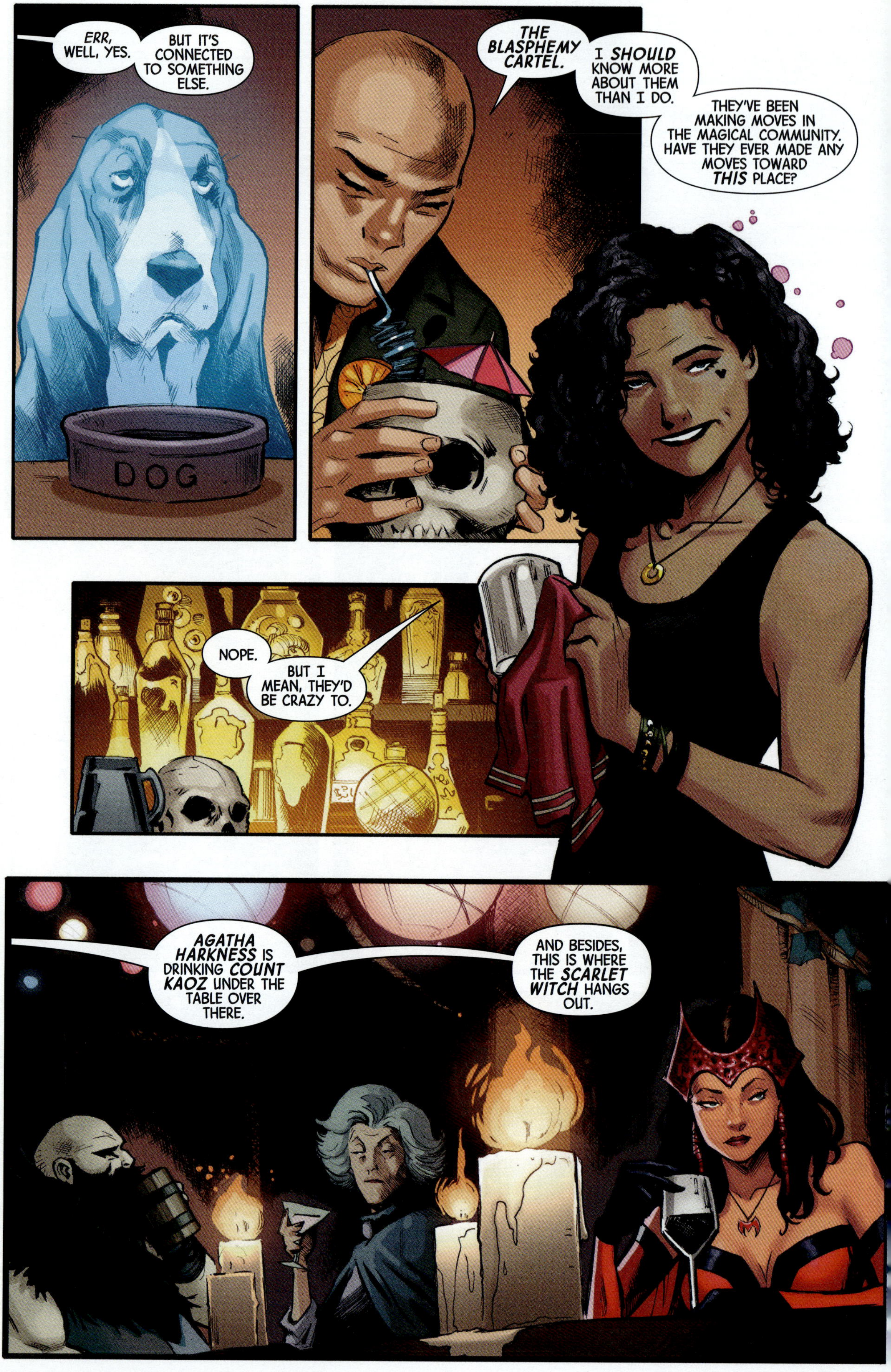
ERR, WELL, YES.
BUT IT'S CONNECTED TO SOMETHING ELSE.
DOG
THE BLASPHEMY CARTEL.
I SHOULD KNOW MORE ABOUT THEM THAN I DO.
THEY'VE BEEN MAKING MOVES IN THE MAGICAL COMMUNITY. HAVE THEY EVER MADE ANY MOVES TOWARD THIS PLACE?
NOPE.
BUT I MEAN, THEY'D BE CRAZY TO.
AGATHA HARKNESS IS DRINKING COUNT KAOZ UNDER THE TABLE OVER THERE.
AND BESIDES, THIS IS WHERE THE SCARLET WITCH HANGS OUT.

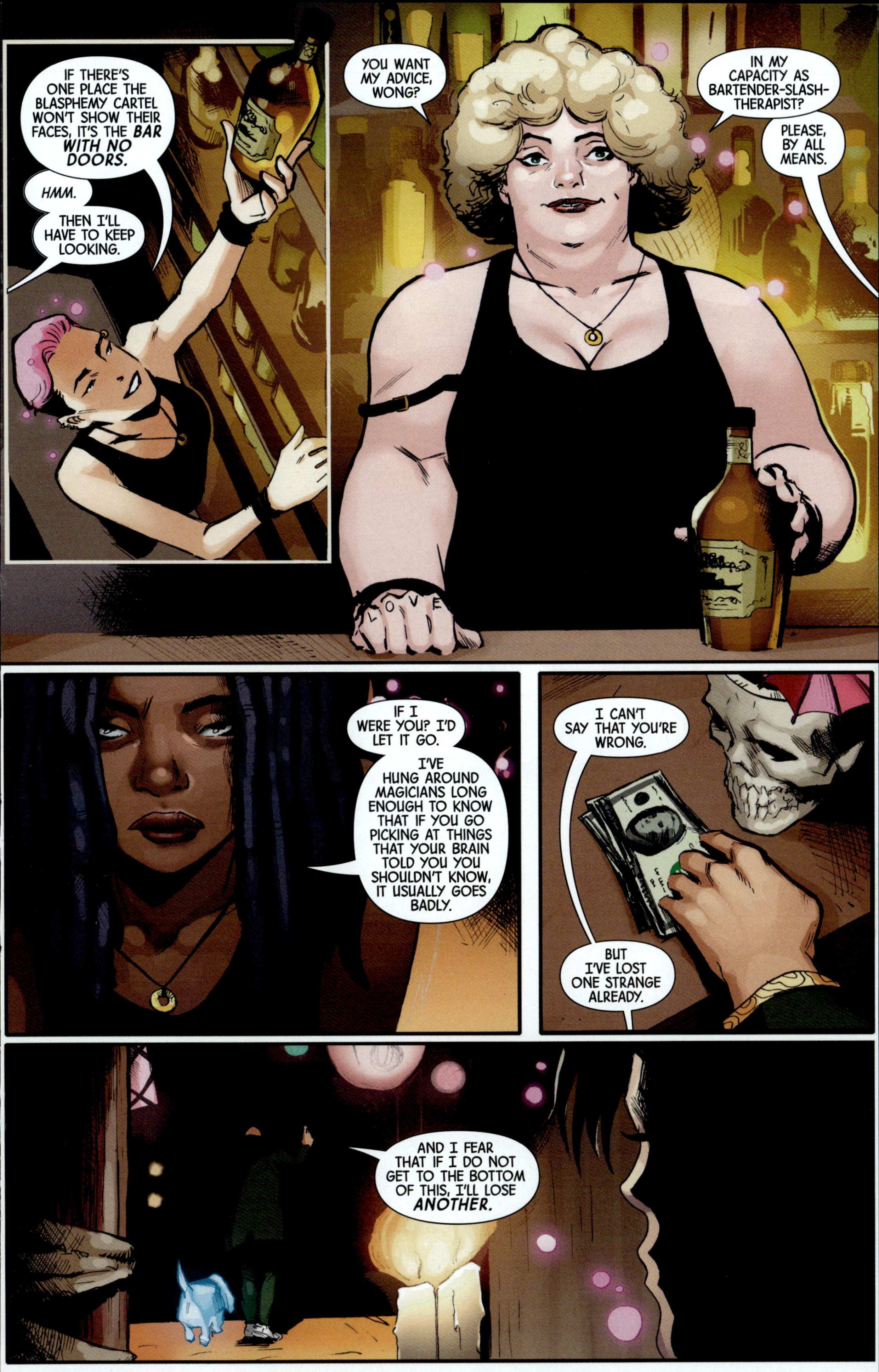

IF THERE'S ONE PLACE THE BLASPHEMY CARTEL WON'T SHOW THEIR FACES, IT'S THE ***BAR WITH NO DOORS.***
HMM.
THEN I'LL HAVE TO KEEP LOOKING.
YOU WANT MY ADVICE, WONG?
IN MY CAPACITY AS BARTENDER-SLASH-THERAPIST?
PLEASE, BY ALL MEANS.
LOVE
IF I WERE YOU? I'D LET IT GO.
I'VE HUNG AROUND MAGICIANS LONG ENOUGH TO KNOW THAT IF YOU GO PICKING AT THINGS THAT YOUR BRAIN TOLD YOU YOU SHOULDN'T KNOW, IT USUALLY GOES BADLY.
I CAN'T SAY THAT YOU'RE WRONG.
BUT I'VE LOST ONE STRANGE ALREADY.
AND I FEAR THAT IF I DO NOT GET TO THE BOTTOM OF THIS, I'LL LOSE ***ANOTHER.***

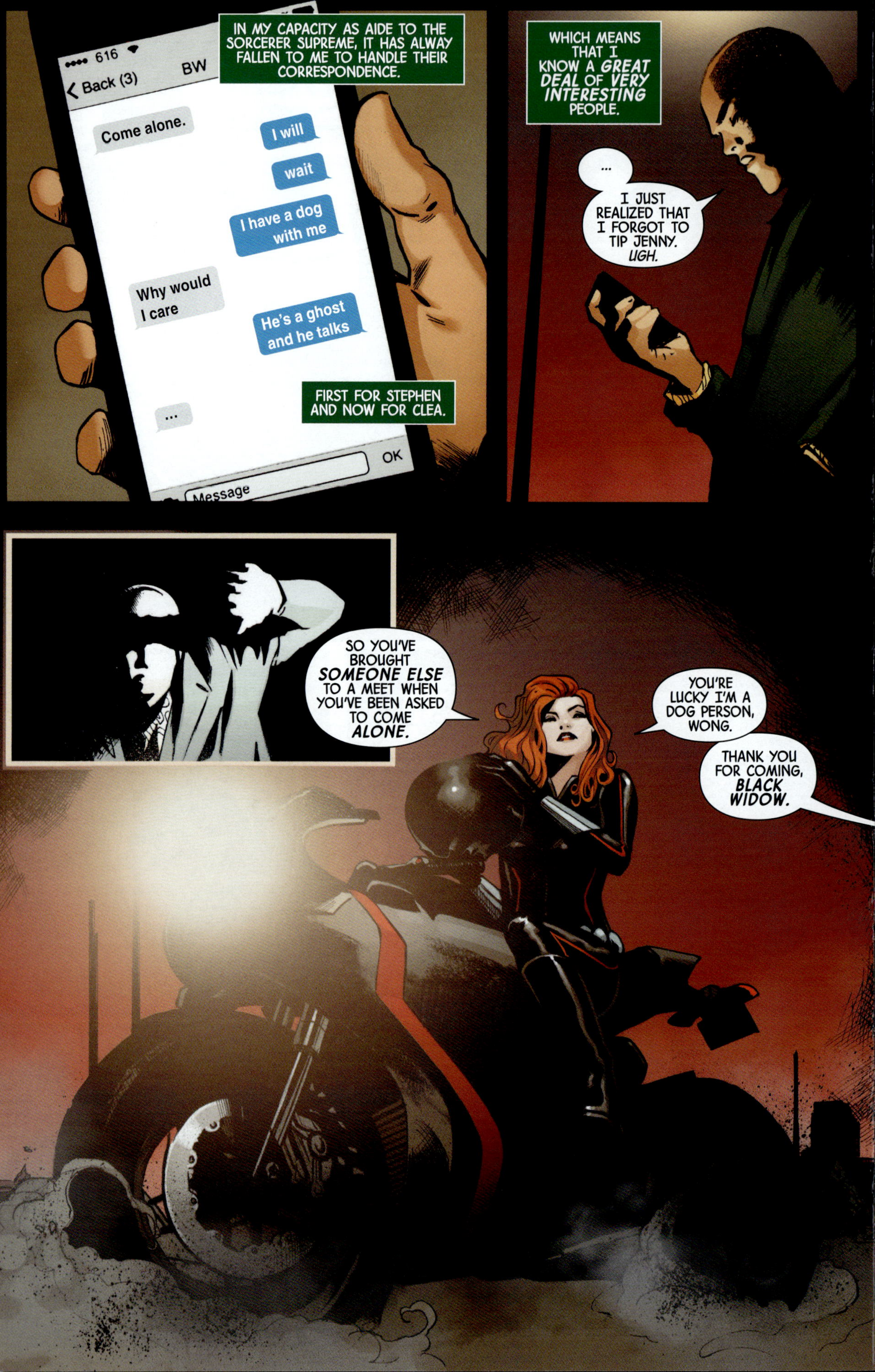

IN MY CAPACITY AS AIDE TO THE SORCERER SUPREME, IT HAS ALWAY FALLEN TO ME TO HANDLE THEIR CORRESPONDENCE.
616
BW
Back (3)
Come alone.
I will
wait
I have a dog with me
Why would I care
He's a ghost and he talks
...
Message
OK
FIRST FOR STEPHEN AND NOW FOR CLEA.
WHICH MEANS THAT I KNOW A GREAT DEAL OF VERY INTERESTING PEOPLE.
...
I JUST REALIZED THAT I FORGOT TO TIP JENNY. UGH.
SO YOU'VE BROUGHT SOMEONE ELSE TO A MEET WHEN YOU'VE BEEN ASKED TO COME ALONE.
YOU'RE LUCKY I'M A DOG PERSON, WONG.
THANK YOU FOR COMING, BLACK WIDOW.

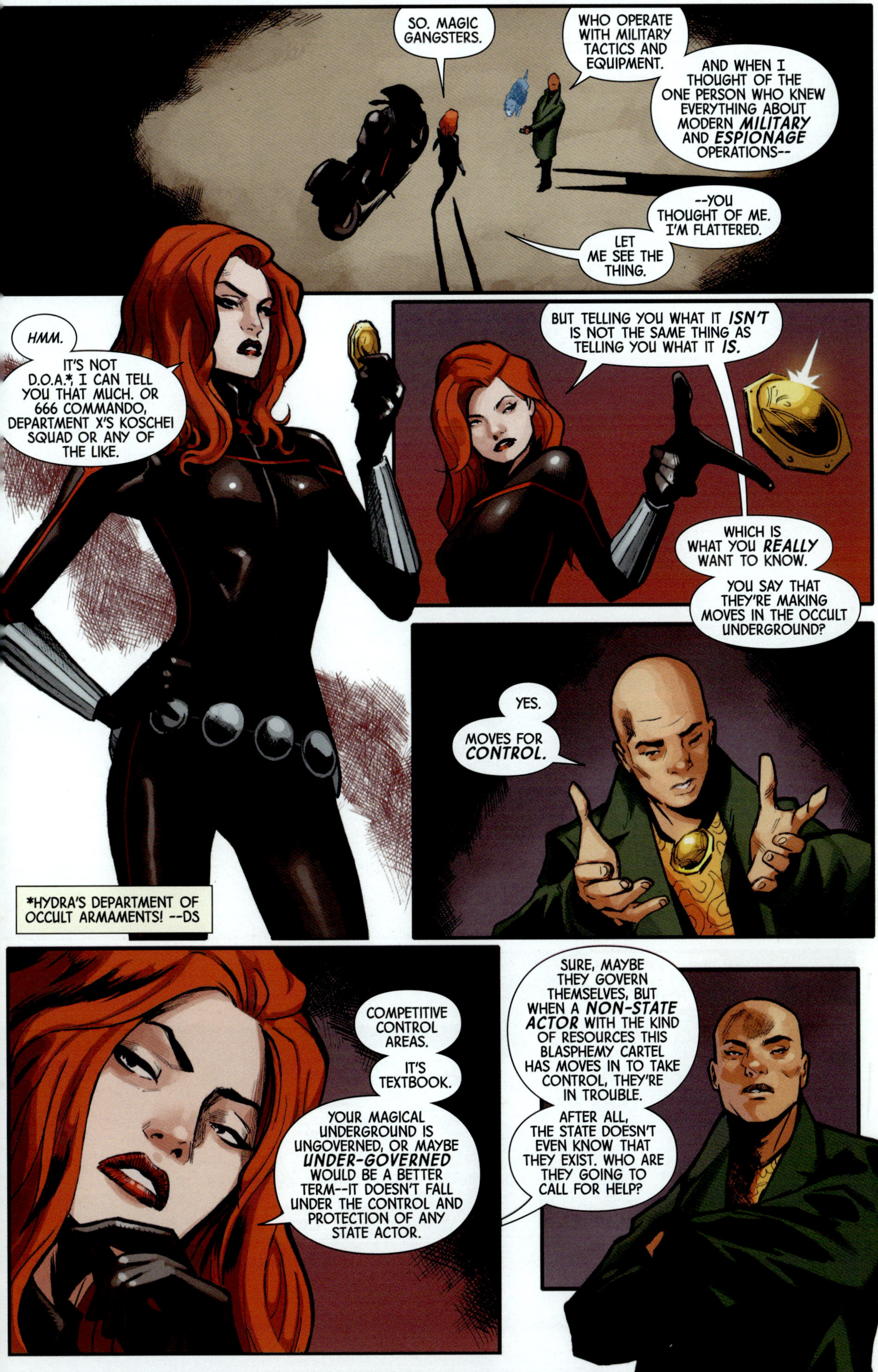
SO. MAGIC GANGSTERS.
WHO OPERATE WITH MILITARY TACTICS AND EQUIPMENT.
AND WHEN I THOUGHT OF THE ONE PERSON WHO KNEW EVERYTHING ABOUT MODERN MILITARY AND ESPIONAGE OPERATIONS--
--YOU THOUGHT OF ME. I'M FLATTERED.
LET ME SEE THE THING.
HMM.
IT'S NOT D.O.A.*, I CAN TELL YOU THAT MUCH. OR 666 COMMANDO, DEPARTMENT X'S KOSCHEI SQUAD OR ANY OF THE LIKE.
*HYDRA'S DEPARTMENT OF OCCULT ARMAMENTS! --DS
BUT TELLING YOU WHAT IT ISN'T IS NOT THE SAME THING AS TELLING YOU WHAT IT IS.
WHICH IS WHAT YOU REALLY WANT TO KNOW.
YOU SAY THAT THEY'RE MAKING MOVES IN THE OCCULT UNDERGROUND?
YES.
MOVES FOR CONTROL.
COMPETITIVE CONTROL AREAS.
IT'S TEXTBOOK.
YOUR MAGICAL UNDERGROUND IS UNGOVERNED, OR MAYBE UNDER-GOVERNED WOULD BE A BETTER TERM--IT DOESN'T FALL UNDER THE CONTROL AND PROTECTION OF ANY STATE ACTOR.
SURE, MAYBE THEY GOVERN THEMSELVES, BUT WHEN A NON-STATE ACTOR WITH THE KIND OF RESOURCES THIS BLASPHEMY CARTEL HAS MOVES IN TO TAKE CONTROL, THEY'RE IN TROUBLE.
AFTER ALL, THE STATE DOESN'T EVEN KNOW THAT THEY EXIST. WHO ARE THEY GOING TO CALL FOR HELP?

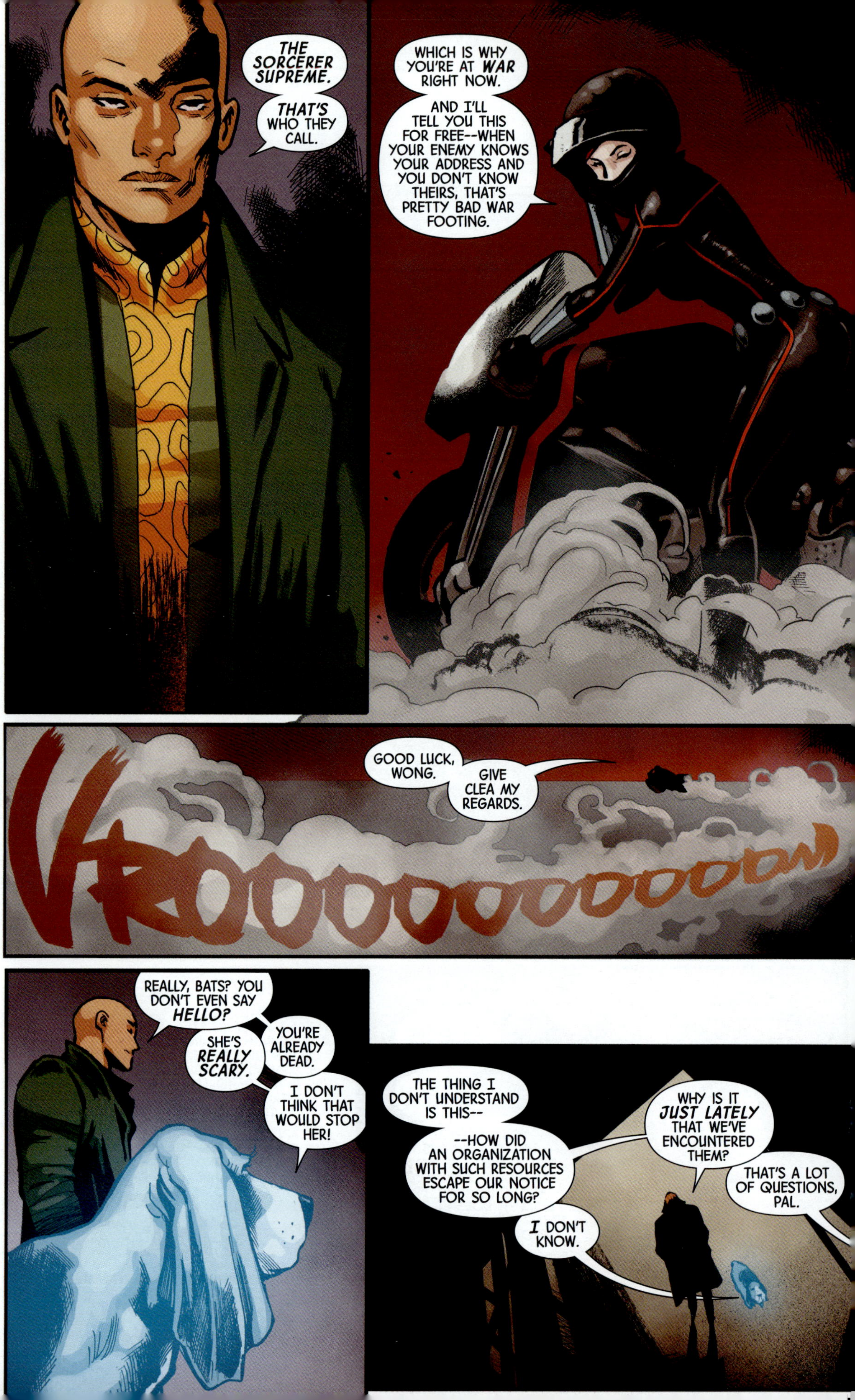
THE SORCERER SUPREME.
THAT'S WHO THEY CALL.
WHICH IS WHY YOU'RE AT WAR RIGHT NOW.
AND I'LL TELL YOU THIS FOR FREE--WHEN YOUR ENEMY KNOWS YOUR ADDRESS AND YOU DON'T KNOW THEIRS, THAT'S PRETTY BAD WAR FOOTING.
GOOD LUCK, WONG.
GIVE CLEA MY REGARDS.
VROOOOOOOOOOM
REALLY, BATS? YOU DON'T EVEN SAY HELLO?
YOU'RE ALREADY DEAD.
SHE'S REALLY SCARY.
I DON'T THINK THAT WOULD STOP HER!
THE THING I DON'T UNDERSTAND IS THIS--
--HOW DID AN ORGANIZATION WITH SUCH RESOURCES ESCAPE OUR NOTICE FOR SO LONG?
WHY IS IT JUST LATELY THAT WE'VE ENCOUNTERED THEM?
THAT'S A LOT OF QUESTIONS, PAL.
I DON'T KNOW.

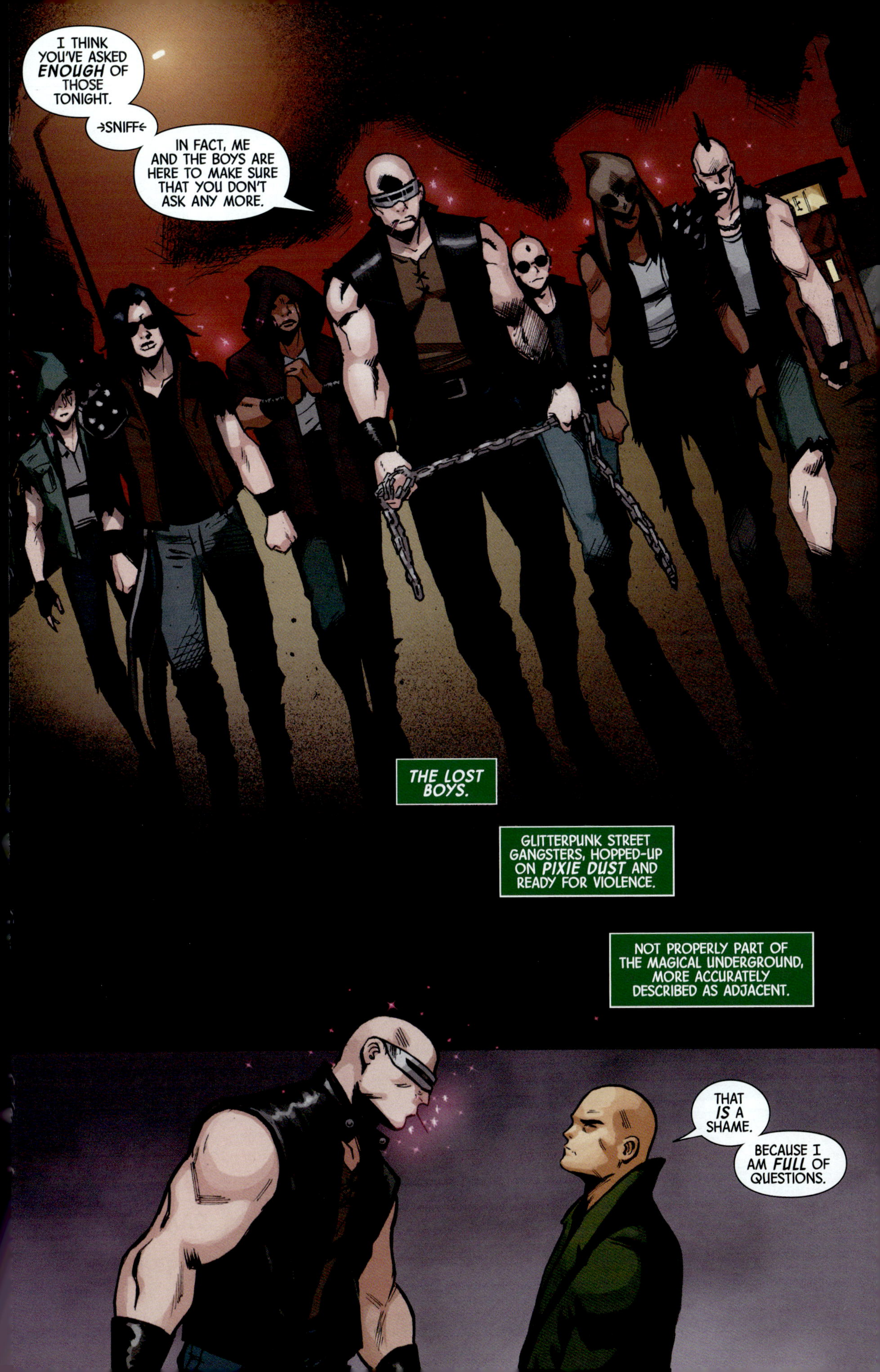
I THINK YOU'VE ASKED ENOUGH OF THOSE TONIGHT.
→SNIFF←
IN FACT, ME AND THE BOYS ARE HERE TO MAKE SURE THAT YOU DON'T ASK ANY MORE.
THE LOST BOYS.
GLITTERPUNK STREET GANGSTERS, HOPPED-UP ON PIXIE DUST AND READY FOR VIOLENCE.
NOT PROPERLY PART OF THE MAGICAL UNDERGROUND, MORE ACCURATELY DESCRIBED AS ADJACENT.
THAT IS A SHAME.
BECAUSE I AM FULL OF QUESTIONS.

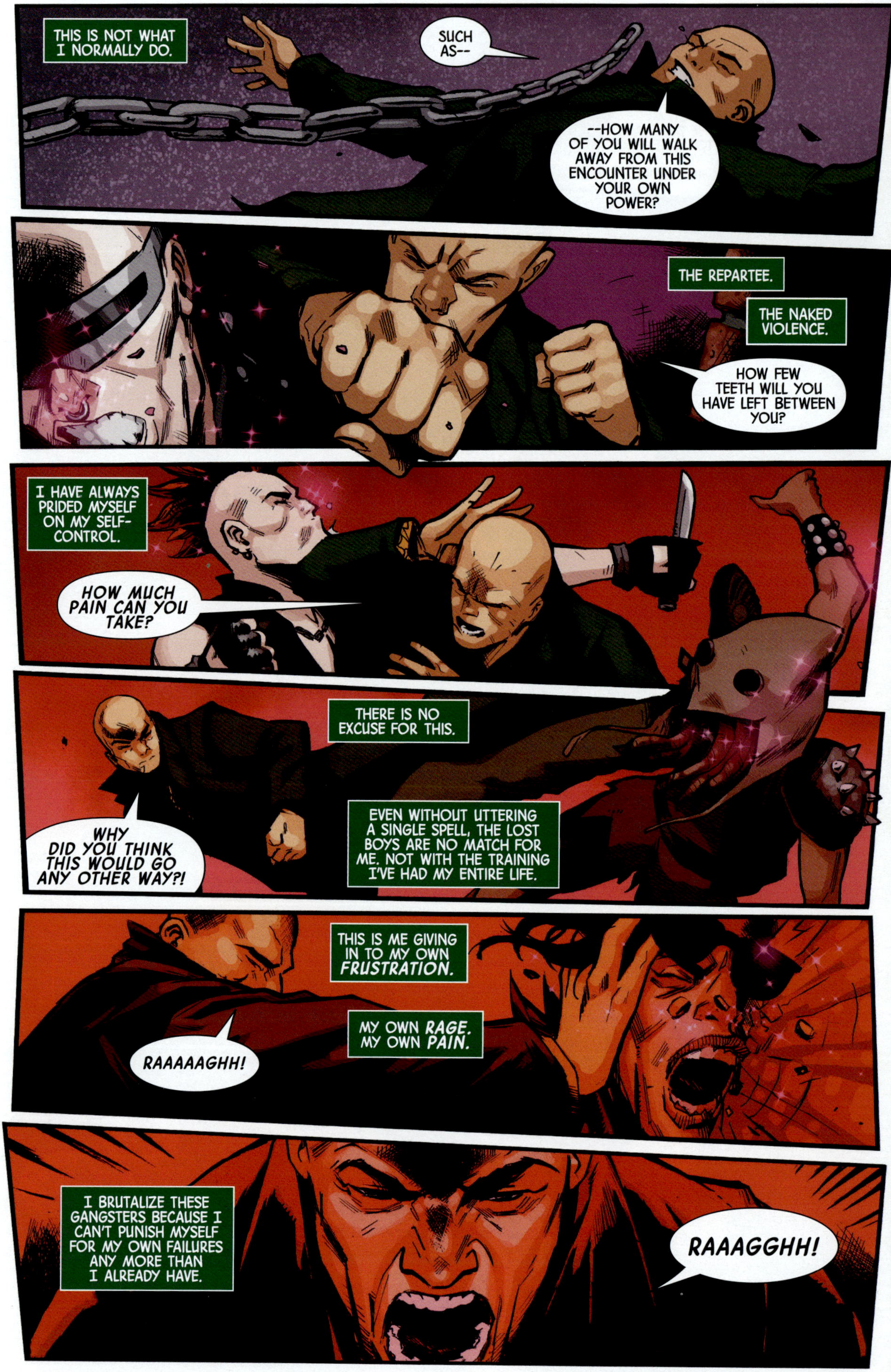
THIS IS NOT WHAT I NORMALLY DO.
SUCH AS--
--HOW MANY OF YOU WILL WALK AWAY FROM THIS ENCOUNTER UNDER YOUR OWN POWER?
THE REPARTEE.
THE NAKED VIOLENCE.
HOW FEW TEETH WILL YOU HAVE LEFT BETWEEN YOU?
I HAVE ALWAYS PRIDED MYSELF ON MY SELF-CONTROL.
HOW MUCH PAIN CAN YOU TAKE?
THERE IS NO EXCUSE FOR THIS.
WHY DID YOU THINK THIS WOULD GO ANY OTHER WAY?!
EVEN WITHOUT UTTERING A SINGLE SPELL, THE LOST BOYS ARE NO MATCH FOR ME. NOT WITH THE TRAINING I'VE HAD MY ENTIRE LIFE.
THIS IS ME GIVING IN TO MY OWN FRUSTRATION.
MY OWN RAGE. MY OWN PAIN.
RAAAAAGHH!
I BRUTALIZE THESE GANGSTERS BECAUSE I CAN'T PUNISH MYSELF FOR MY OWN FAILURES ANY MORE THAN I ALREADY HAVE.
RAAAGGHH!

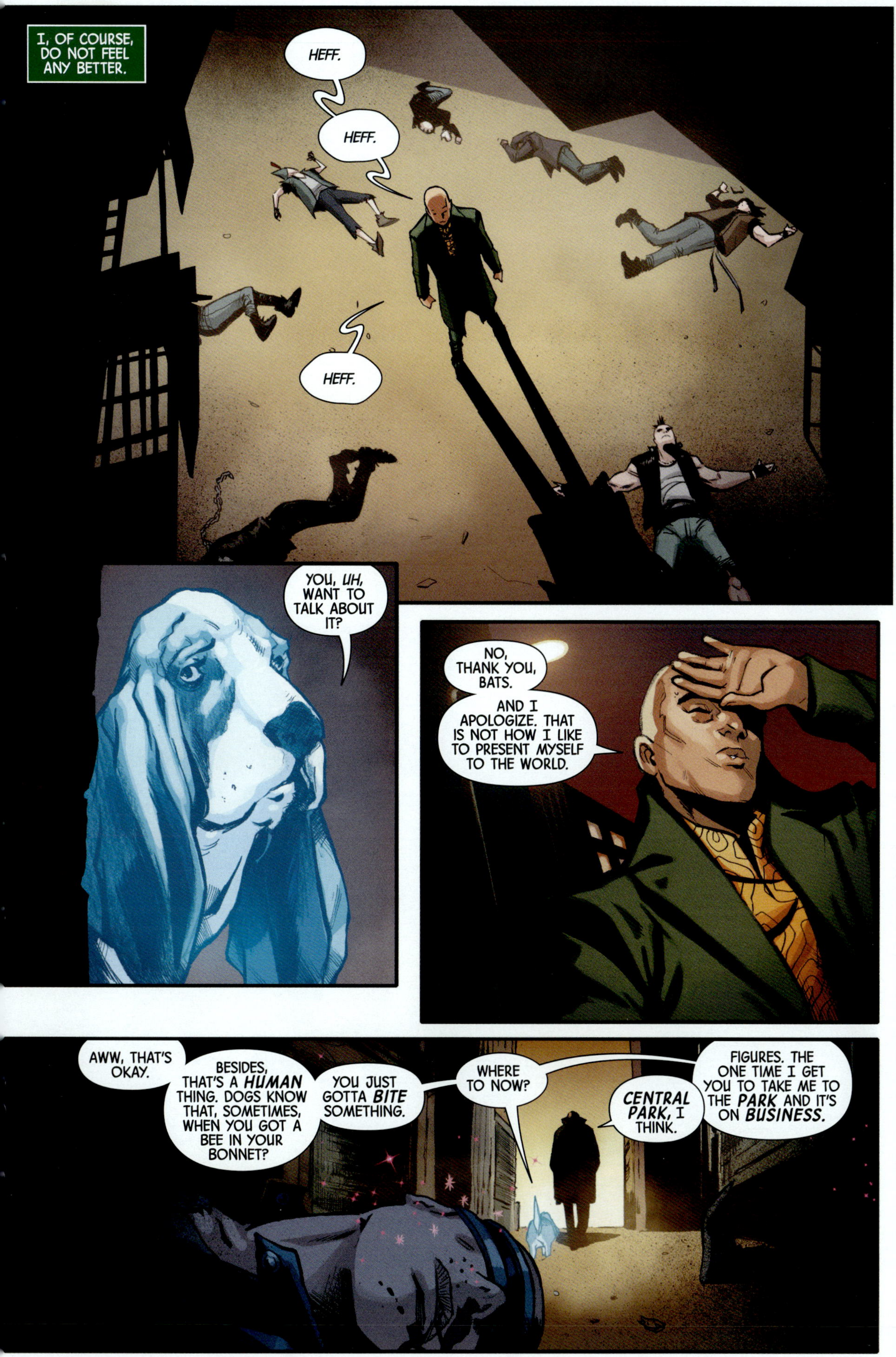

I, OF COURSE, DO NOT FEEL ANY BETTER.
HEFF.
HEFF.
HEFF.
YOU, UH, WANT TO TALK ABOUT IT?
NO, THANK YOU, BATS.
AND I APOLOGIZE. THAT IS NOT HOW I LIKE TO PRESENT MYSELF TO THE WORLD.
AWW, THAT'S OKAY.
BESIDES, THAT'S A HUMAN THING. DOGS KNOW THAT, SOMETIMES, WHEN YOU GOT A BEE IN YOUR BONNET?
YOU JUST GOTTA BITE SOMETHING.
WHERE TO NOW?
CENTRAL PARK, I THINK.
FIGURES. THE ONE TIME I GET YOU TO TAKE ME TO THE PARK AND IT'S ON BUSINESS.

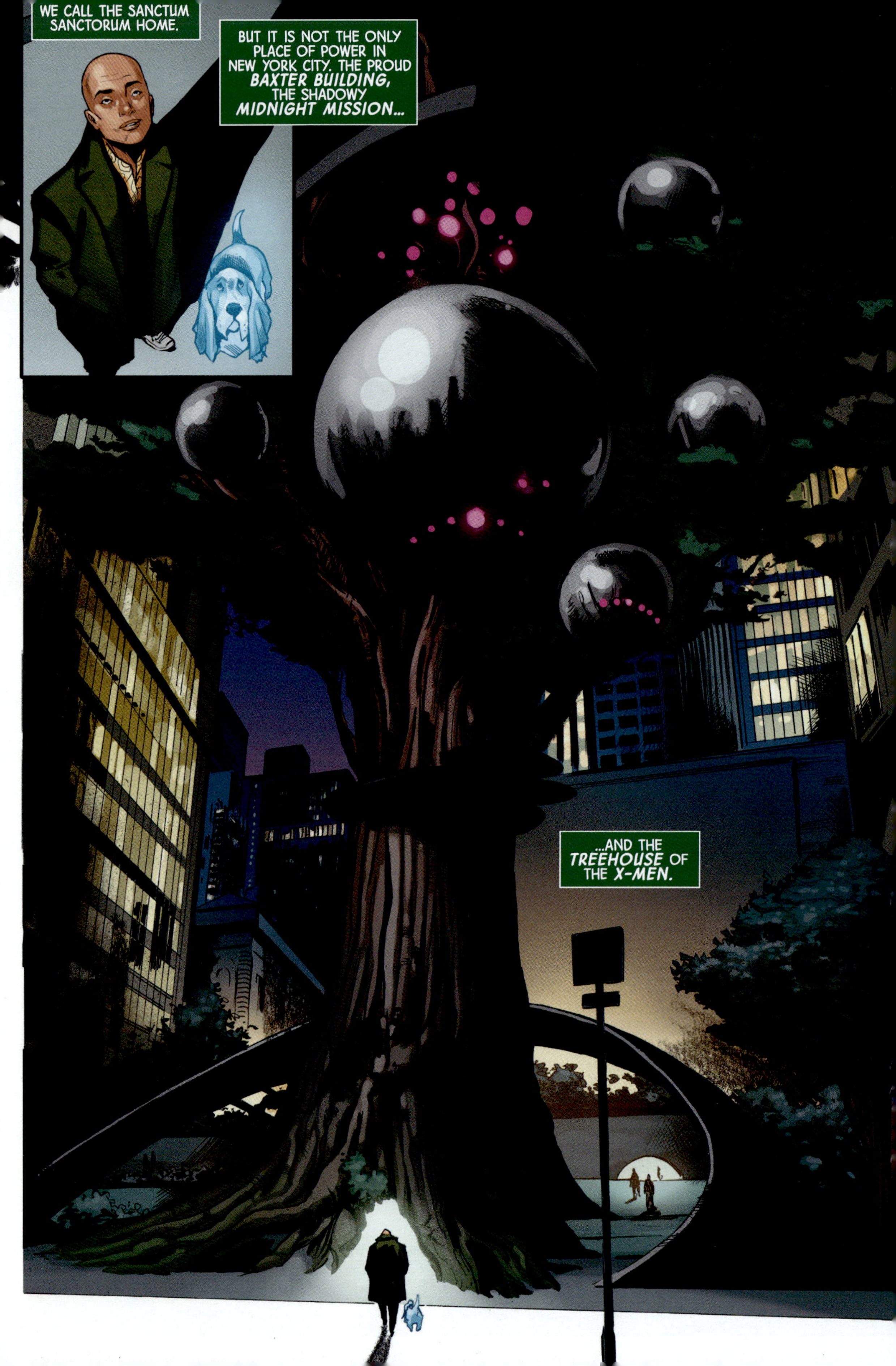
WE CALL THE SANCTUM SANCTORUM HOME.
BUT IT IS NOT THE ONLY PLACE OF POWER IN NEW YORK CITY. THE PROUD BAXTER BUILDING, THE SHADOWY MIDNIGHT MISSION...
...AND THE TREEHOUSE OF THE X-MEN.

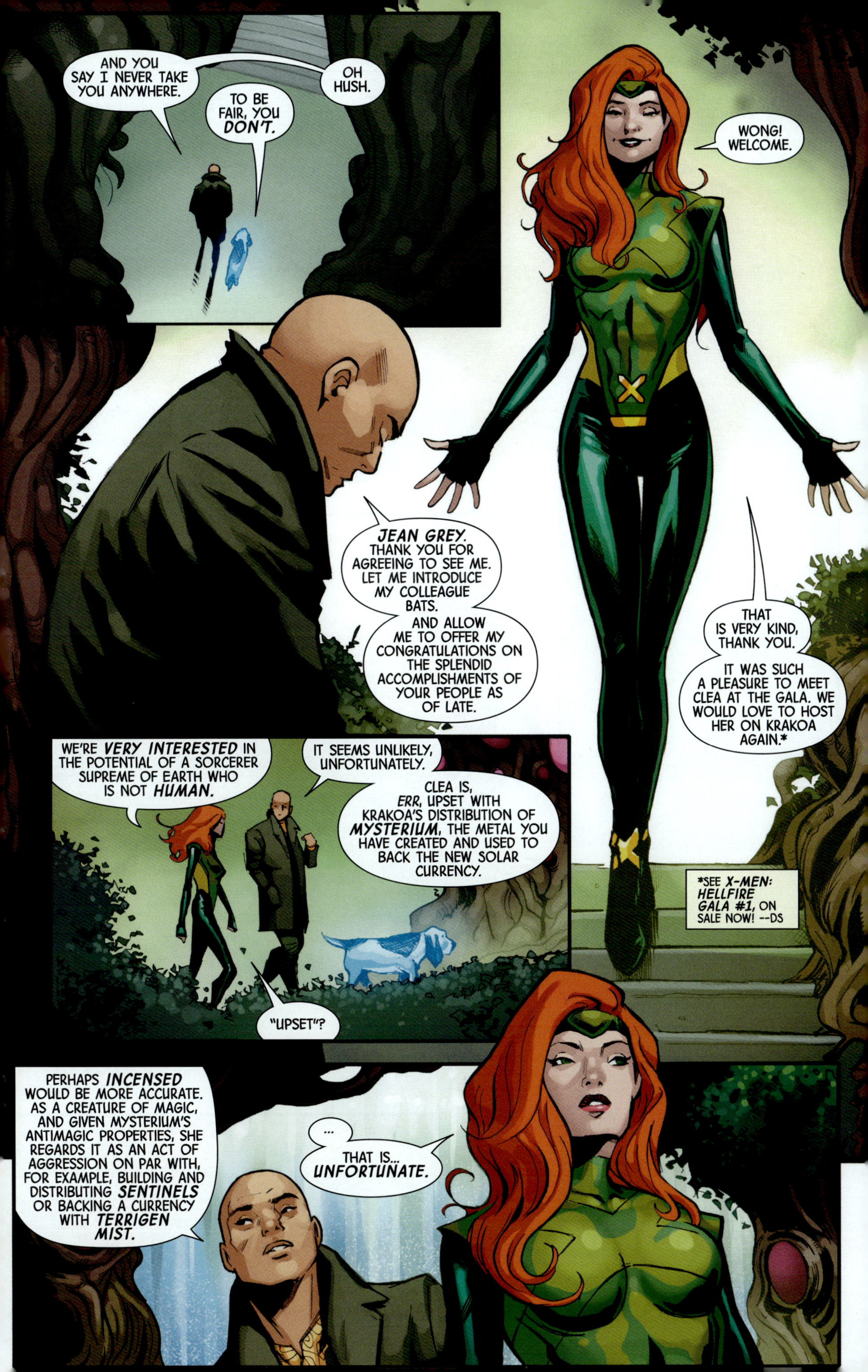
AND YOU SAY I NEVER TAKE YOU ANYWHERE.
OH HUSH.
TO BE FAIR, YOU DON'T.
WONG! WELCOME.
JEAN GREY. THANK YOU FOR AGREEING TO SEE ME. LET ME INTRODUCE MY COLLEAGUE BATS.
AND ALLOW ME TO OFFER MY CONGRATULATIONS ON THE SPLENDID ACCOMPLISHMENTS OF YOUR PEOPLE AS OF LATE.
THAT IS VERY KIND, THANK YOU.
IT WAS SUCH A PLEASURE TO MEET CLEA AT THE GALA. WE WOULD LOVE TO HOST HER ON KRAKOA AGAIN.*
WE'RE VERY INTERESTED IN THE POTENTIAL OF A SORCERER SUPREME OF EARTH WHO IS NOT HUMAN.
IT SEEMS UNLIKELY, UNFORTUNATELY.
CLEA IS, ERR, UPSET WITH KRAKOA'S DISTRIBUTION OF MYSTERIUM, THE METAL YOU HAVE CREATED AND USED TO BACK THE NEW SOLAR CURRENCY.
"UPSET"?
*SEE X-MEN: HELLFIRE GALA #1, ON SALE NOW! --DS
PERHAPS INCENSED WOULD BE MORE ACCURATE. AS A CREATURE OF MAGIC, AND GIVEN MYSTERIUM'S ANTIMAGIC PROPERTIES, SHE REGARDS IT AS AN ACT OF AGGRESSION ON PAR WITH, FOR EXAMPLE, BUILDING AND DISTRIBUTING SENTINELS OR BACKING A CURRENCY WITH TERRIGEN MIST.
...
THAT IS... UNFORTUNATE.

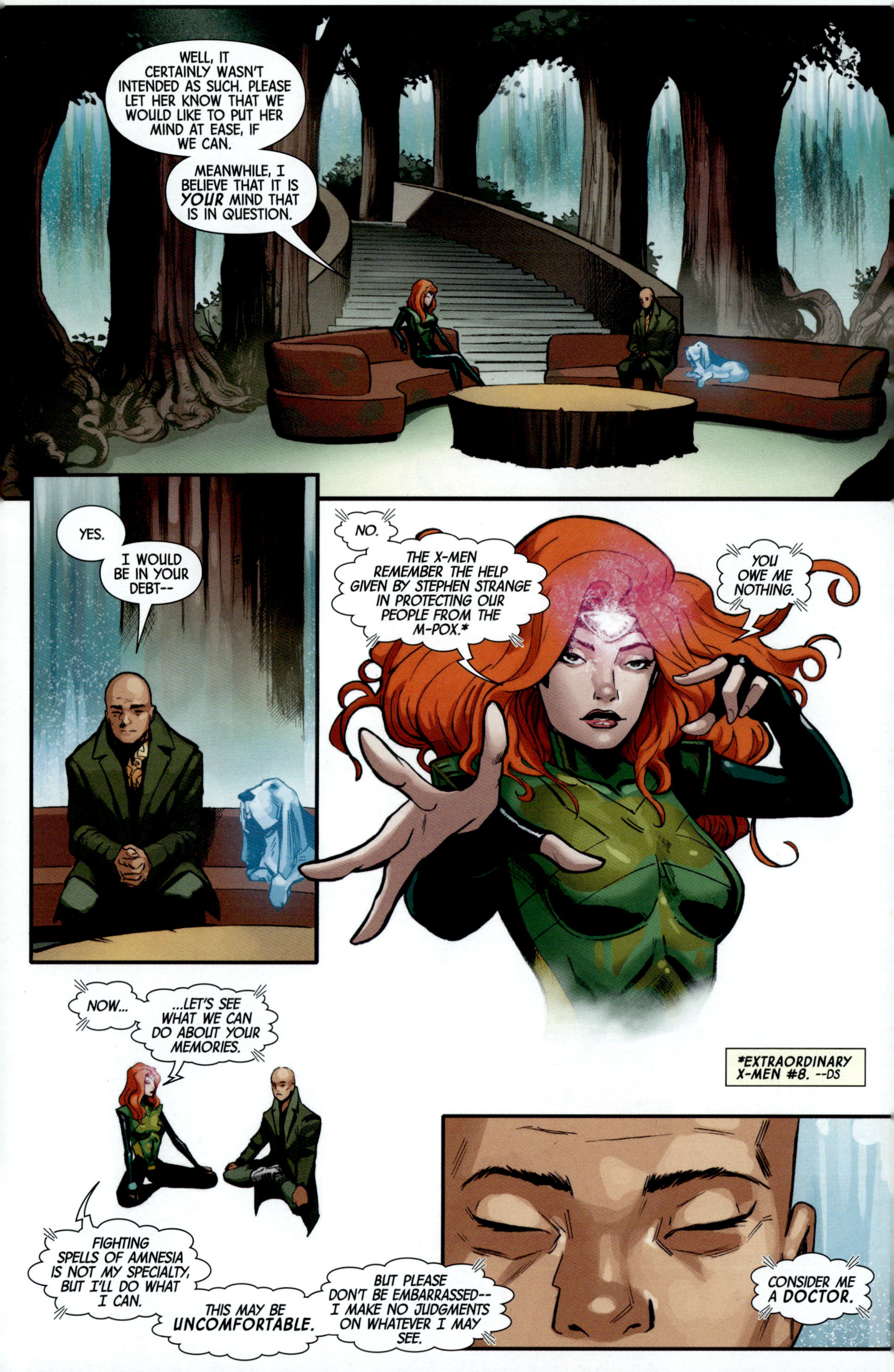
WELL, IT CERTAINLY WASN'T INTENDED AS SUCH. PLEASE LET HER KNOW THAT WE WOULD LIKE TO PUT HER MIND AT EASE, IF WE CAN.
MEANWHILE, I BELIEVE THAT IT IS YOUR MIND THAT IS IN QUESTION.
YES.
I WOULD BE IN YOUR DEBT--
NO.
THE X-MEN REMEMBER THE HELP GIVEN BY STEPHEN STRANGE IN PROTECTING OUR PEOPLE FROM THE M-POX.*
YOU OWE ME NOTHING.
*EXTRAORDINARY X-MEN #8. --DS
NOW...
...LET'S SEE WHAT WE CAN DO ABOUT YOUR MEMORIES.
FIGHTING SPELLS OF AMNESIA IS NOT MY SPECIALTY, BUT I'LL DO WHAT I CAN.
THIS MAY BE UNCOMFORTABLE.
BUT PLEASE DON'T BE EMBARRASSED-- I MAKE NO JUDGMENTS ON WHATEVER I MAY SEE.
CONSIDER ME A DOCTOR.

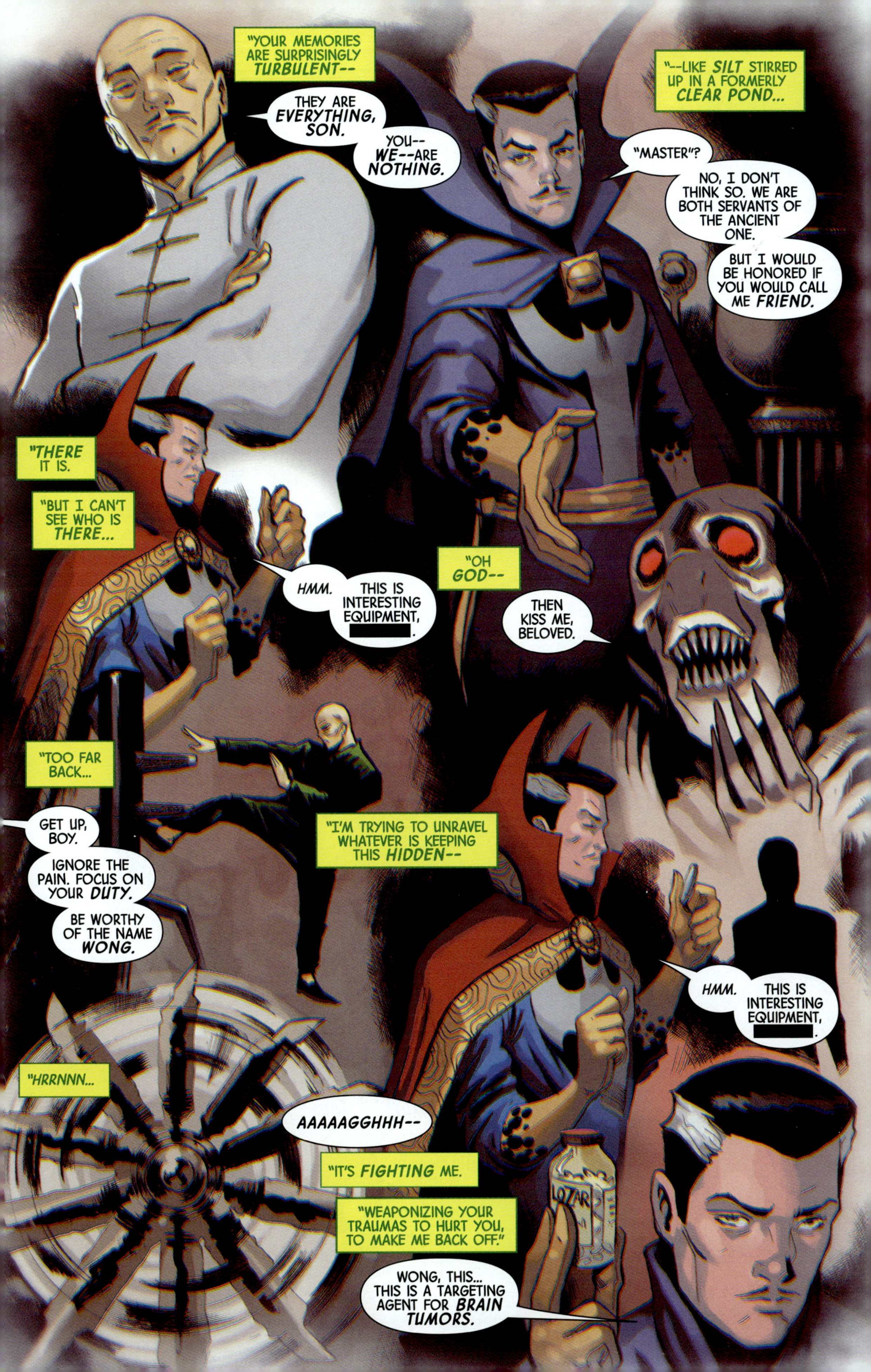
"YOUR MEMORIES ARE SURPRISINGLY TURBULENT--
THEY ARE EVERYTHING, SON.
YOU-- WE--ARE NOTHING.
"--LIKE SILT STIRRED UP IN A FORMERLY CLEAR POND...
"MASTER"?
NO, I DON'T THINK SO. WE ARE BOTH SERVANTS OF THE ANCIENT ONE.
BUT I WOULD BE HONORED IF YOU WOULD CALL ME FRIEND.
"THERE IT IS.
"BUT I CAN'T SEE WHO IS THERE...
HMM.
THIS IS INTERESTING EQUIPMENT, [redacted].
"OH GOD--
THEN KISS ME, BELOVED.
"TOO FAR BACK...
GET UP, BOY.
IGNORE THE PAIN. FOCUS ON YOUR DUTY.
BE WORTHY OF THE NAME WONG.
"I'M TRYING TO UNRAVEL WHATEVER IS KEEPING THIS HIDDEN--
HMM.
THIS IS INTERESTING EQUIPMENT, [redacted].
"HRRNNN...
AAAAAGGHHH--
"IT'S FIGHTING ME.
"WEAPONIZING YOUR TRAUMAS TO HURT YOU, TO MAKE ME BACK OFF."
WONG, THIS... THIS IS A TARGETING AGENT FOR BRAIN TUMORS.
LOZAR

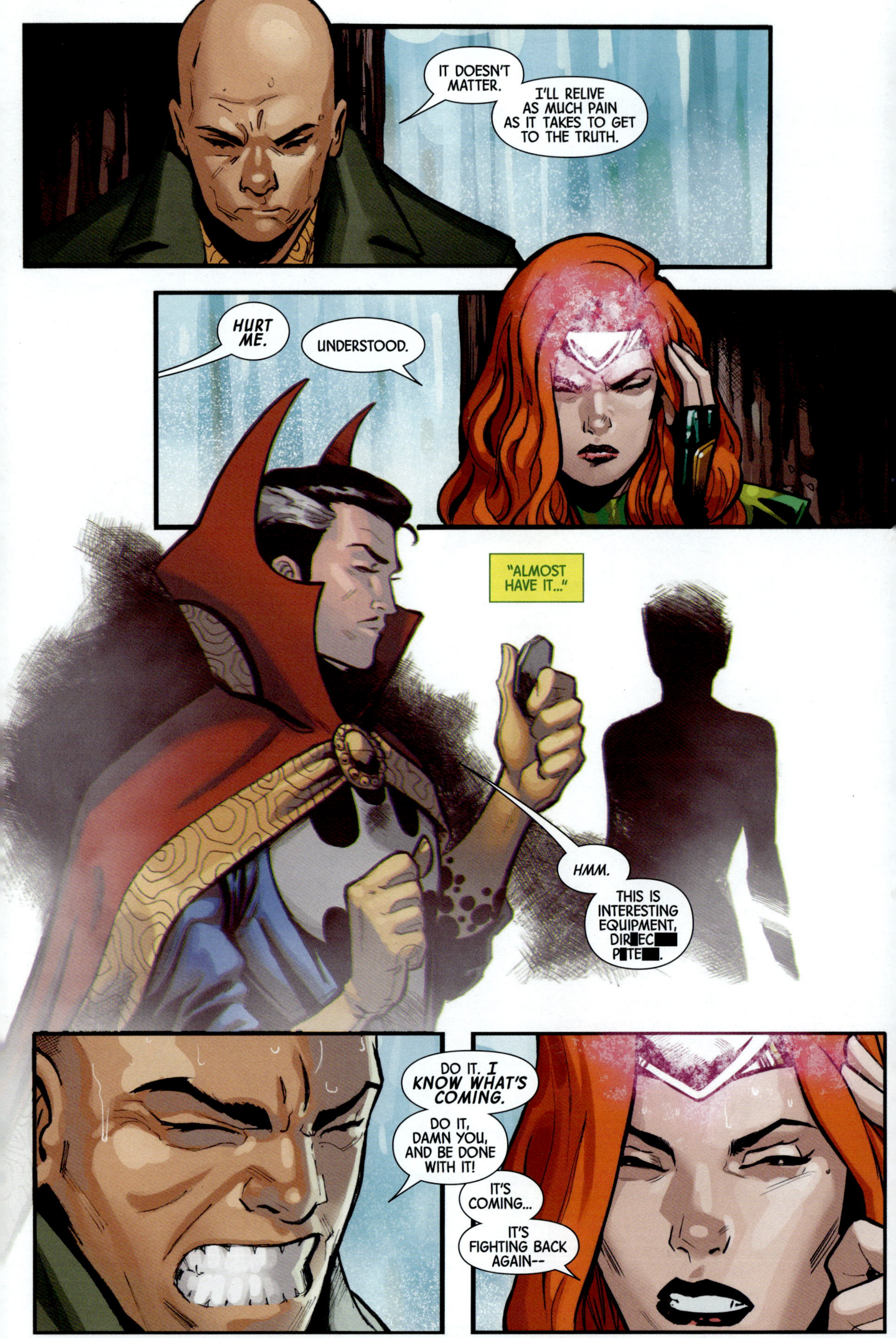
IT DOESN'T MATTER.
I'LL RELIVE AS MUCH PAIN AS IT TAKES TO GET TO THE TRUTH.
HURT ME.
UNDERSTOOD.
"ALMOST HAVE IT..."
HMM.
THIS IS INTERESTING EQUIPMENT,
DIR[redacted]EC[redacted]
P[redacted]TE[redacted].
DO IT. I KNOW WHAT'S COMING.
DO IT, DAMN YOU, AND BE DONE WITH IT!
IT'S COMING...
IT'S FIGHTING BACK AGAIN--

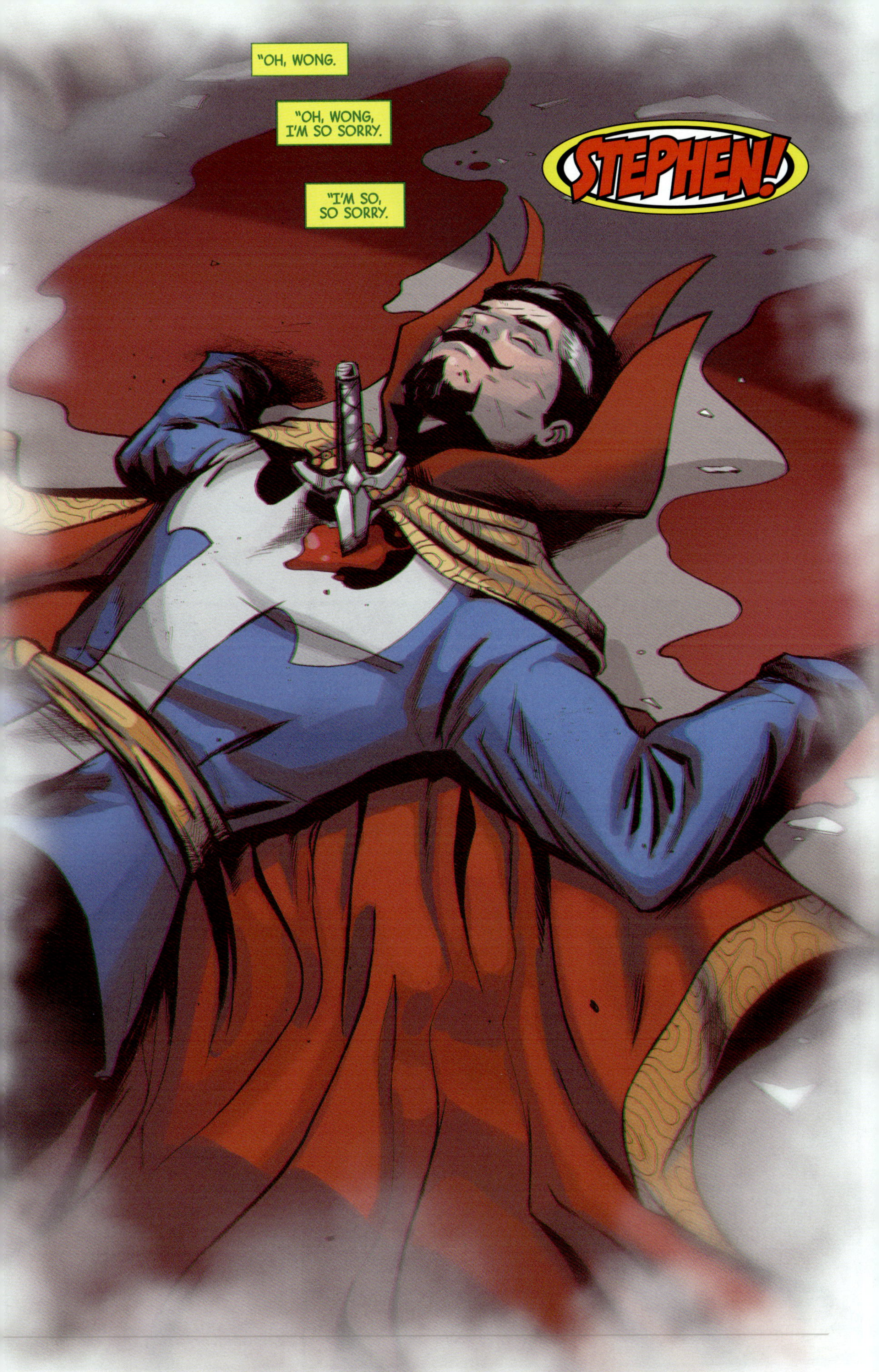
"OH, WONG.
"OH, WONG, I'M SO SORRY.
"I'M SO, SO SORRY.
STEPHEN!

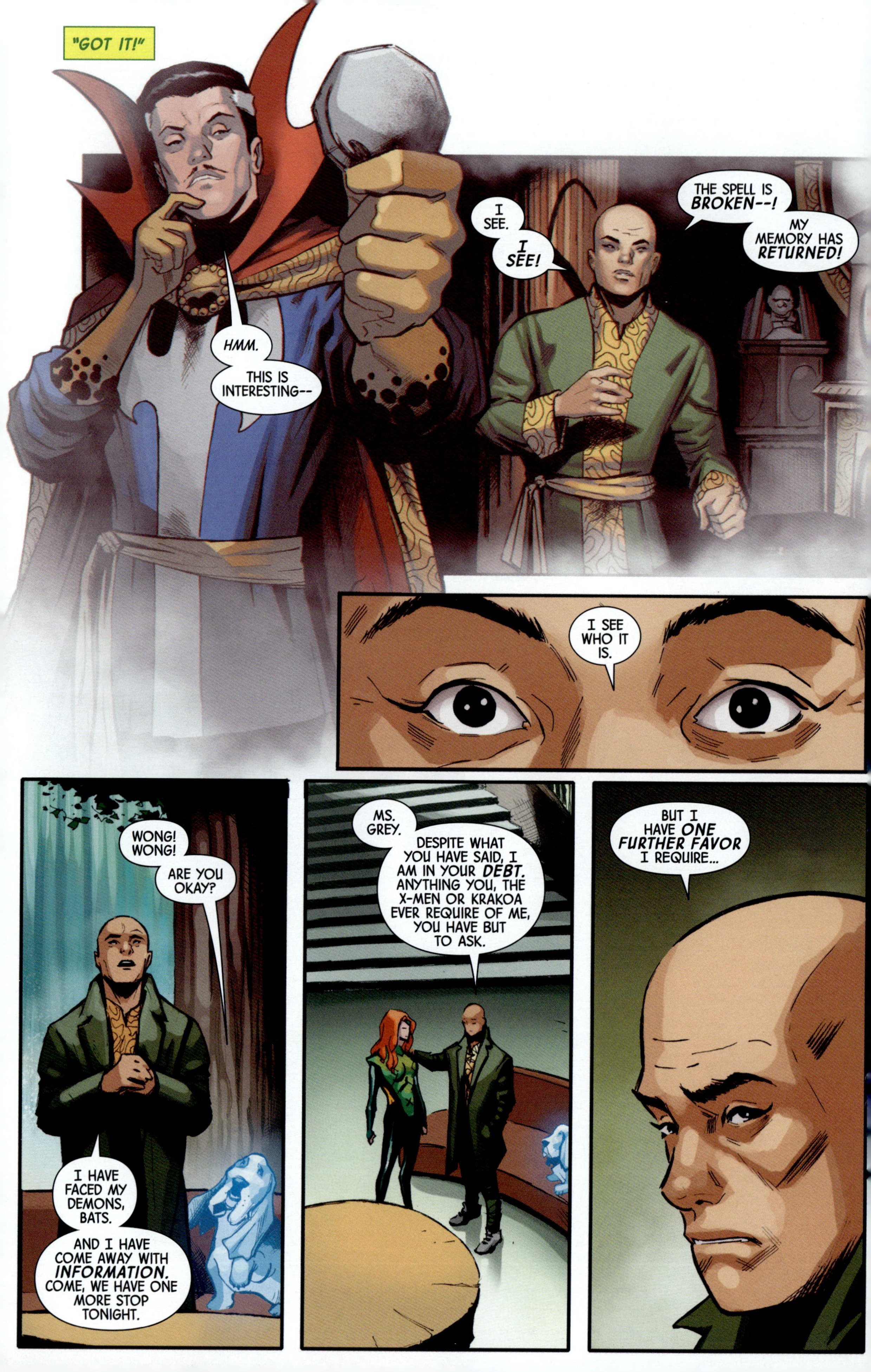
"GOT IT!"
HMM.
THIS IS INTERESTING--
I SEE.
I SEE!
THE SPELL IS BROKEN--!
MY MEMORY HAS RETURNED!
I SEE WHO IT IS.
WONG! WONG!
ARE YOU OKAY?
I HAVE FACED MY DEMONS, BATS.
AND I HAVE COME AWAY WITH INFORMATION. COME, WE HAVE ONE MORE STOP TONIGHT.
MS. GREY.
DESPITE WHAT YOU HAVE SAID, I AM IN YOUR DEBT. ANYTHING YOU, THE X-MEN OR KRAKOA EVER REQUIRE OF ME, YOU HAVE BUT TO ASK.
BUT I HAVE ONE FURTHER FAVOR I REQUIRE...

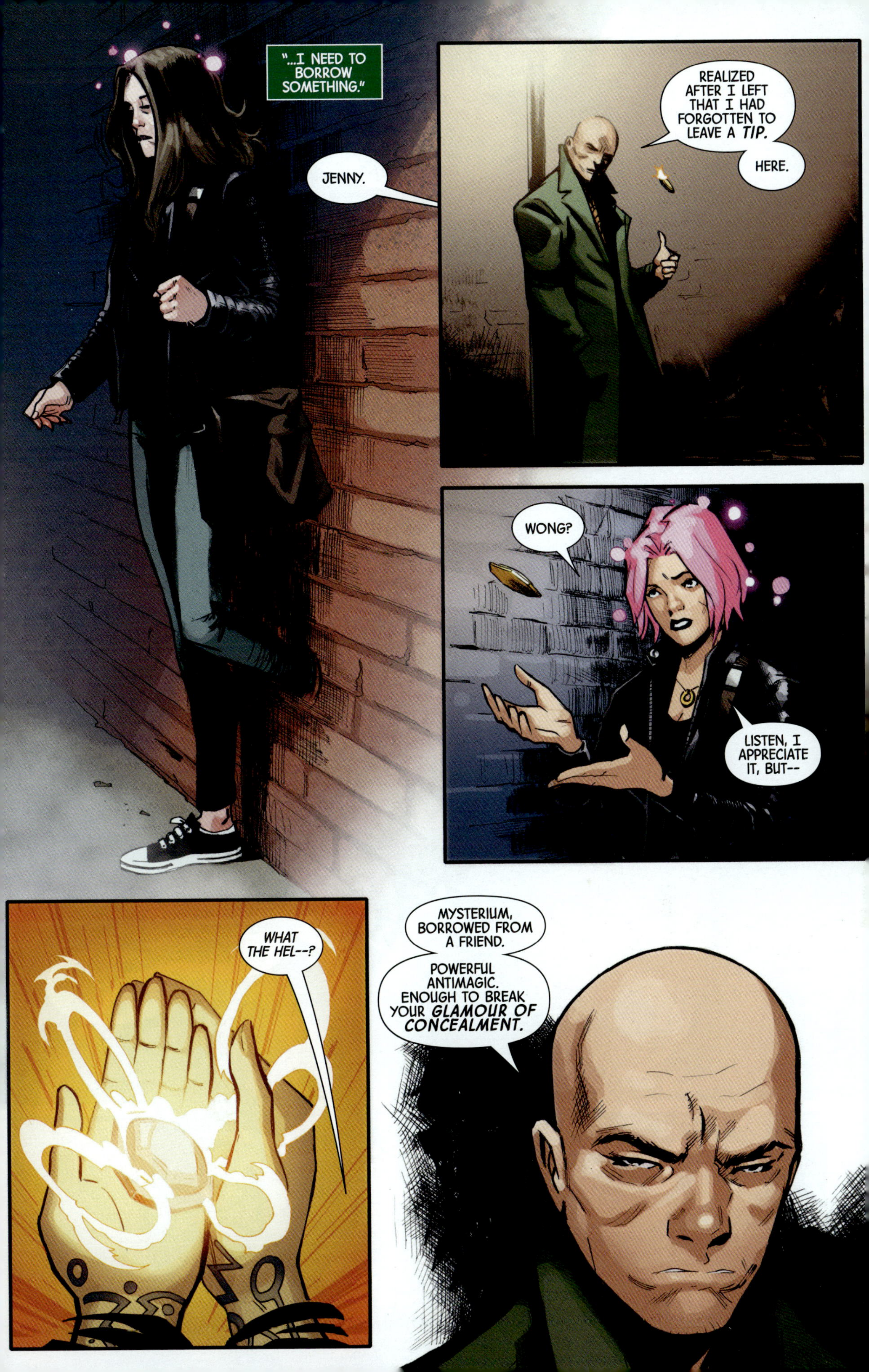
"...I NEED TO BORROW SOMETHING."
JENNY.
REALIZED AFTER I LEFT THAT I HAD FORGOTTEN TO LEAVE A *TIP*.
HERE.
WONG?
LISTEN, I APPRECIATE IT, BUT--
WHAT THE HEL--?
MYSTERIUM, BORROWED FROM A FRIEND.
POWERFUL ANTIMAGIC. ENOUGH TO BREAK YOUR *GLAMOUR OF CONCEALMENT*.

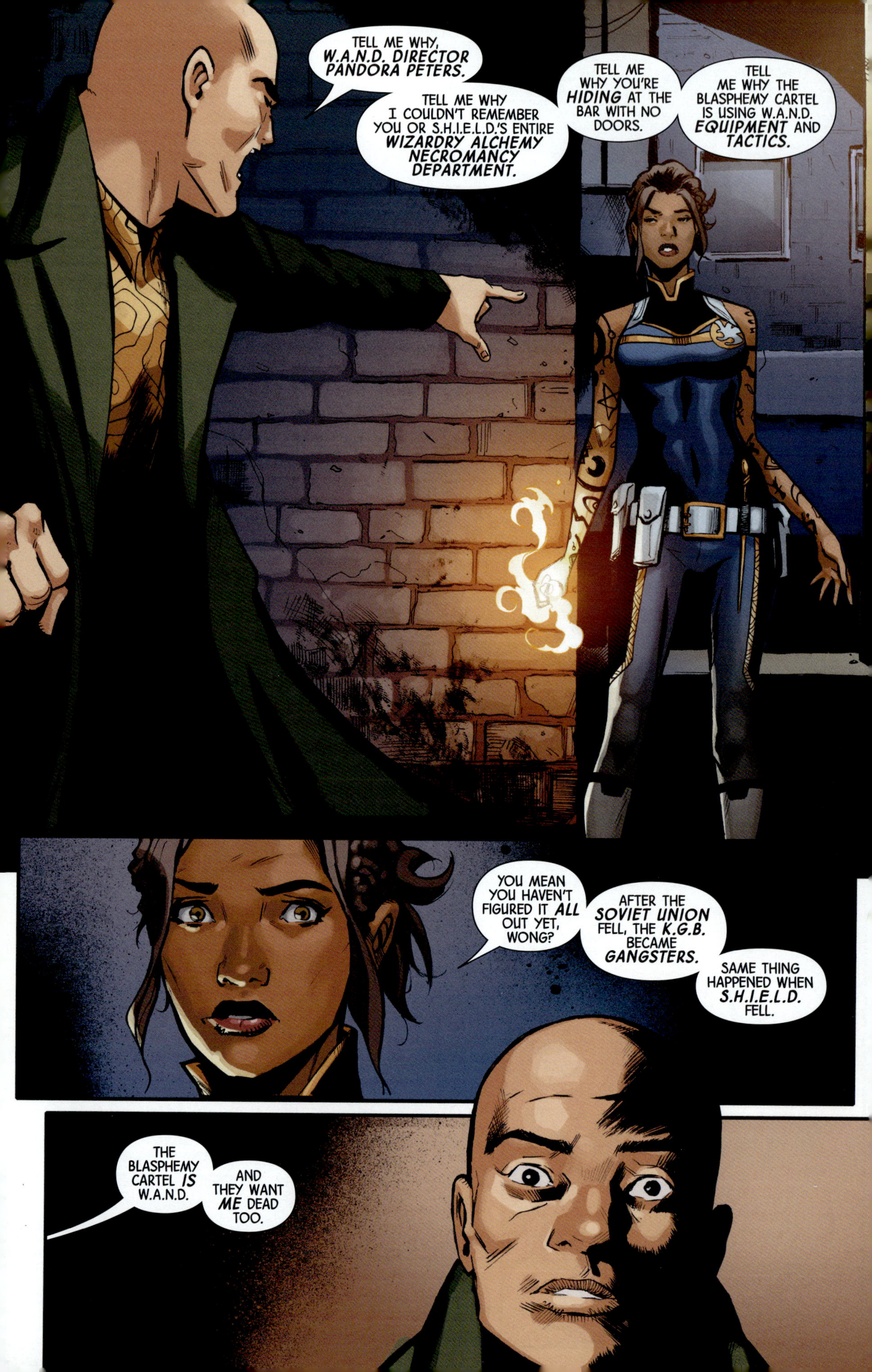
TELL ME WHY, W.A.N.D. DIRECTOR PANDORA PETERS.
TELL ME WHY I COULDN'T REMEMBER YOU OR S.H.I.E.L.D.'S ENTIRE WIZARDRY ALCHEMY NECROMANCY DEPARTMENT.
TELL ME WHY YOU'RE HIDING AT THE BAR WITH NO DOORS.
TELL ME WHY THE BLASPHEMY CARTEL IS USING W.A.N.D. EQUIPMENT AND TACTICS.
YOU MEAN YOU HAVEN'T FIGURED IT ALL OUT YET, WONG?
AFTER THE SOVIET UNION FELL, THE K.G.B. BECAME GANGSTERS.
SAME THING HAPPENED WHEN S.H.I.E.L.D. FELL.
THE BLASPHEMY CARTEL IS W.A.N.D.
AND THEY WANT ME DEAD TOO.

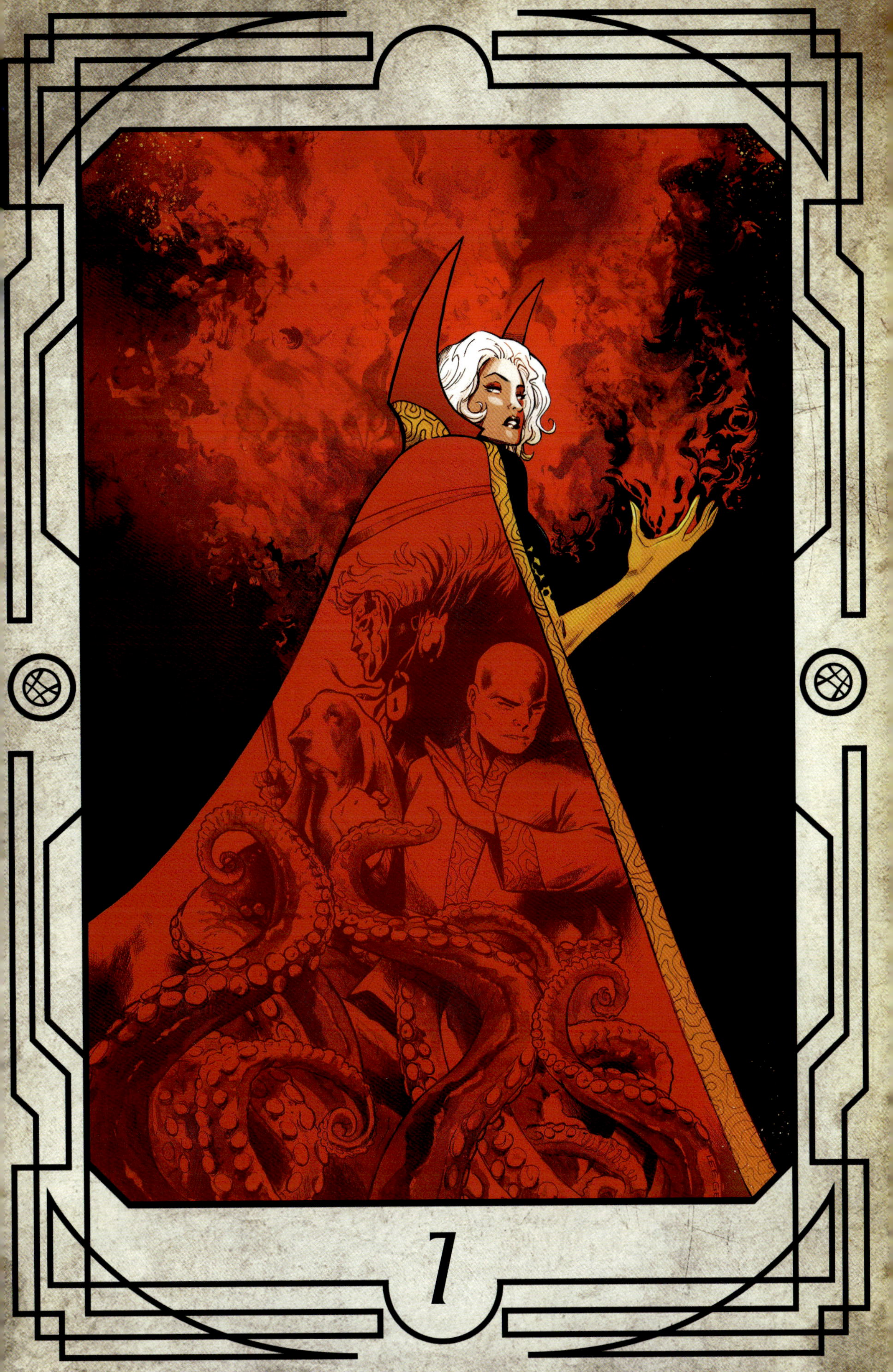
7

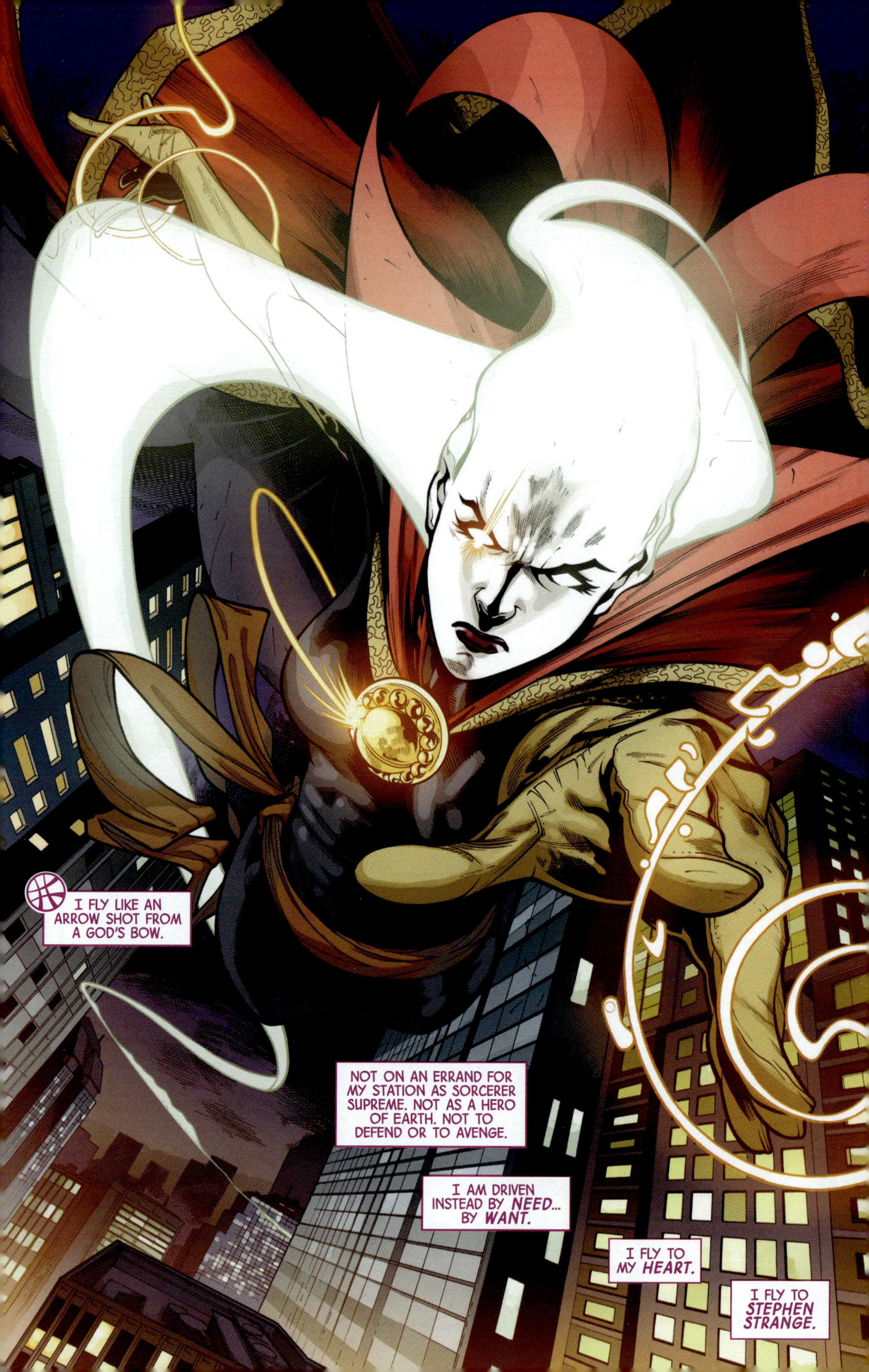
I FLY LIKE AN ARROW SHOT FROM A GOD'S BOW.
NOT ON AN ERRAND FOR MY STATION AS SORCERER SUPREME. NOT AS A HERO OF EARTH. NOT TO DEFEND OR TO AVENGE.
I AM DRIVEN INSTEAD BY *NEED*... BY *WANT*.
I FLY TO MY *HEART*.
I FLY TO *STEPHEN STRANGE*.

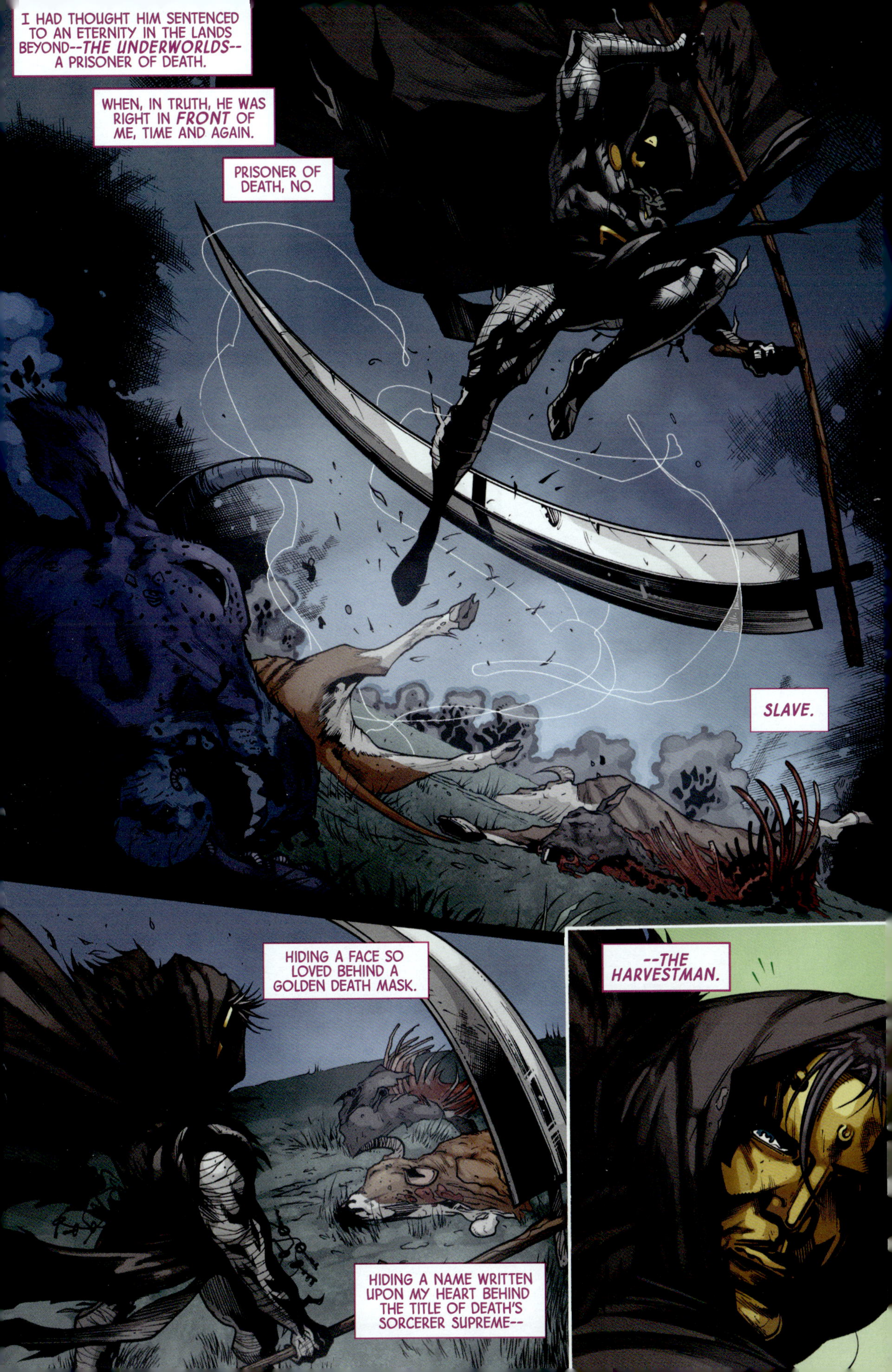
I HAD THOUGHT HIM SENTENCED TO AN ETERNITY IN THE LANDS BEYOND--*THE UNDERWORLDS*-- A PRISONER OF DEATH.
WHEN, IN TRUTH, HE WAS RIGHT IN *FRONT* OF ME, TIME AND AGAIN.
PRISONER OF DEATH, NO.
SLAVE.
HIDING A FACE SO LOVED BEHIND A GOLDEN DEATH MASK.
HIDING A NAME WRITTEN UPON MY HEART BEHIND THE TITLE OF DEATH'S SORCERER SUPREME--
--THE HARVESTMAN.

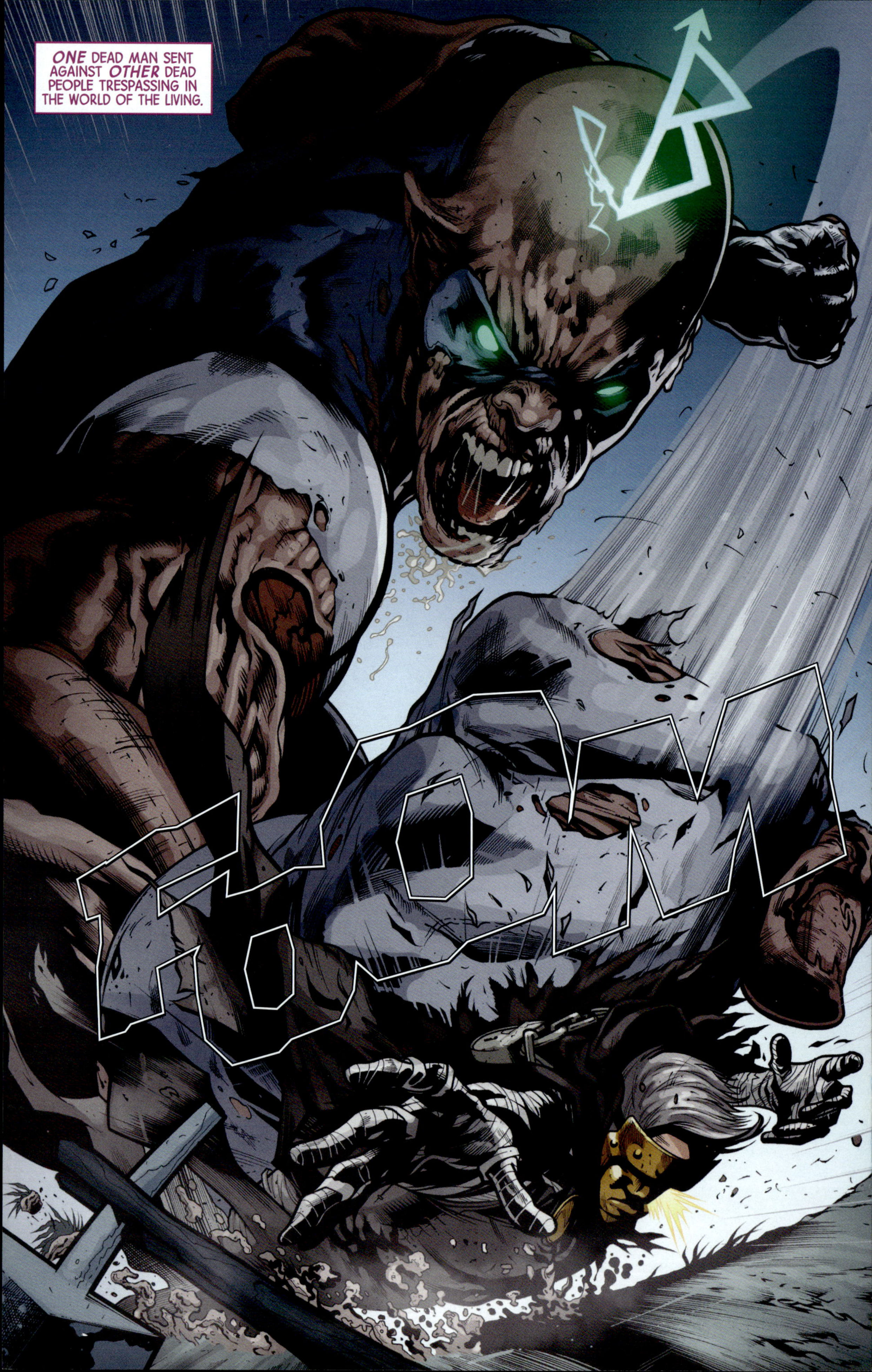
ONE DEAD MAN SENT AGAINST *OTHER* DEAD PEOPLE TRESPASSING IN THE WORLD OF THE LIVING.
FOOM

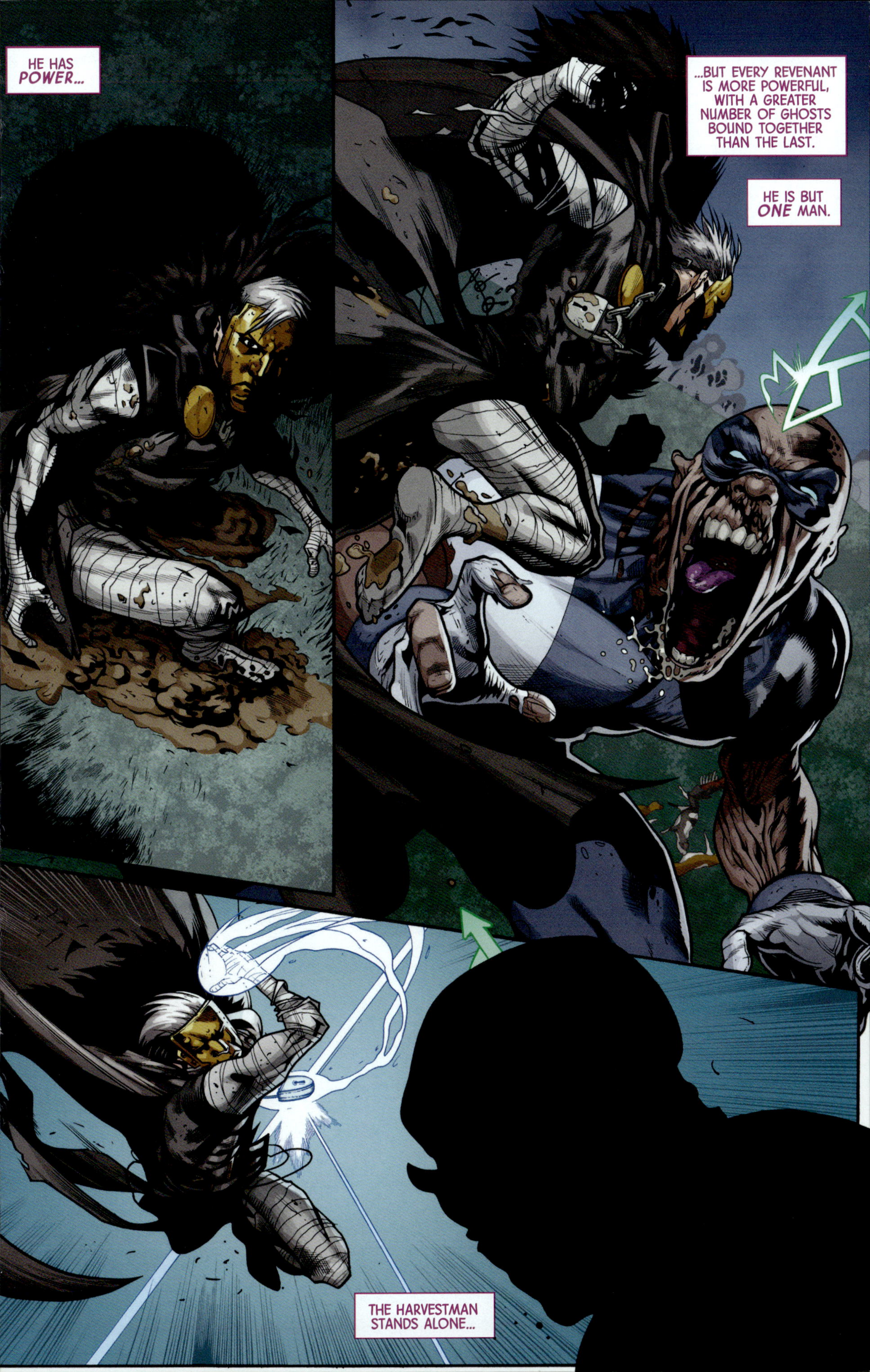

HE HAS *POWER*...
...BUT EVERY REVENANT IS MORE POWERFUL, WITH A GREATER NUMBER OF GHOSTS BOUND TOGETHER THAN THE LAST.
HE IS BUT *ONE* MAN.
THE HARVESTMAN STANDS ALONE...

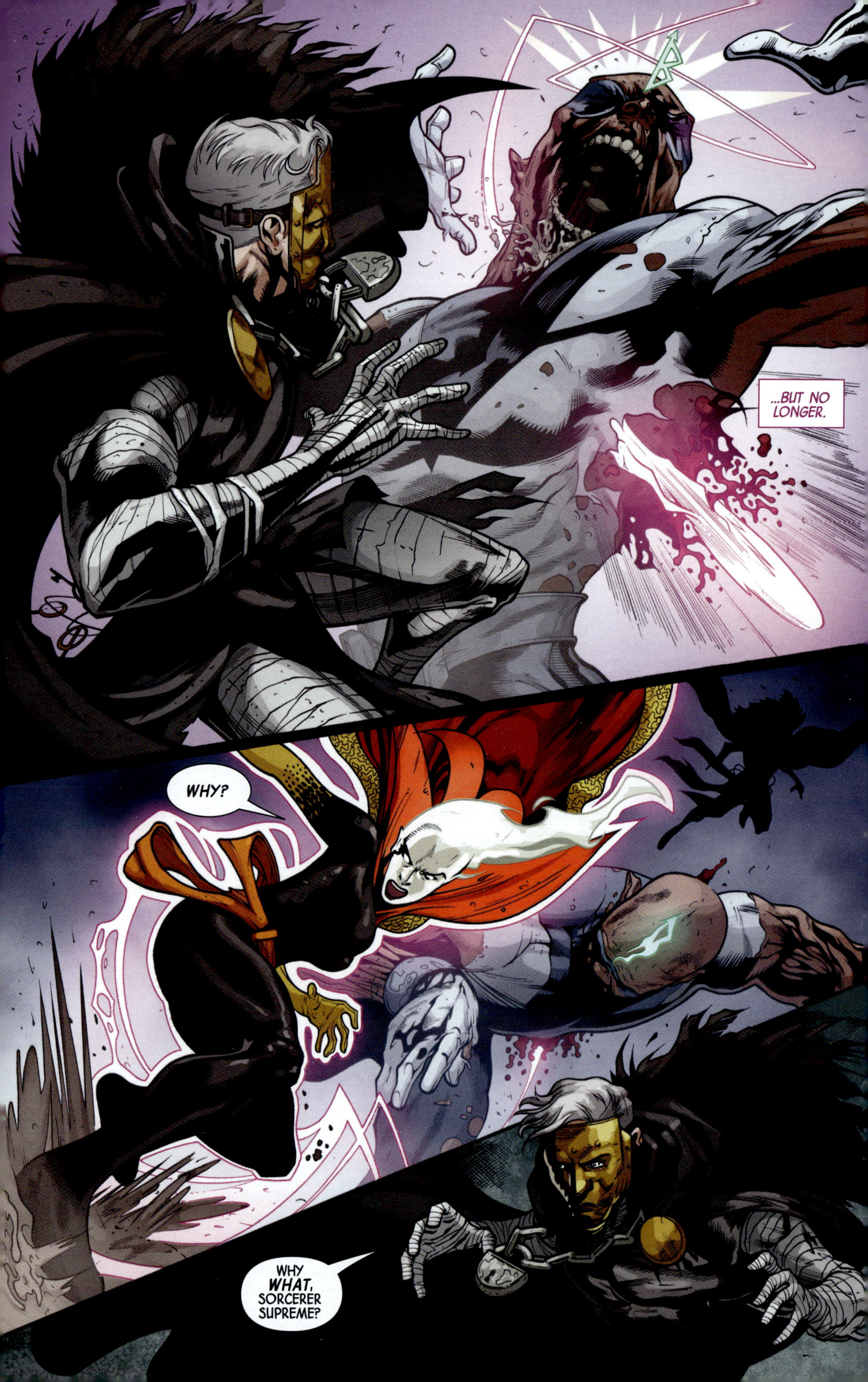
...BUT NO LONGER.
WHY?
WHY *WHAT*, SORCERER SUPREME?

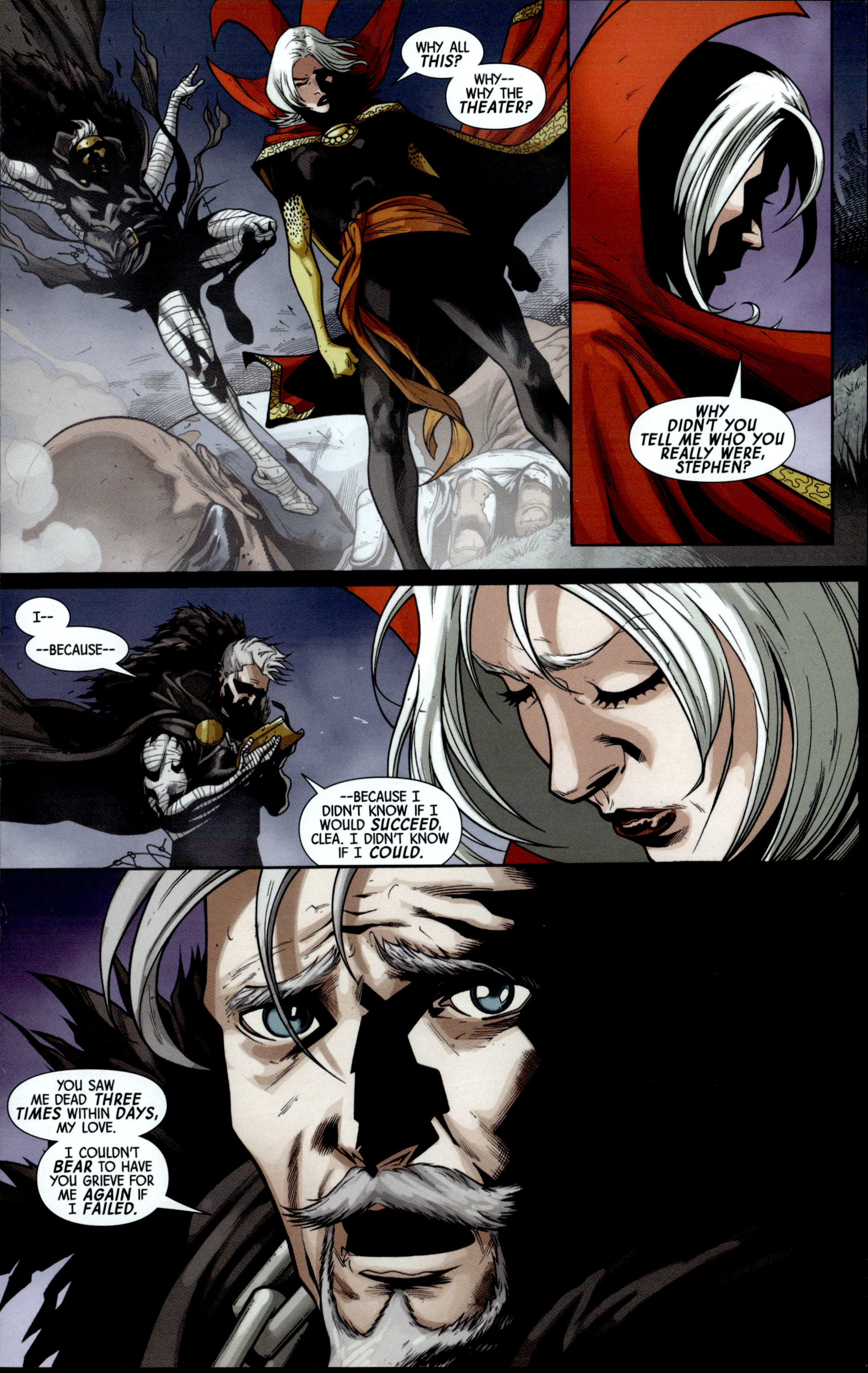
WHY ALL THIS?
WHY-- WHY THE THEATER?
WHY DIDN'T YOU TELL ME WHO YOU REALLY WERE, STEPHEN?
I--
--BECAUSE--
--BECAUSE I DIDN'T KNOW IF I WOULD SUCCEED, CLEA. I DIDN'T KNOW IF I COULD.
YOU SAW ME DEAD THREE TIMES WITHIN DAYS, MY LOVE.
I COULDN'T BEAR TO HAVE YOU GRIEVE FOR ME AGAIN IF I FAILED.

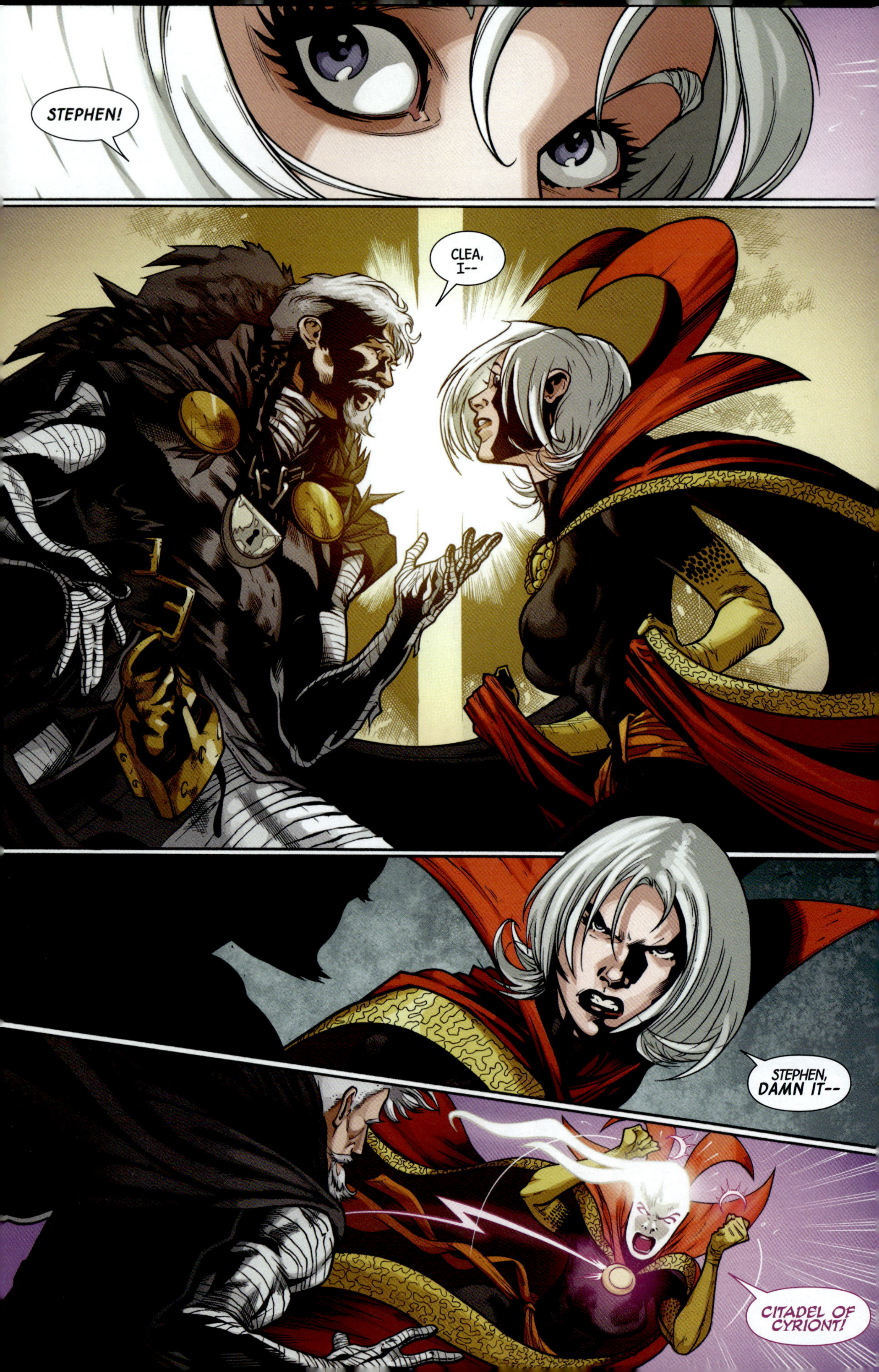
STEPHEN!
CLEA, I--
STEPHEN, DAMN IT--
CITADEL OF CYRIONT!

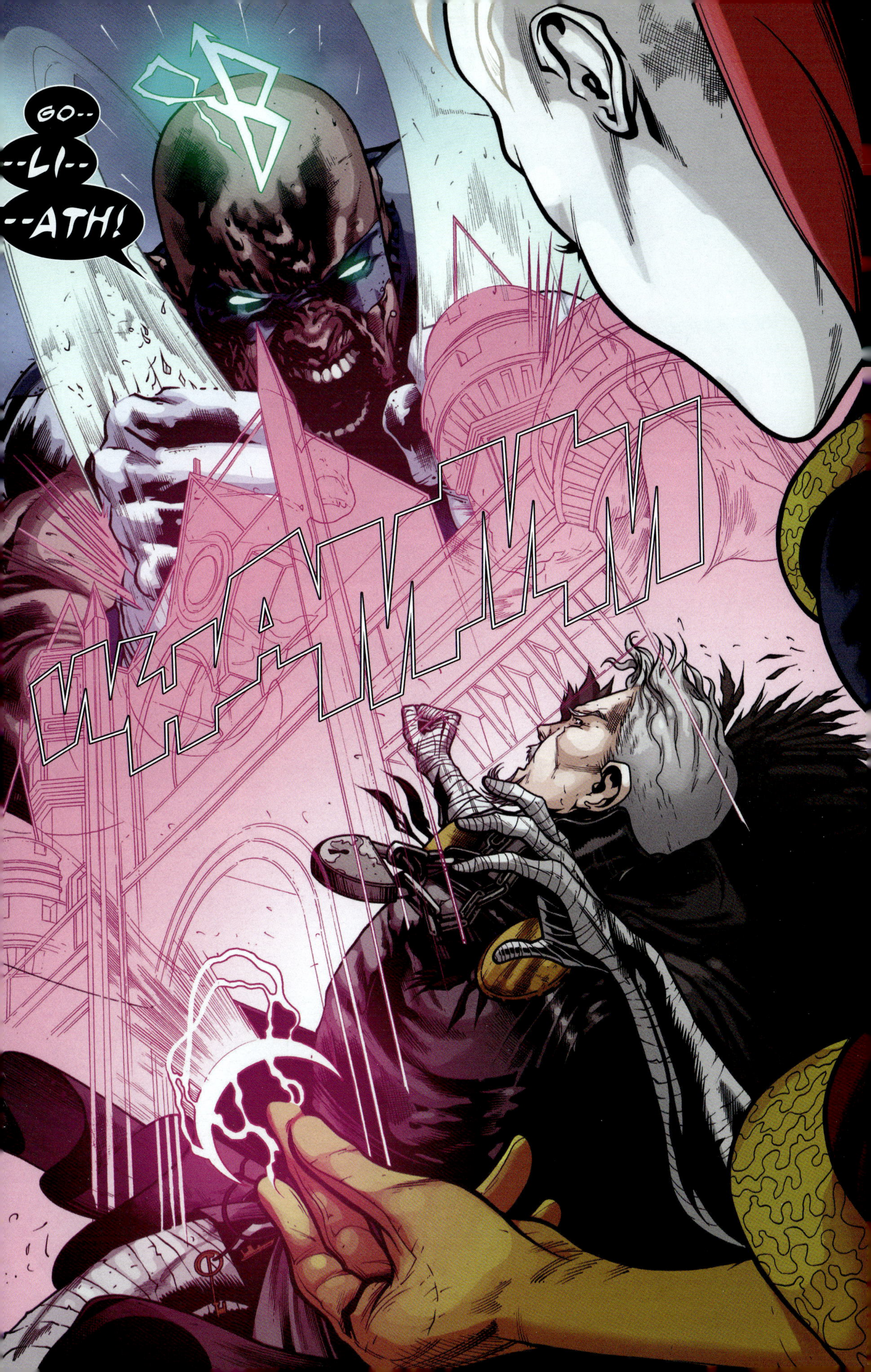
GO--
--LI--
--ATH!
WHAMMM

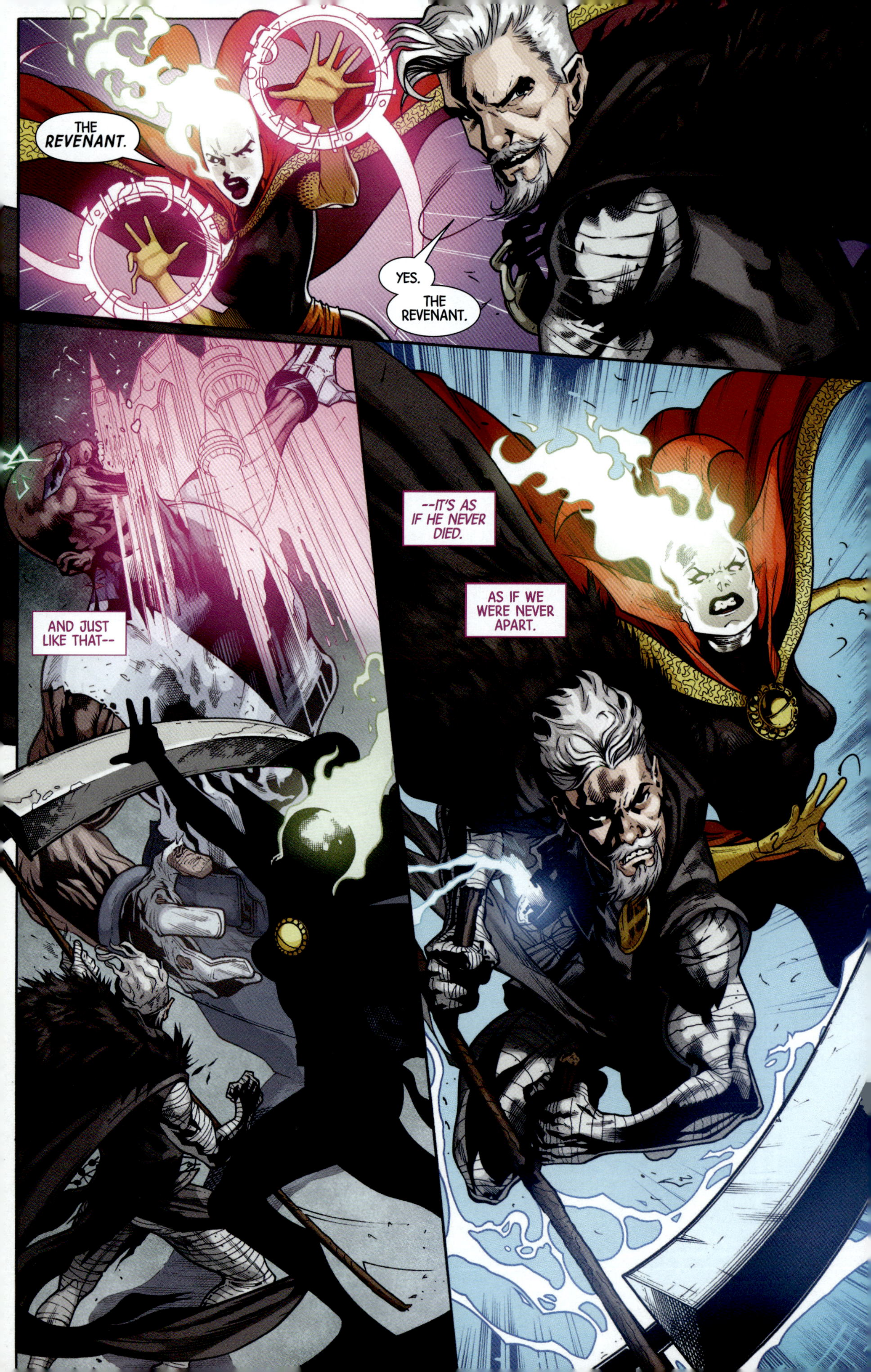
THE REVENANT.
YES.
THE REVENANT.
AND JUST LIKE THAT--
--IT'S AS IF HE NEVER DIED.
AS IF WE WERE NEVER APART.

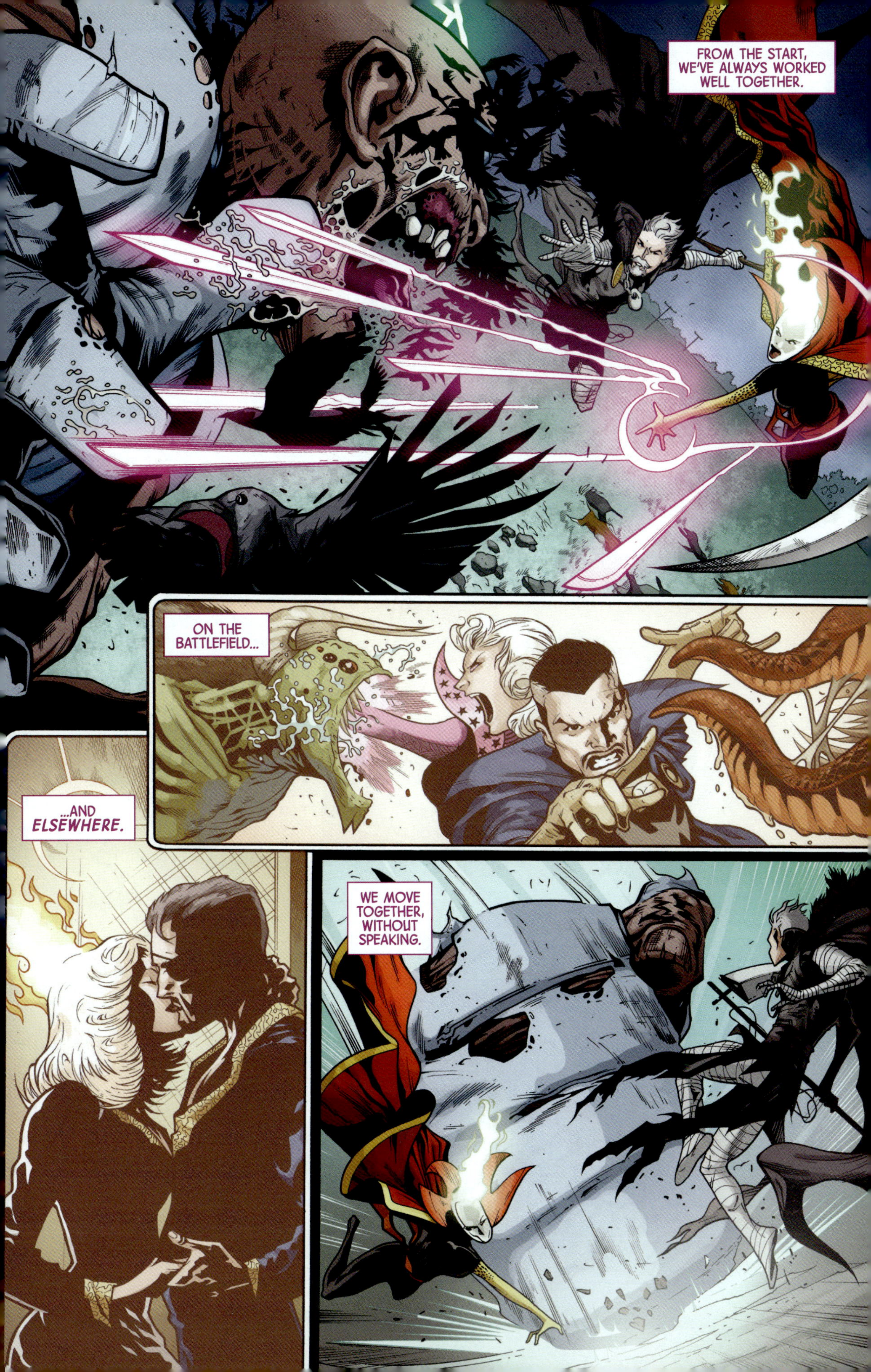
FROM THE START, WE'VE ALWAYS WORKED WELL TOGETHER.
ON THE BATTLEFIELD...
...AND *ELSEWHERE.*
WE MOVE TOGETHER, WITHOUT SPEAKING.

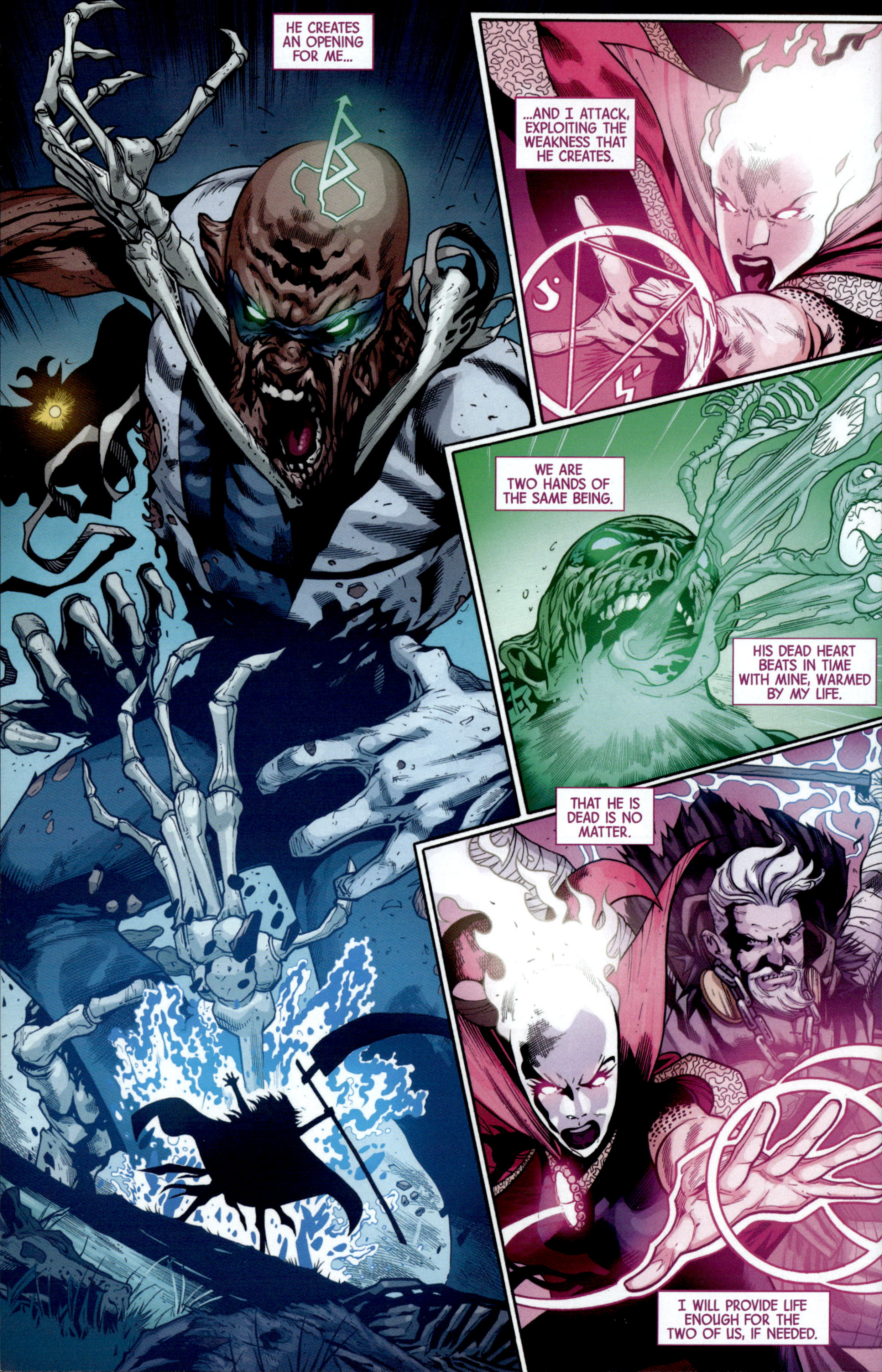
HE CREATES AN OPENING FOR ME...
...AND I ATTACK, EXPLOITING THE WEAKNESS THAT HE CREATES.
WE ARE TWO HANDS OF THE SAME BEING.
HIS DEAD HEART BEATS IN TIME WITH MINE, WARMED BY MY LIFE.
THAT HE IS DEAD IS NO MATTER.
I WILL PROVIDE LIFE ENOUGH FOR THE TWO OF US, IF NEEDED.

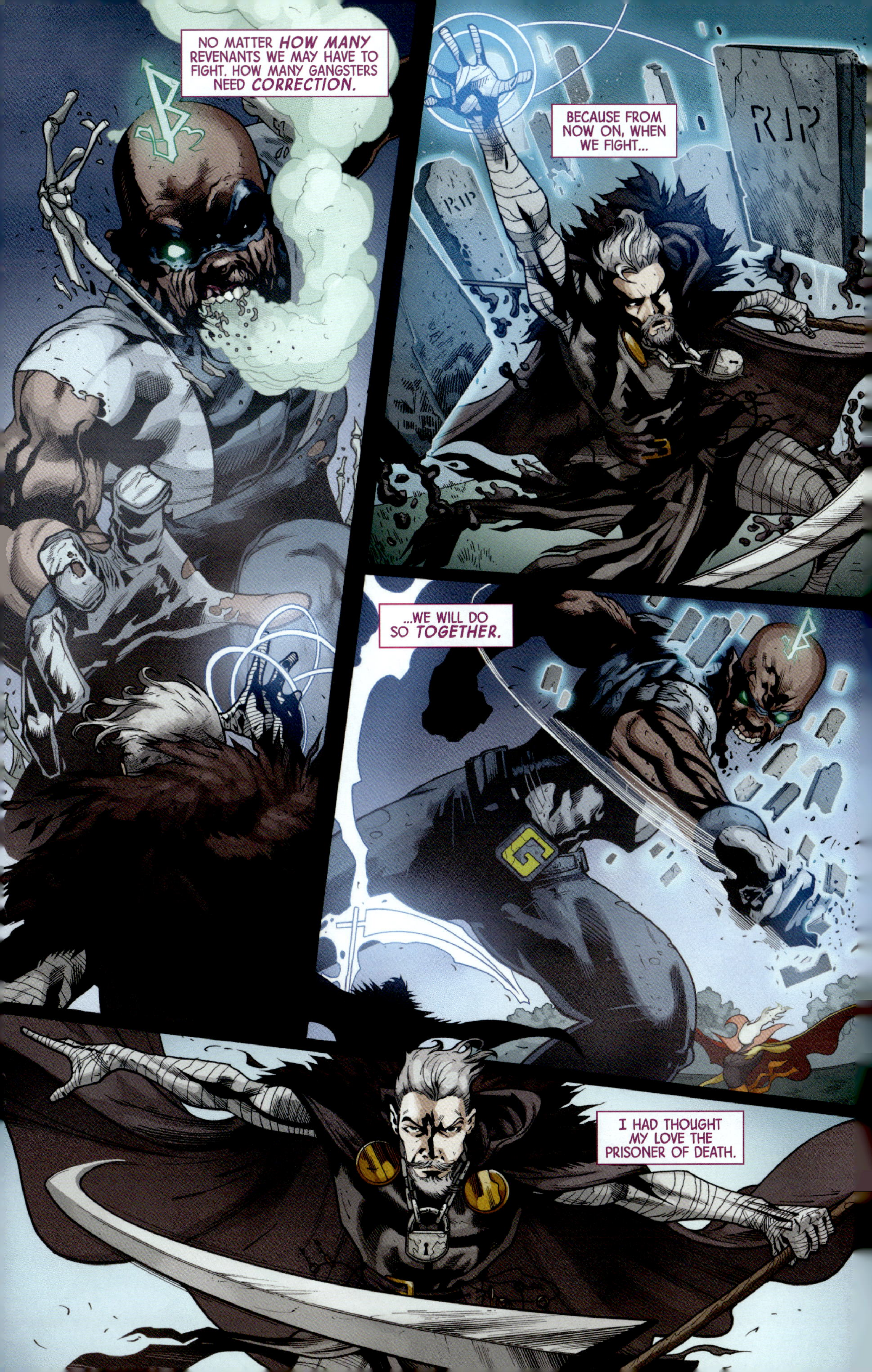
NO MATTER HOW MANY REVENANTS WE MAY HAVE TO FIGHT. HOW MANY GANGSTERS NEED CORRECTION.
RIP
BECAUSE FROM NOW ON, WHEN WE FIGHT...
...WE WILL DO SO TOGETHER.
I HAD THOUGHT MY LOVE THE PRISONER OF DEATH.

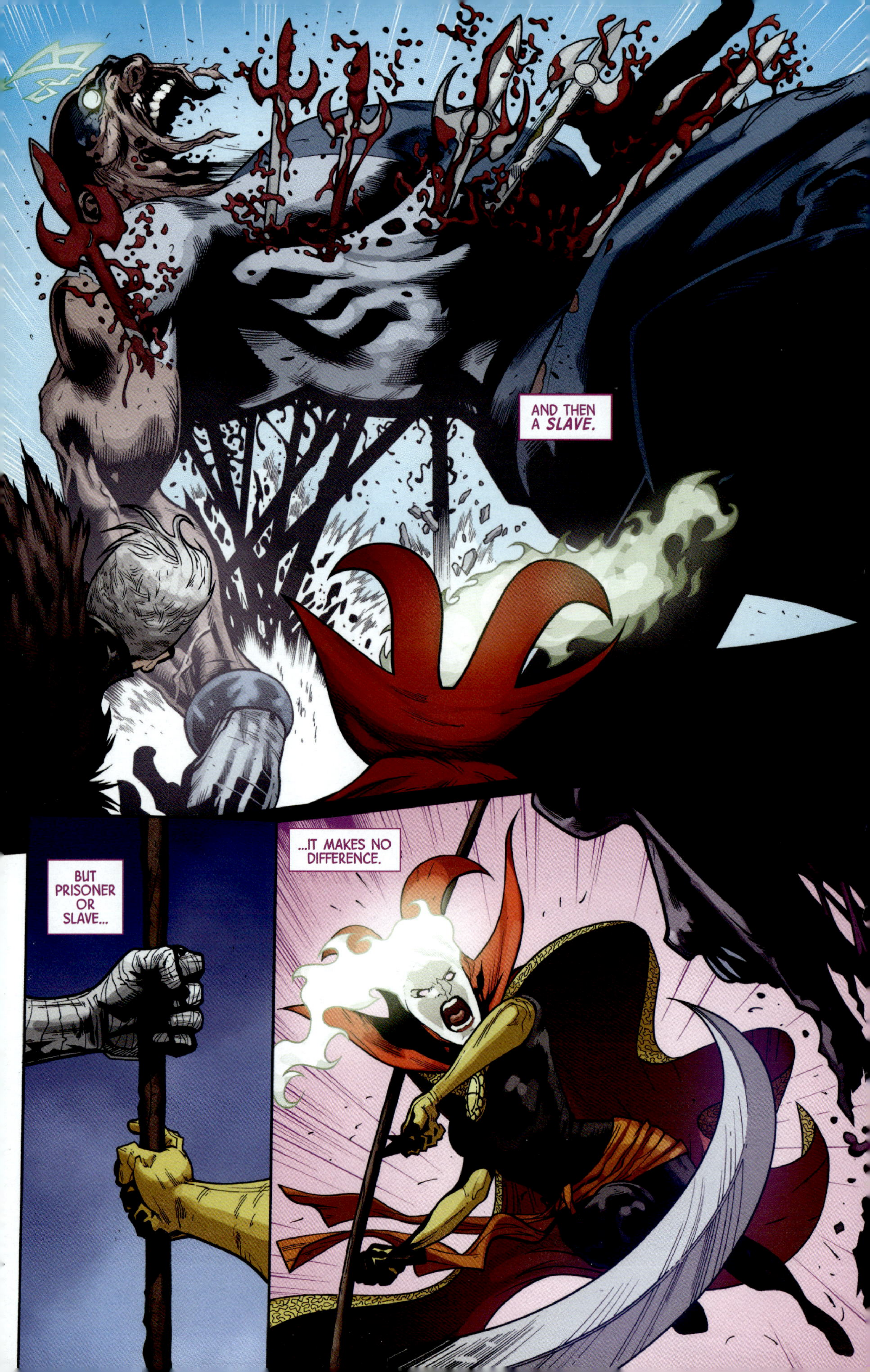
AND THEN A *SLAVE.*
BUT PRISONER OR SLAVE...
...IT MAKES NO DIFFERENCE.

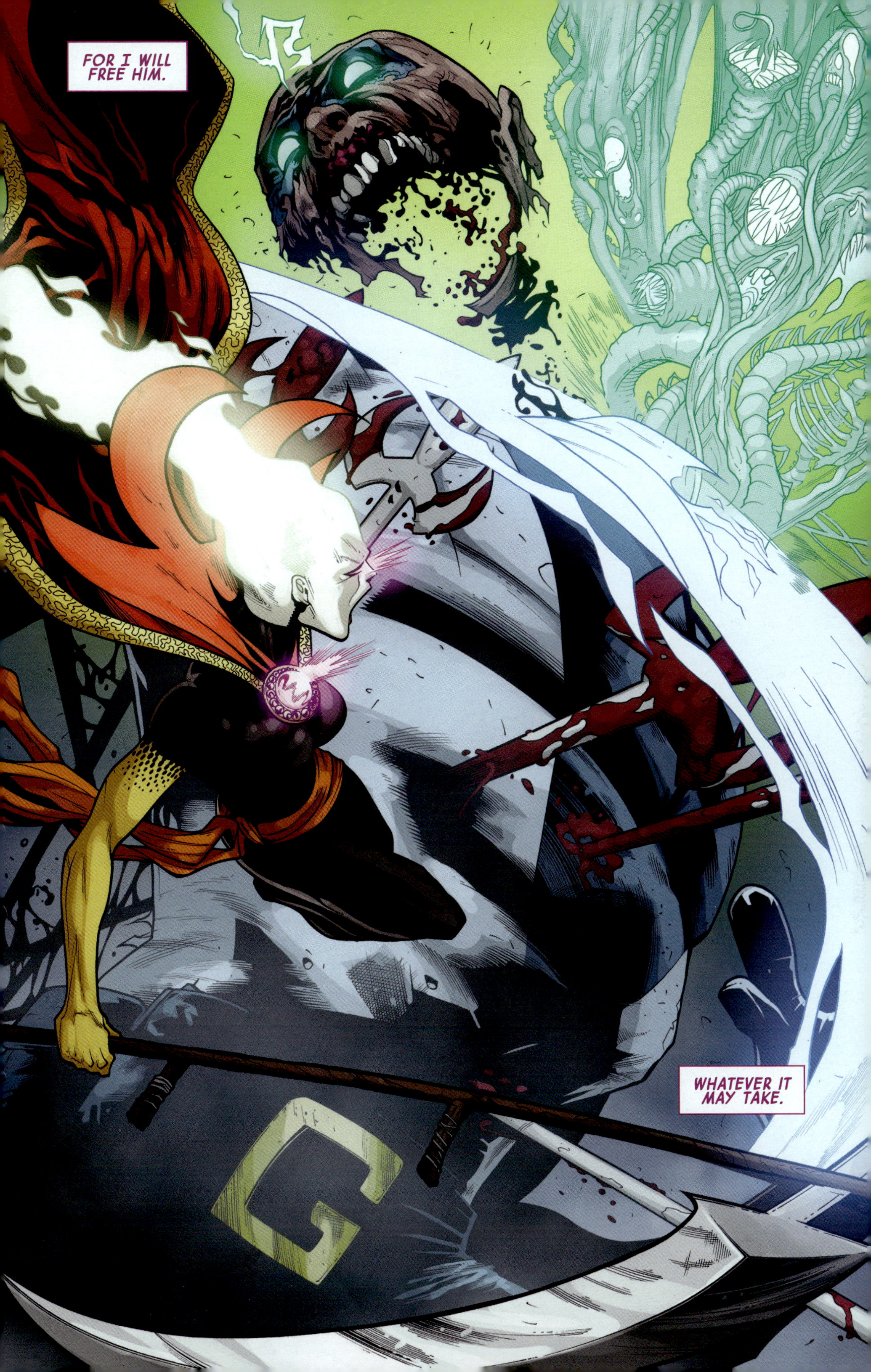
FOR I WILL FREE HIM.
WHATEVER IT MAY TAKE.

IT IS DONE.
DAMN IT, STEPHEN--
--DO YOU HAVE ANY IDEA HOW MUCH I'VE MISSED YOU?
CLEA, NO--
WHAT--?
WE CANNOT *TOUCH,* MY LOVE.
THINK ABOUT IT.
YOU ARE THE SORCERER SUPREME. YOU ARE *LIFE,* BECAUSE MAGIC IS *LIFE.*
I AM THE HARVESTMAN. AND I BELONG TO *DEATH* AND AM *SUFFUSED* WITH HER COLD POWER.
OUR MAGICS ARE IN *OPPOSITION.*
WE ARE POSITIVE AND NEGATIVE. MATTER AND ANTIMATTER.
YOUR TOUCH IS THE BEATING HEART OF THE WORLD, AND I'VE NEVER WISHED FOR ANYTHING MORE THAN IT.
BUT MINE IS THE CHILL OF GRAVEYARD MIST.
TO BRING THOSE TWO POWERFUL MAGICS INTO CONTACT WITH ONE ANOTHER COULD BE... DISASTROUS.

AND THIS IS WHY YOU DID NOT REVEAL YOURSELF TO ME?
YES, THOUGH IT BROKE MY HEART TO DO SO.
AND AS I SAID BEFORE-- I COULD NOT BRING YOU ANY MORE PAIN IF I FAILED IN MY MISSION.
AS MY MISSION IS THE RETURN OF MY HUSBAND, THEN I AM WITH YOU.
TELL ME OF OUR MISSION, MY LOVE.
THE REVENANTS.
DEATH IS BEING DISRESPECTED, AND SHE WILL HAVE NO MORE OF IT. SHE MADE ME AN OFFER--TO RE-CREATE ME AS HER AGENT IN ORDER TO END THE REVENANT MENACE.
IF I SUCCEED IN ENDING THIS AFFRONT TO HER POWER...
...THEN I WILL HAVE EARNED MY RETURN.
TO LIFE. TO YOU.

NO!
NO, IT CANNOT BE!
...CLEA?
MY MOTHER TOLD ME THAT I HAD TERRIBLE TASTE IN MEN JUST THE OTHER NIGHT AND YOU...YOU PROVE HER, UMAR THE UNRELENTING, RIGHT?!
I DON'T--
YOU.
YOU STUBBORN, FOOLISH, PROUD--
YOU WOULD RATHER DO ALL THIS ON YOUR OWN THAN ASK ME FOR HELP? ASK WONG FOR HELP?
ALL OUT OF CONCERN FOR MY FEELINGS?
I HAVE KNOWN HURT, STEPHEN STRANGE.
SOME OF IT FROM YOUR OWN ACTIONS.
BUT I AM THE SORCERER SUPREME OF EARTH AND THE DARK DIMENSION.
AND I DO NOT NEED YOUR PROTECTION.
I ONLY NEED YOU.

ENOUGH OF THIS. IT IS TIME YOU CAME HOME, MY LOVE.
CALL IT A "DIPLOMATIC MISSION" TO YOUR COLD MISTRESS IF YOU MUST.
YOU AND WONG AND I... WE WILL SCHEME, AND WE WILL PLAN.
AND WE WILL DRINK SOME WINE, AND YOU WILL PET POOR BATS, WHO HAS BEEN INCONSOLABLE.
AND WE WILL ELIMINATE THESE REVENANTS TOGETHER, AND I WILL HAVE YOU BACK.
BECAUSE THE SORCERER SUPREME AND WARLORD OF MANHATTAN DOES NOT LET ANYONE, EVEN DEATH, TELL HER WHOM SHE MAY AND MAY NOT TOUCH.

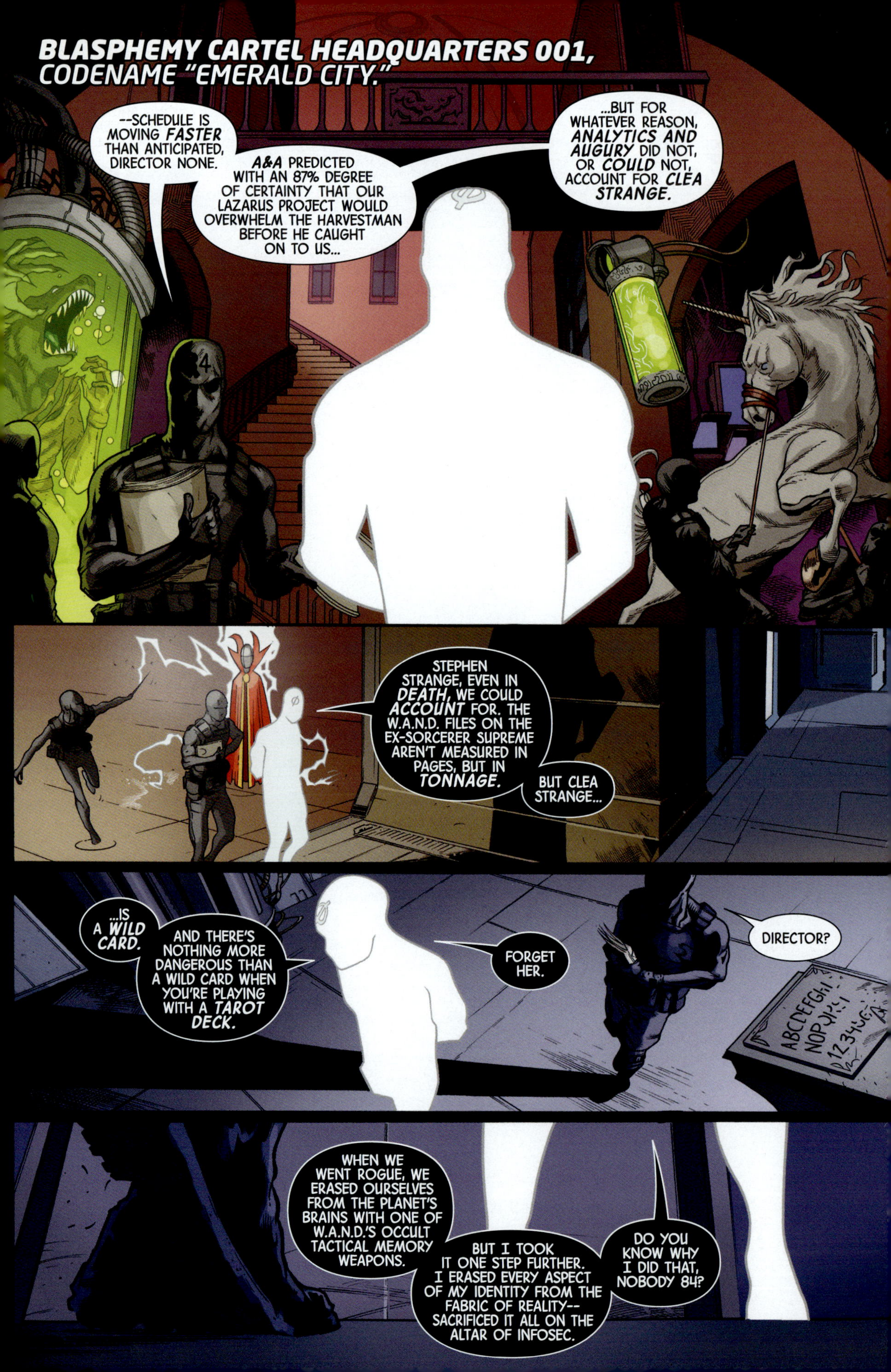
BLASPHEMY CARTEL HEADQUARTERS 001, CODENAME "EMERALD CITY."
--SCHEDULE IS MOVING FASTER THAN ANTICIPATED, DIRECTOR NONE.
A&A PREDICTED WITH AN 87% DEGREE OF CERTAINTY THAT OUR LAZARUS PROJECT WOULD OVERWHELM THE HARVESTMAN BEFORE HE CAUGHT ON TO US...
...BUT FOR WHATEVER REASON, ANALYTICS AND AUGURY DID NOT, OR COULD NOT, ACCOUNT FOR CLEA STRANGE.
STEPHEN STRANGE, EVEN IN DEATH, WE COULD ACCOUNT FOR. THE W.A.N.D. FILES ON THE EX-SORCERER SUPREME AREN'T MEASURED IN PAGES, BUT IN TONNAGE.
BUT CLEA STRANGE...
...IS A WILD CARD.
AND THERE'S NOTHING MORE DANGEROUS THAN A WILD CARD WHEN YOU'RE PLAYING WITH A TAROT DECK.
FORGET HER.
DIRECTOR?
WHEN WE WENT ROGUE, WE ERASED OURSELVES FROM THE PLANET'S BRAINS WITH ONE OF W.A.N.D.'S OCCULT TACTICAL MEMORY WEAPONS.
BUT I TOOK IT ONE STEP FURTHER. I ERASED EVERY ASPECT OF MY IDENTITY FROM THE FABRIC OF REALITY-- SACRIFICED IT ALL ON THE ALTAR OF INFOSEC.
DO YOU KNOW WHY I DID THAT, NOBODY 84?

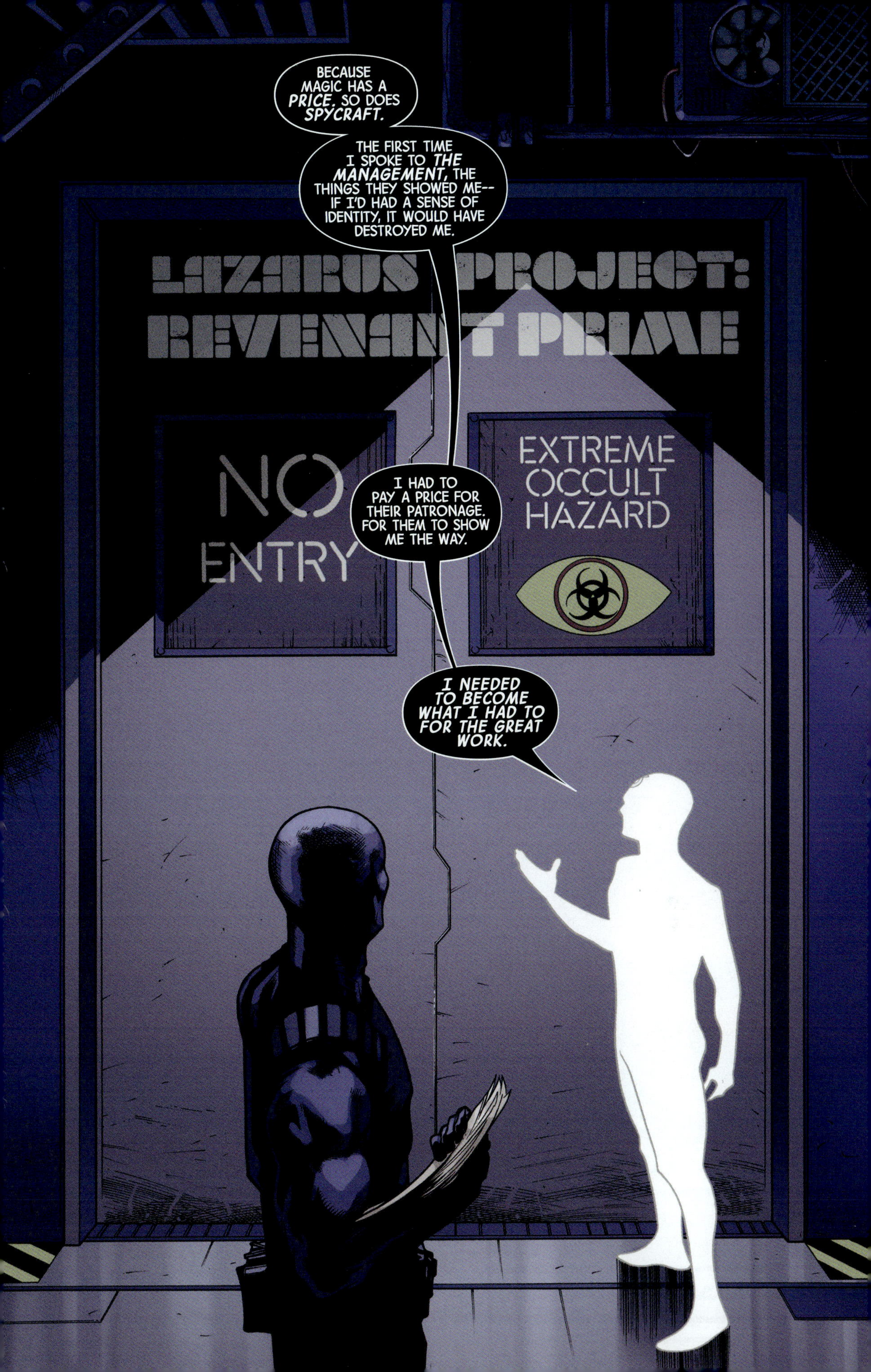
BECAUSE MAGIC HAS A PRICE. SO DOES SPYCRAFT.
THE FIRST TIME I SPOKE TO THE MANAGEMENT, THE THINGS THEY SHOWED ME-- IF I'D HAD A SENSE OF IDENTITY, IT WOULD HAVE DESTROYED ME.
LAZARUS PROJECT: REVENANT PRIME
NO ENTRY
EXTREME OCCULT HAZARD
I HAD TO PAY A PRICE FOR THEIR PATRONAGE. FOR THEM TO SHOW ME THE WAY.
I NEEDED TO BECOME WHAT I HAD TO FOR THE GREAT WORK.

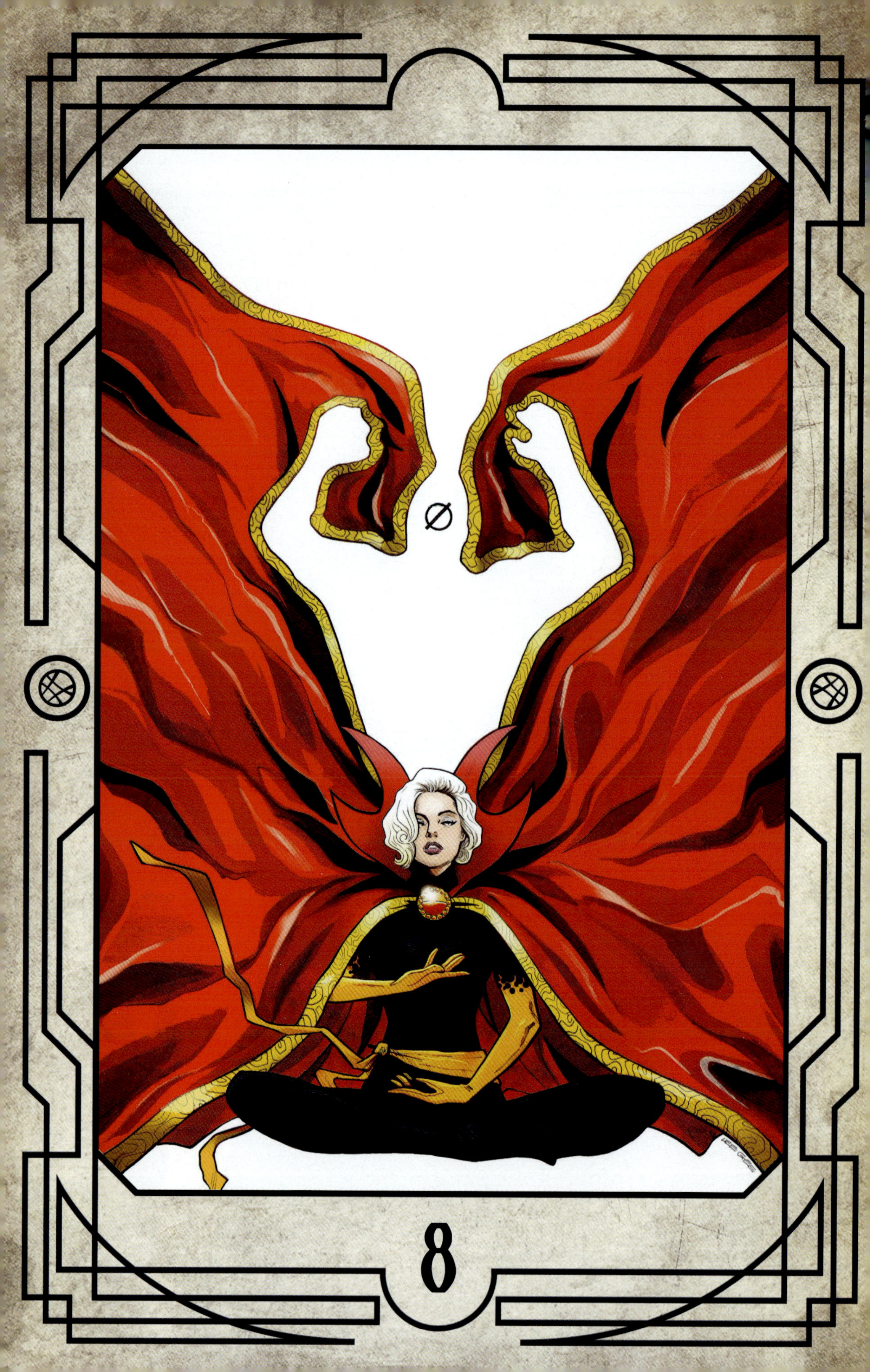
8

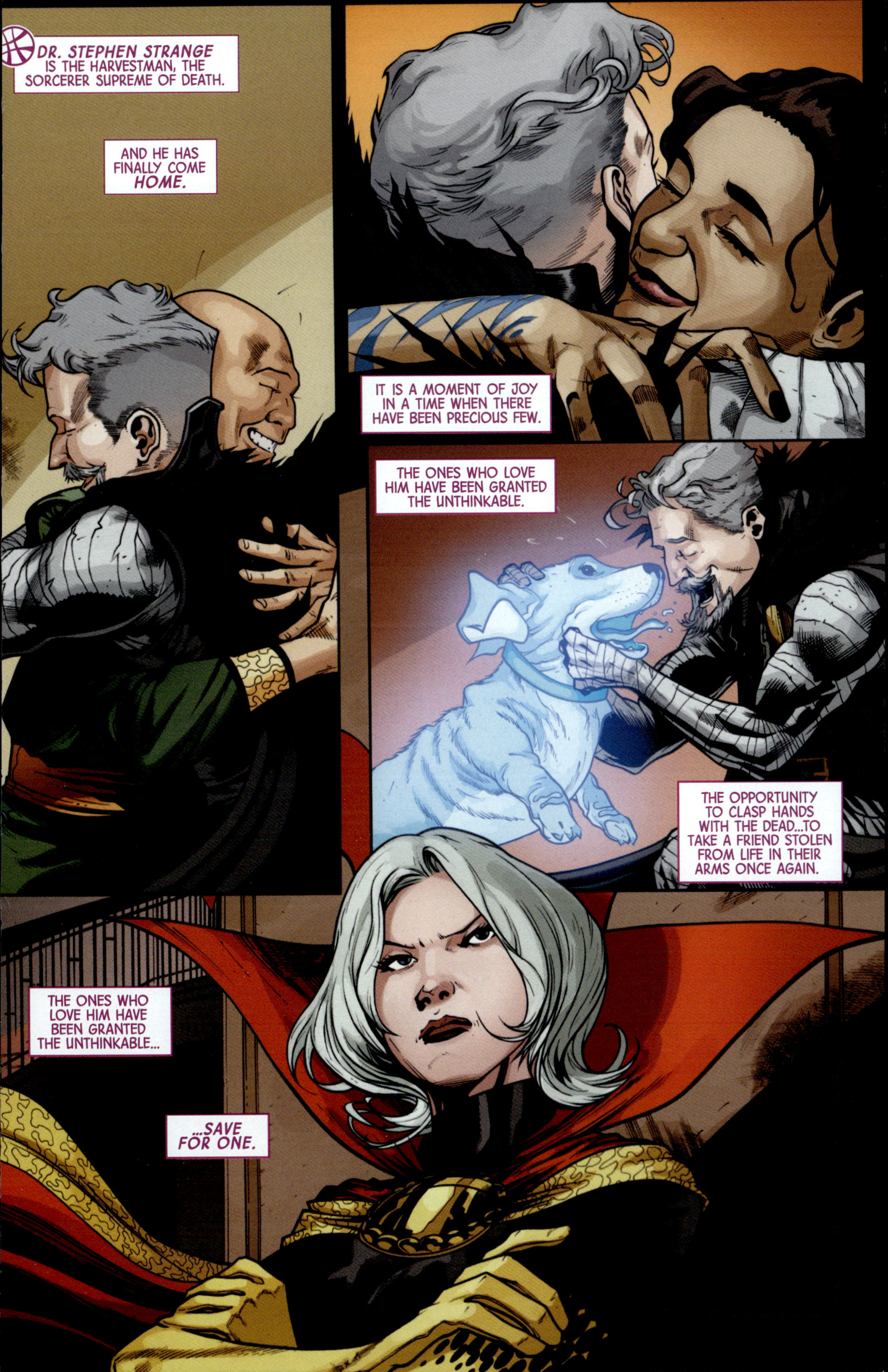
DR. STEPHEN STRANGE IS THE HARVESTMAN, THE SORCERER SUPREME OF DEATH.
AND HE HAS FINALLY COME HOME.
IT IS A MOMENT OF JOY IN A TIME WHEN THERE HAVE BEEN PRECIOUS FEW.
THE ONES WHO LOVE HIM HAVE BEEN GRANTED THE UNTHINKABLE.
THE OPPORTUNITY TO CLASP HANDS WITH THE DEAD...TO TAKE A FRIEND STOLEN FROM LIFE IN THEIR ARMS ONCE AGAIN.
THE ONES WHO LOVE HIM HAVE BEEN GRANTED THE UNTHINKABLE...
...SAVE FOR ONE.

FOR THE SORCERER SUPREME IS OF LIFE...
...AND THE HARVESTMAN BELONGS TO DEATH.
IF THOSE OPPOSITE ENERGIES, EACH ANATHEMA TO ONE ANOTHER, WERE TO TOUCH, TO COME IN CONTACT...
...THE BAREST BRUSH OF LIPS ON LIPS, ONE HAND FURTIVELY SEEKING THE ONE IT FIT BEST IN...
...THE RESULT WOULD BE CATASTROPHE.
FURTHER JOYOUS REUNIONS WILL HAVE TO WAIT, I FEAR.
WONG.
PLEASE TELL ME WHO THIS IS YOU'VE INVITED TO OUR WAR COUNCIL. FOR MAKE NO MISTAKE--
--WE ARE AT WAR.
MY APOLOGIES, CLEA. THIS IS--

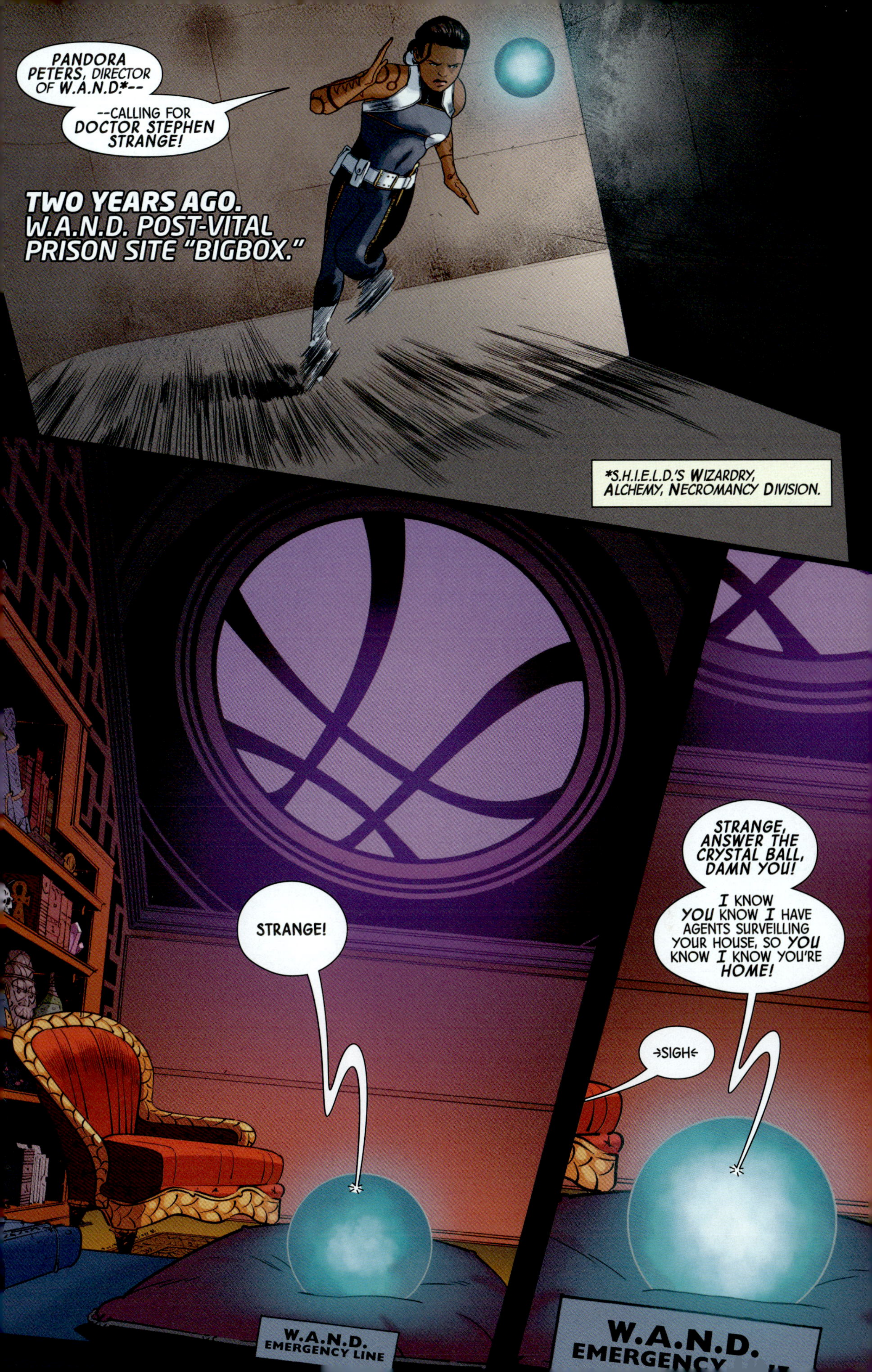
PANDORA PETERS, DIRECTOR OF W.A.N.D.*--
--CALLING FOR DOCTOR STEPHEN STRANGE!
TWO YEARS AGO. W.A.N.D. POST-VITAL PRISON SITE "BIGBOX."
*S.H.I.E.L.D.'S WIZARDRY, ALCHEMY, NECROMANCY DIVISION.
STRANGE!
W.A.N.D. EMERGENCY LINE
STRANGE, ANSWER THE CRYSTAL BALL, DAMN YOU!
I KNOW YOU KNOW I HAVE AGENTS SURVEILLING YOUR HOUSE, SO YOU KNOW I KNOW YOU'RE HOME!
SIGH
W.A.N.D. EMERGENCY

YES, DIRECTOR PETERS? WHAT CAN I DO FOR YOU?
WE'VE GOT A SITUATION AT BIGBOX, STRANGE!
IS THAT NOT NORMAL? YOU ARE, OF COURSE, IN A DANGEROUS LINE OF WORK.
YOU'RE GOING TO MAKE ME SAY IT, AREN'T YOU?
NO ONE CAN MAKE YOU SAY ANYTHING, DIRECTOR PETERS.
THIS IS BECAUSE OF THAT THING IN HOBOKEN.
A "THING" IN HOBOKEN?
YOU GOT AN OFFICIAL, FORMAL APOLOGY! FROM S.H.I.E.L.D. AND EVERYTHING! ON STATIONARY!
AH. BUT I DIDN'T RECEIVE AN APOLOGY FROM W.A.N.D., AND I DIDN'T RECEIVE AN APOLOGY FROM THE COMMANDING OFFICER ON THE HOBOKEN INCIDENT...YOU.
RRRRRRRR...

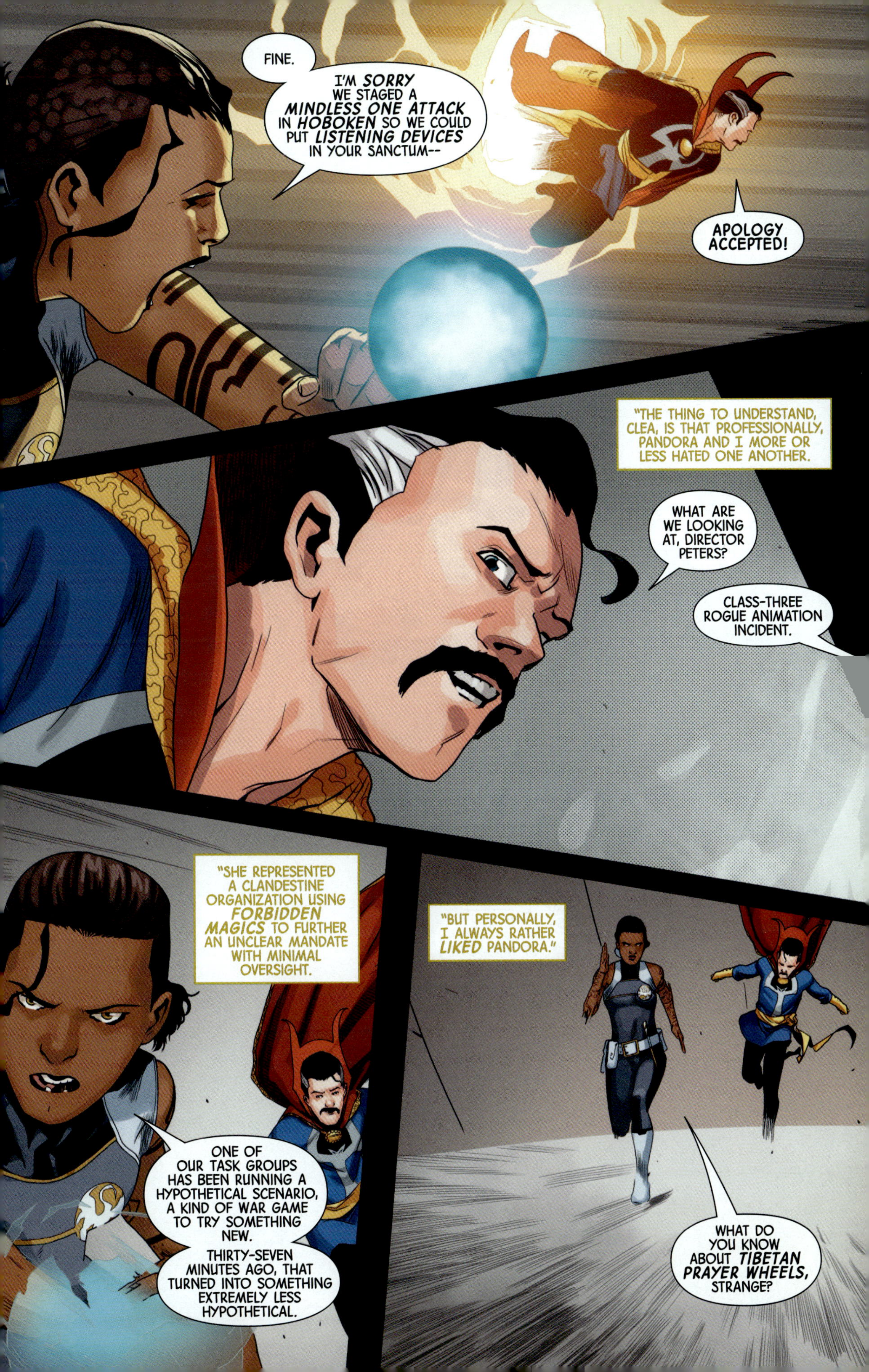
FINE.
I'M SORRY WE STAGED A MINDLESS ONE ATTACK IN HOBOKEN SO WE COULD PUT LISTENING DEVICES IN YOUR SANCTUM--
APOLOGY ACCEPTED!
"THE THING TO UNDERSTAND, CLEA, IS THAT PROFESSIONALLY, PANDORA AND I MORE OR LESS HATED ONE ANOTHER.
WHAT ARE WE LOOKING AT, DIRECTOR PETERS?
CLASS-THREE ROGUE ANIMATION INCIDENT.
"SHE REPRESENTED A CLANDESTINE ORGANIZATION USING FORBIDDEN MAGICS TO FURTHER AN UNCLEAR MANDATE WITH MINIMAL OVERSIGHT.
ONE OF OUR TASK GROUPS HAS BEEN RUNNING A HYPOTHETICAL SCENARIO, A KIND OF WAR GAME TO TRY SOMETHING NEW.
THIRTY-SEVEN MINUTES AGO, THAT TURNED INTO SOMETHING EXTREMELY LESS HYPOTHETICAL.
"BUT PERSONALLY, I ALWAYS RATHER LIKED PANDORA."
WHAT DO YOU KNOW ABOUT TIBETAN PRAYER WHEELS, STRANGE?

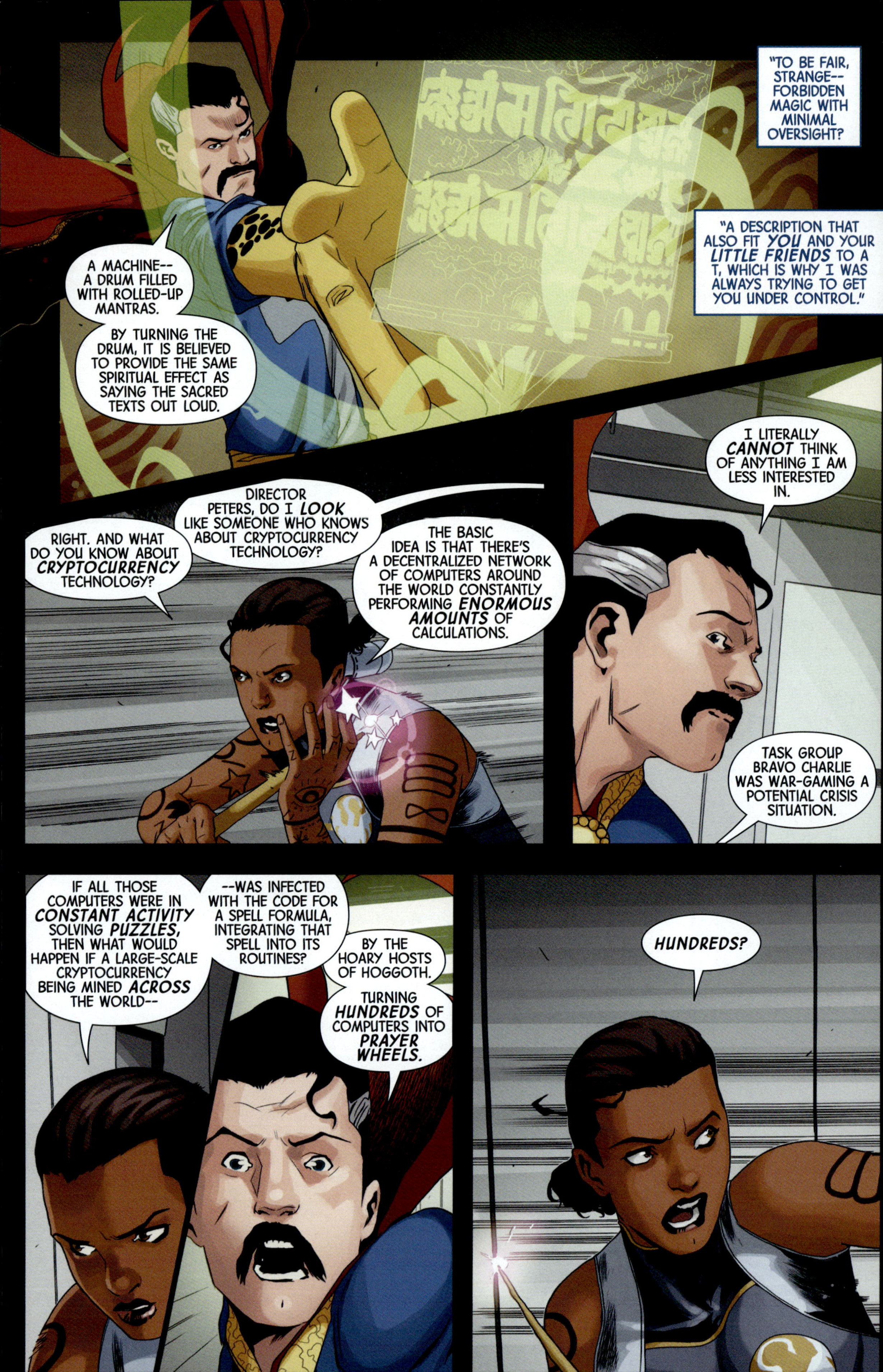
"TO BE FAIR, STRANGE-- FORBIDDEN MAGIC WITH MINIMAL OVERSIGHT?
"A DESCRIPTION THAT ALSO FIT YOU AND YOUR LITTLE FRIENDS TO A T, WHICH IS WHY I WAS ALWAYS TRYING TO GET YOU UNDER CONTROL."
A MACHINE-- A DRUM FILLED WITH ROLLED-UP MANTRAS.
BY TURNING THE DRUM, IT IS BELIEVED TO PROVIDE THE SAME SPIRITUAL EFFECT AS SAYING THE SACRED TEXTS OUT LOUD.
RIGHT. AND WHAT DO YOU KNOW ABOUT CRYPTOCURRENCY TECHNOLOGY?
DIRECTOR PETERS, DO I LOOK LIKE SOMEONE WHO KNOWS ABOUT CRYPTOCURRENCY TECHNOLOGY?
THE BASIC IDEA IS THAT THERE'S A DECENTRALIZED NETWORK OF COMPUTERS AROUND THE WORLD CONSTANTLY PERFORMING ENORMOUS AMOUNTS OF CALCULATIONS.
I LITERALLY CANNOT THINK OF ANYTHING I AM LESS INTERESTED IN.
TASK GROUP BRAVO CHARLIE WAS WAR-GAMING A POTENTIAL CRISIS SITUATION.
IF ALL THOSE COMPUTERS WERE IN CONSTANT ACTIVITY SOLVING PUZZLES, THEN WHAT WOULD HAPPEN IF A LARGE-SCALE CRYPTOCURRENCY BEING MINED ACROSS THE WORLD--
--WAS INFECTED WITH THE CODE FOR A SPELL FORMULA, INTEGRATING THAT SPELL INTO ITS ROUTINES?
BY THE HOARY HOSTS OF HOGGOTH.
TURNING HUNDREDS OF COMPUTERS INTO PRAYER WHEELS.
HUNDREDS?

YOU'RE OFF BY A FEW ORDERS OF MAGNITUDE, DOC.
TASK GROUP BRAVO CHARLIE'S EXPERIMENT ACCIDENTALLY WENT LIVE.
THEIR SEANCE SPELL SPREAD ACROSS A WIDE BLOCKCHAIN NETWORK AND NOW EVERY PRISONER HERE IS AN UNDEAD MONSTER, POSSESSED BY SCREAMING-MAD GHOSTS.

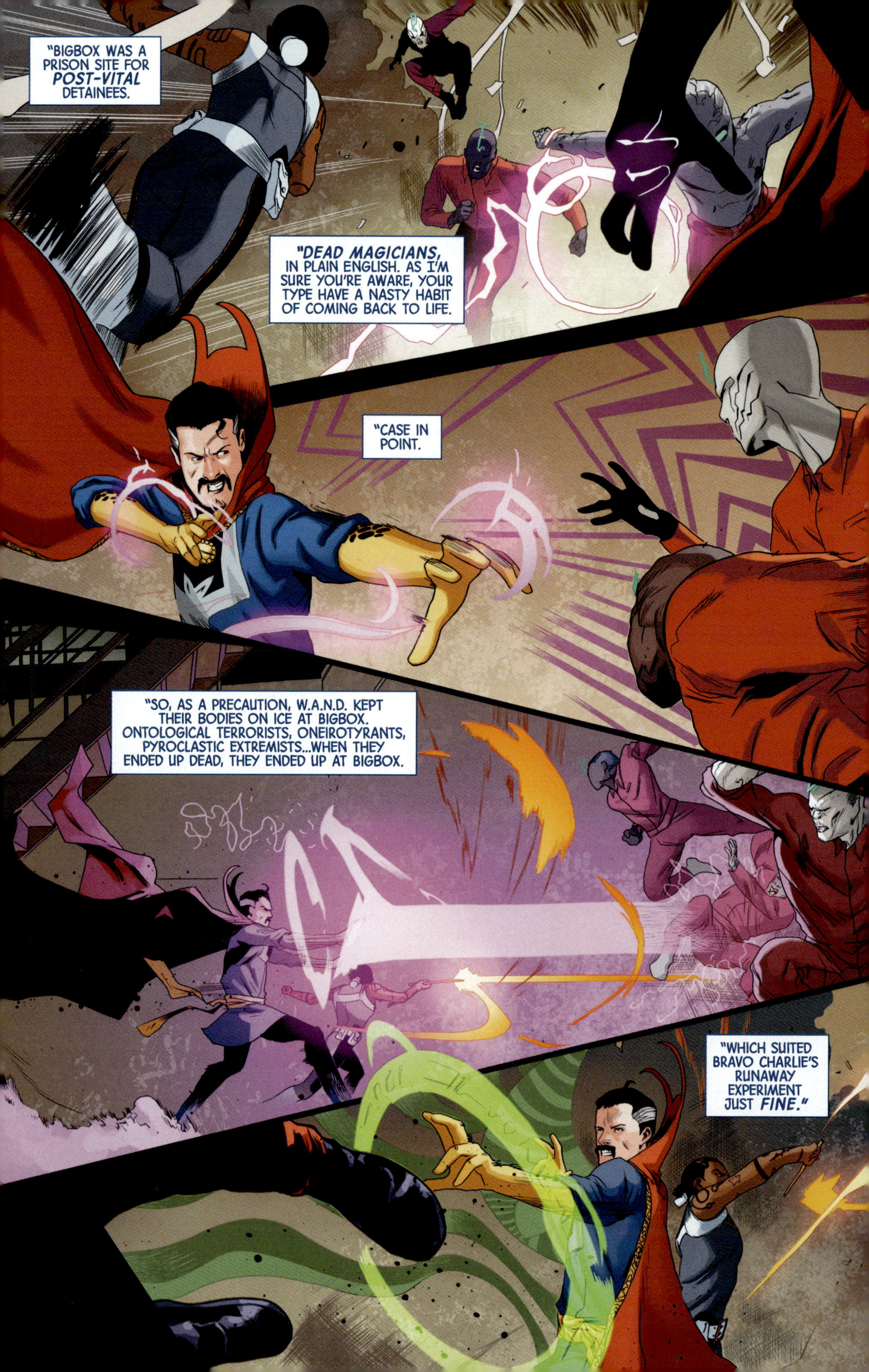
"BIGBOX WAS A PRISON SITE FOR *POST-VITAL* DETAINEES.
"*DEAD MAGICIANS,* IN PLAIN ENGLISH. AS I'M SURE YOU'RE AWARE, YOUR TYPE HAVE A NASTY HABIT OF COMING BACK TO LIFE.
"CASE IN POINT.
"SO, AS A PRECAUTION, W.A.N.D. KEPT THEIR BODIES ON ICE AT BIGBOX. ONTOLOGICAL TERRORISTS, ONEIROTYRANTS, PYROCLASTIC EXTREMISTS...WHEN THEY ENDED UP DEAD, THEY ENDED UP AT BIGBOX.
"WHICH SUITED BRAVO CHARLIE'S RUNAWAY EXPERIMENT JUST *FINE.*"

DIRECTOR PETERS, YOU NEED TO PULL YOUR PEOPLE OUT NOW.
YOU GOT A PLAN, DOC?
YES.
I'M GOING TO ACTIVATE BIGBOX'S FAIL-SAFE.
HOW DO YOU KNOW ABOUT THAT?!
YOU AREN'T THE ONLY ONE KEEPING AN EYE ON THINGS, DIRECTOR PETERS.

FINE. TAKE THIS COMMUNICATION CRYSTAL.
GOD, THIS IS GOING TO BE A BUDGETARY DISASTER.
THIS IS DIRECTOR PANDORA PETERS TO W.A.N.D. COMMAND/EMERALD CITY!
IMMEDIATE EMERGENCY SUMMONING FOR ALL W.A.N.D. PERSONNEL NOW!
GOOD LUCK, STRANGE.
PAFF
LUCK?
PFFT.
I AM A DOCTOR-- SKILL IS ALL I NEED.
SHIELD OF THE SERAPHIM!

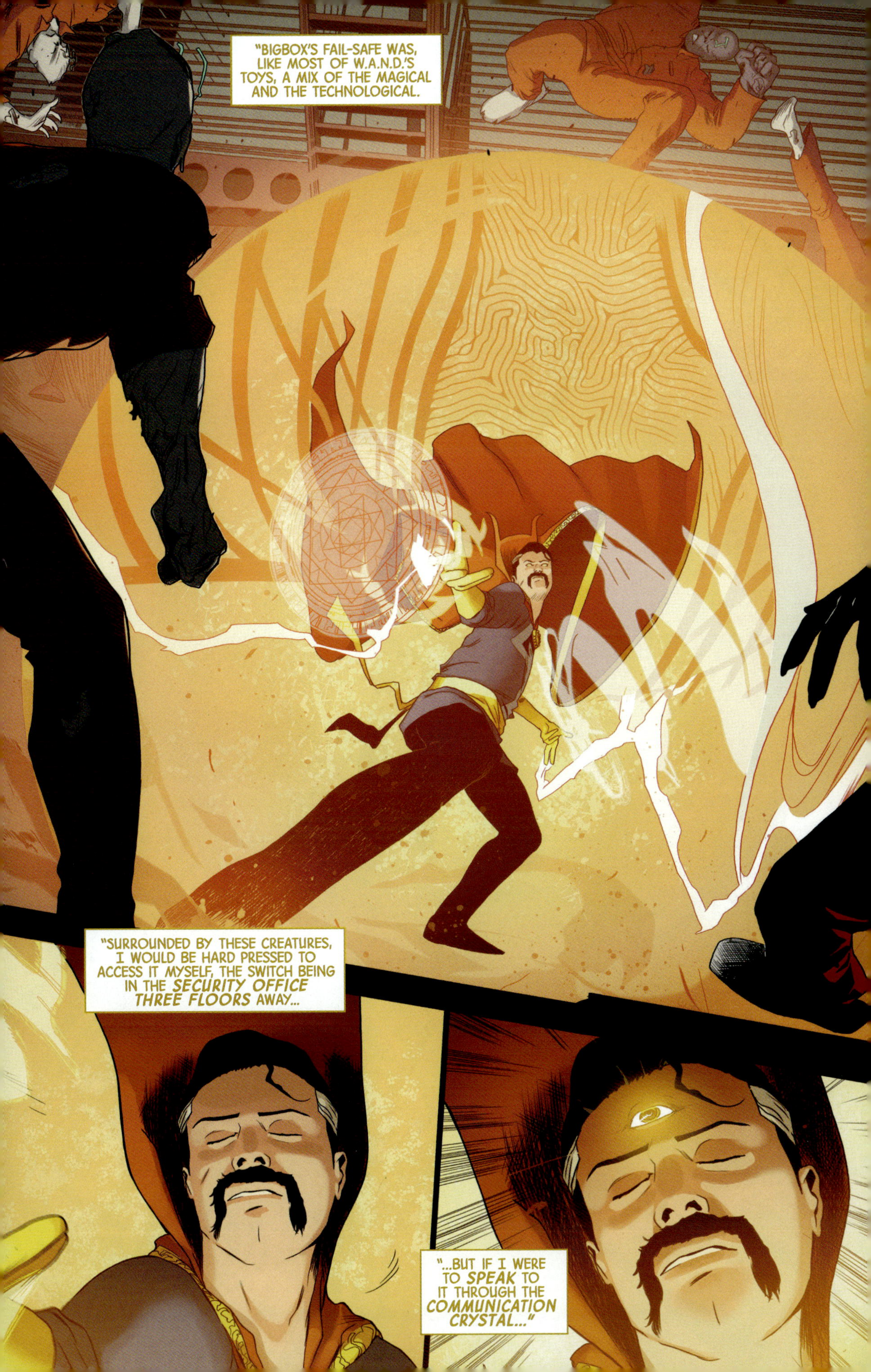
"BIGBOX'S FAIL-SAFE WAS, LIKE MOST OF W.A.N.D.'S TOYS, A MIX OF THE MAGICAL AND THE TECHNOLOGICAL.
"SURROUNDED BY THESE CREATURES, I WOULD BE HARD PRESSED TO ACCESS IT MYSELF, THE SWITCH BEING IN THE SECURITY OFFICE THREE FLOORS AWAY...
"...BUT IF I WERE TO SPEAK TO IT THROUGH THE COMMUNICATION CRYSTAL..."

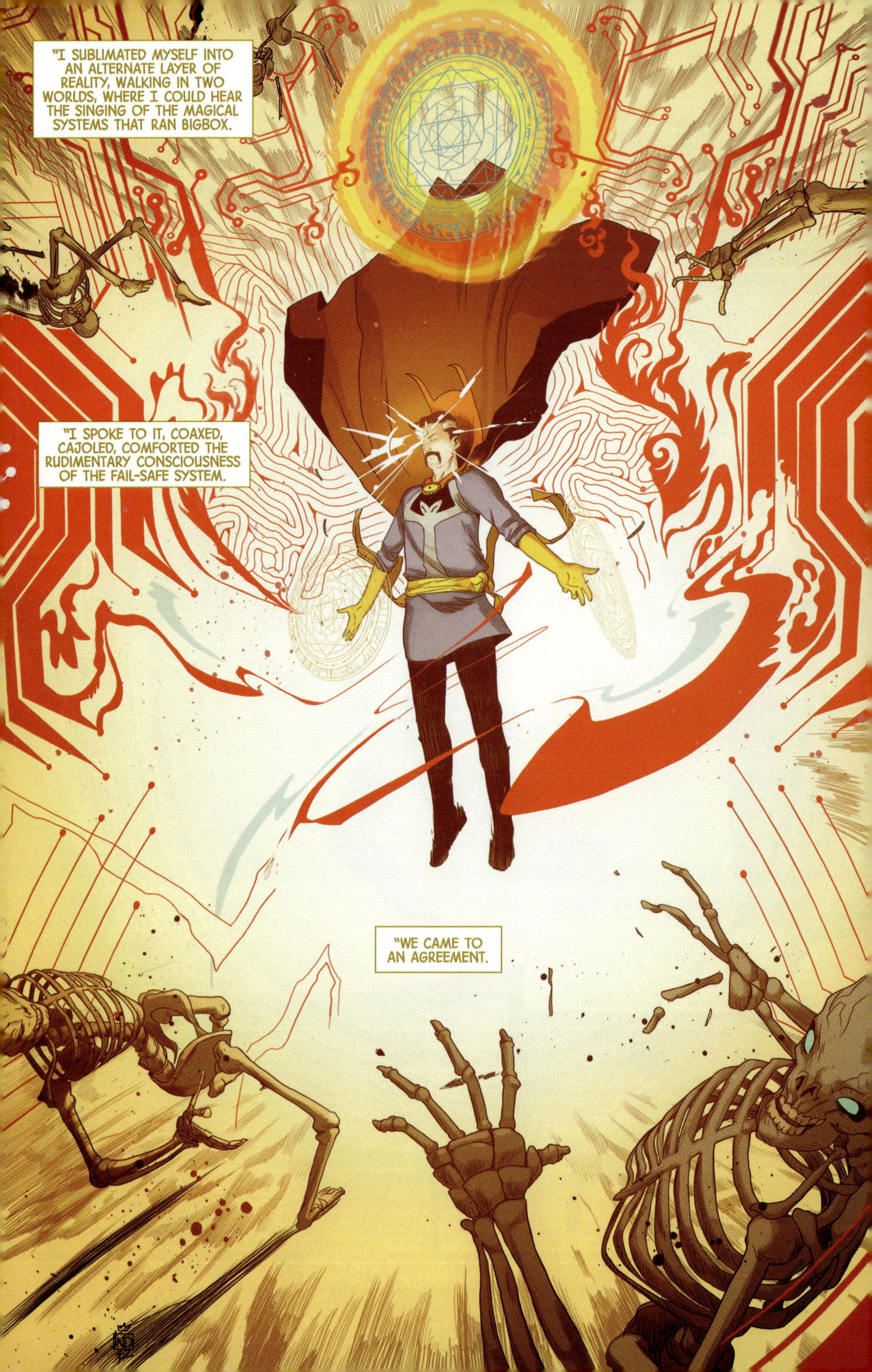
"I SUBLIMATED MYSELF INTO AN ALTERNATE LAYER OF REALITY, WALKING IN TWO WORLDS, WHERE I COULD HEAR THE SINGING OF THE MAGICAL SYSTEMS THAT RAN BIGBOX.
"I SPOKE TO IT, COAXED, CAJOLED, COMFORTED THE RUDIMENTARY CONSCIOUSNESS OF THE FAIL-SAFE SYSTEM.
"WE CAME TO AN AGREEMENT.

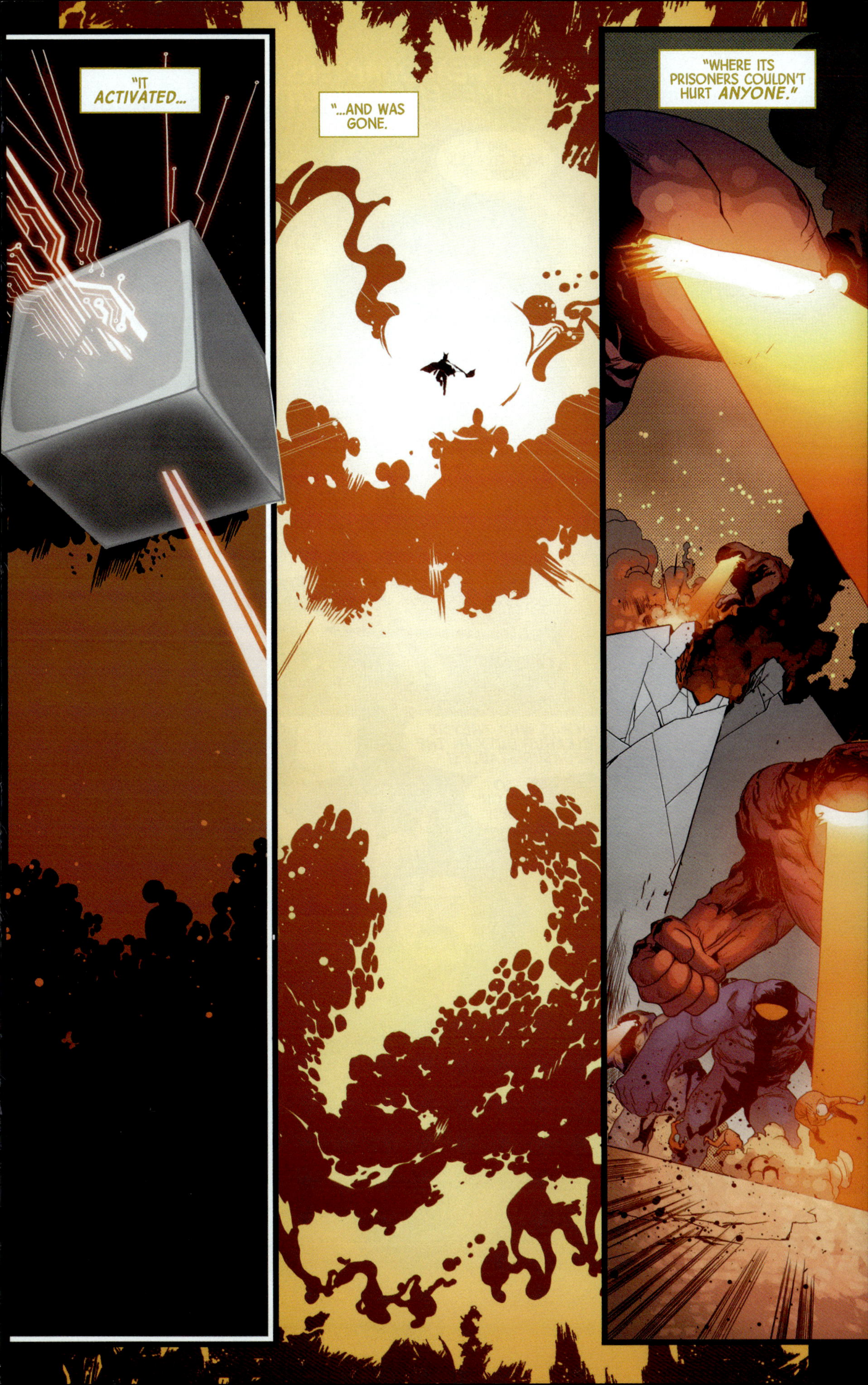
"IT ACTIVATED...
"...AND WAS GONE.
"WHERE ITS PRISONERS COULDN'T HURT ANYONE."

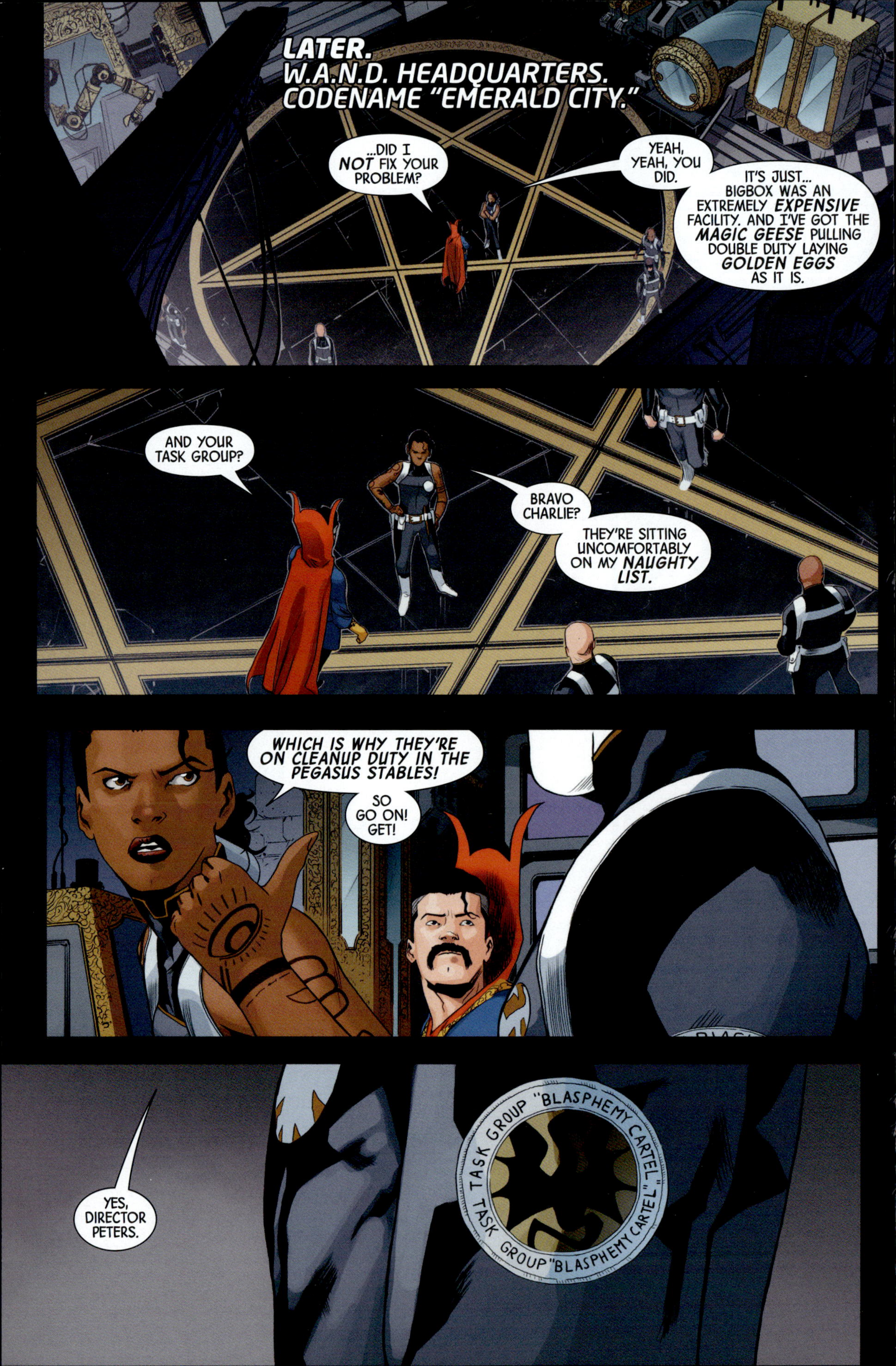
LATER.
W.A.N.D. HEADQUARTERS.
CODENAME "EMERALD CITY."
...DID I NOT FIX YOUR PROBLEM?
YEAH, YEAH, YOU DID.
IT'S JUST... BIGBOX WAS AN EXTREMELY EXPENSIVE FACILITY. AND I'VE GOT THE MAGIC GEESE PULLING DOUBLE DUTY LAYING GOLDEN EGGS AS IT IS.
AND YOUR TASK GROUP?
BRAVO CHARLIE?
THEY'RE SITTING UNCOMFORTABLY ON MY NAUGHTY LIST.
WHICH IS WHY THEY'RE ON CLEANUP DUTY IN THE PEGASUS STABLES!
SO GO ON! GET!
YES, DIRECTOR PETERS.
TASK GROUP "BLASPHEMY CARTEL"
TASK GROUP "BLASPHEMY CARTEL"

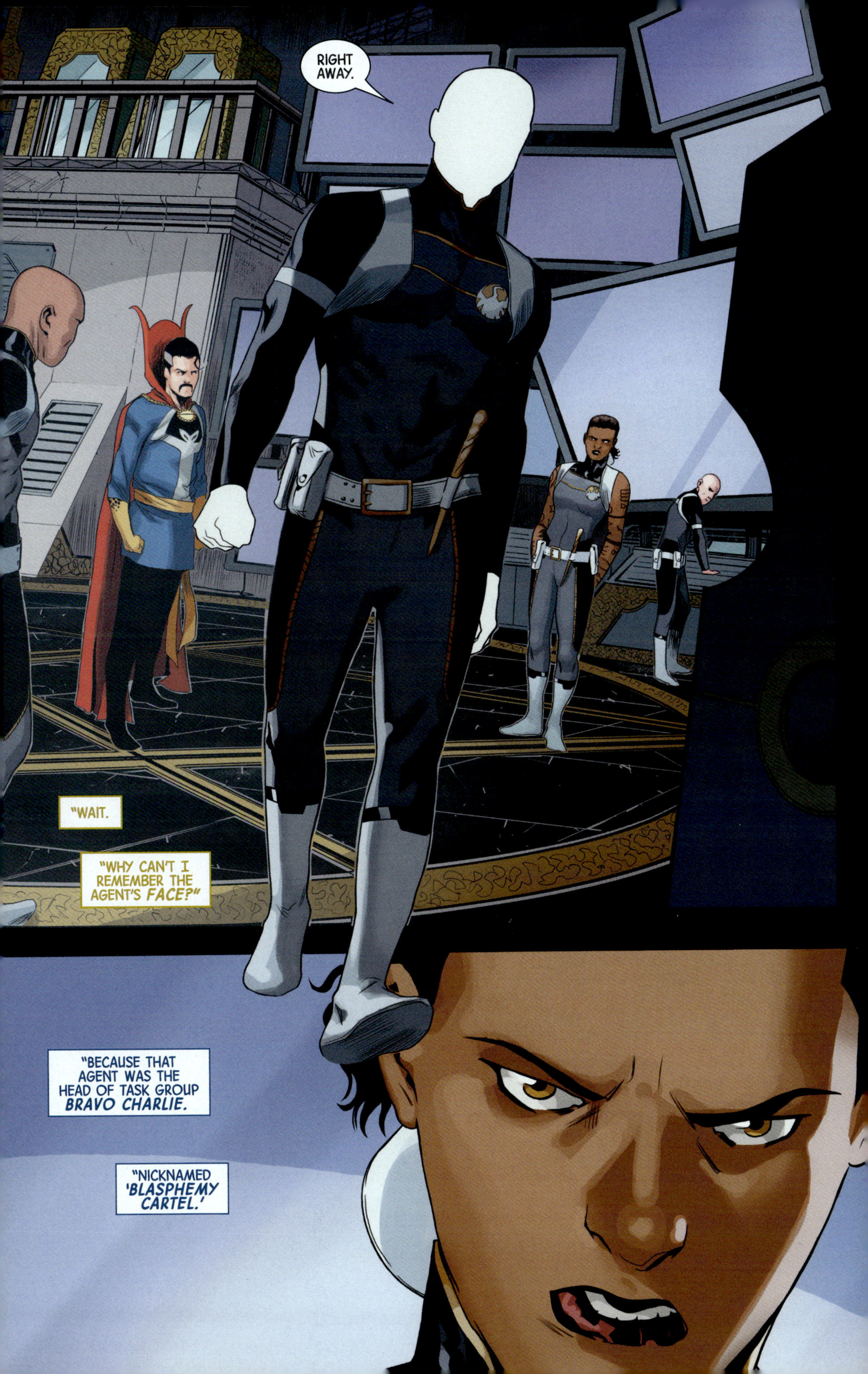
RIGHT AWAY.
"WAIT.
"WHY CAN'T I REMEMBER THE AGENT'S *FACE?*"
"BECAUSE THAT AGENT WAS THE HEAD OF TASK GROUP ***BRAVO CHARLIE.***
"NICKNAMED ***'BLASPHEMY CARTEL.'***

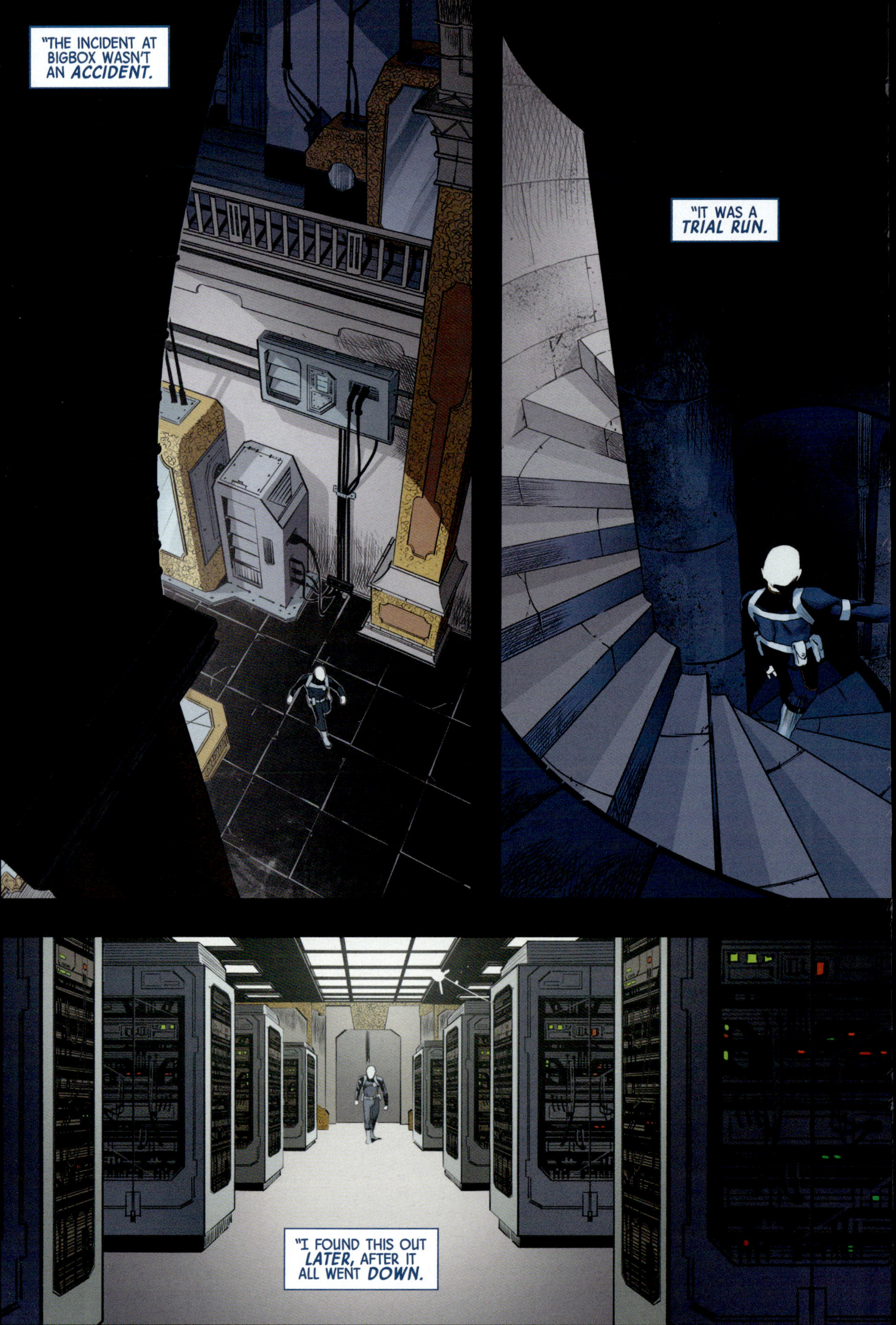
"THE INCIDENT AT BIGBOX WASN'T AN *ACCIDENT.*
"IT WAS A *TRIAL RUN.*
"I FOUND THIS OUT *LATER*, AFTER IT ALL WENT *DOWN.*

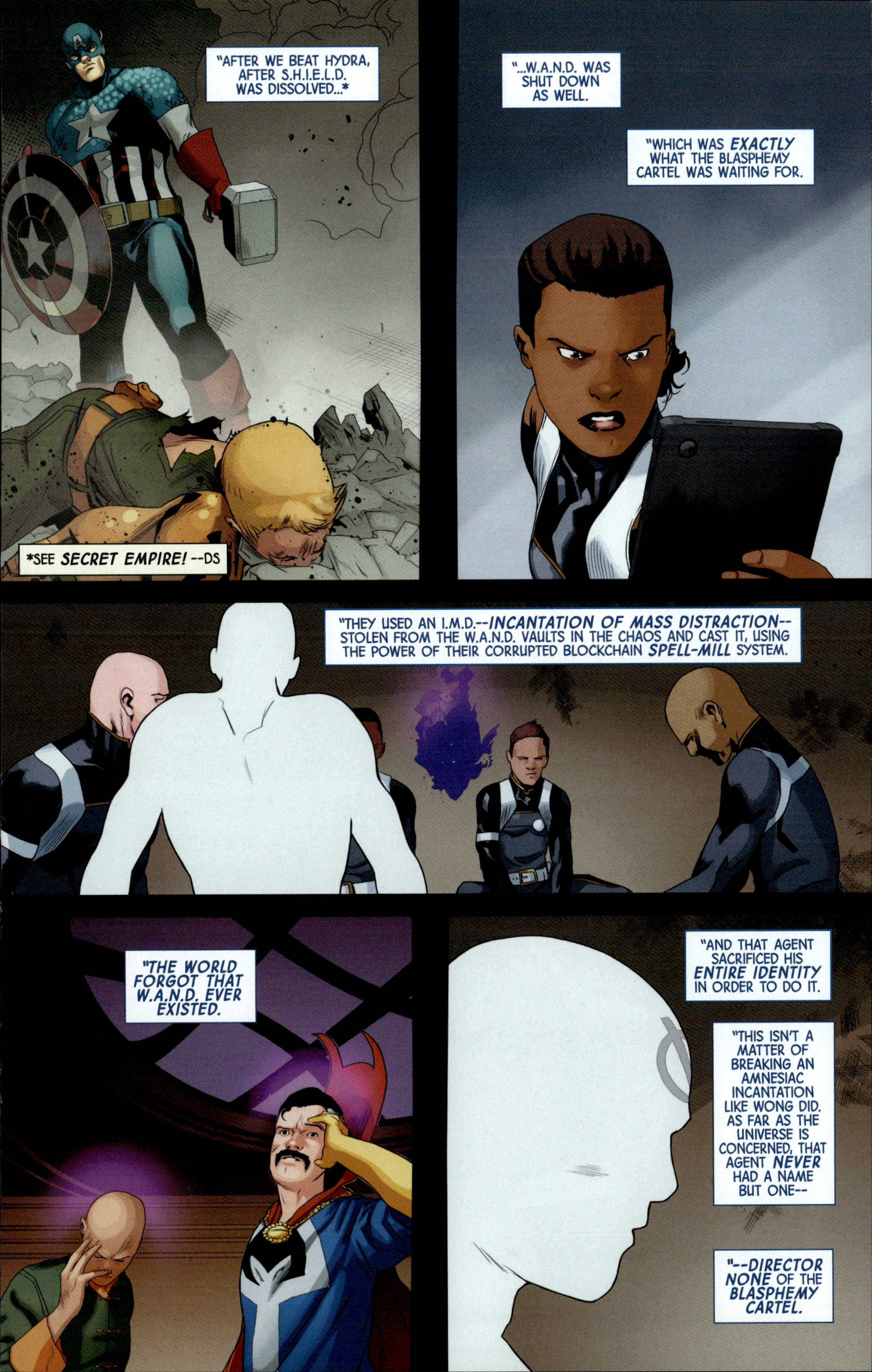
"AFTER WE BEAT HYDRA, AFTER S.H.I.E.L.D. WAS DISSOLVED...*
*SEE SECRET EMPIRE! --DS
"...W.A.N.D. WAS SHUT DOWN AS WELL.
"WHICH WAS EXACTLY WHAT THE BLASPHEMY CARTEL WAS WAITING FOR.
"THEY USED AN I.M.D.--INCANTATION OF MASS DISTRACTION--STOLEN FROM THE W.A.N.D. VAULTS IN THE CHAOS AND CAST IT, USING THE POWER OF THEIR CORRUPTED BLOCKCHAIN SPELL-MILL SYSTEM.
"THE WORLD FORGOT THAT W.A.N.D. EVER EXISTED.
"AND THAT AGENT SACRIFICED HIS ENTIRE IDENTITY IN ORDER TO DO IT.
"THIS ISN'T A MATTER OF BREAKING AN AMNESIAC INCANTATION LIKE WONG DID. AS FAR AS THE UNIVERSE IS CONCERNED, THAT AGENT NEVER HAD A NAME BUT ONE--
"--DIRECTOR NONE OF THE BLASPHEMY CARTEL.

"IN THE CONFUSION, THE BLASPHEMY CARTEL TOOK OVER THE REMAINING W.A.N.D. INFRASTRUCTURE, CONVERTING WHAT AGENTS IT COULD AND KILLING THOSE WHO RESISTED.
"AND NUMBER ONE ON THEIR KILL LIST?
"ME.

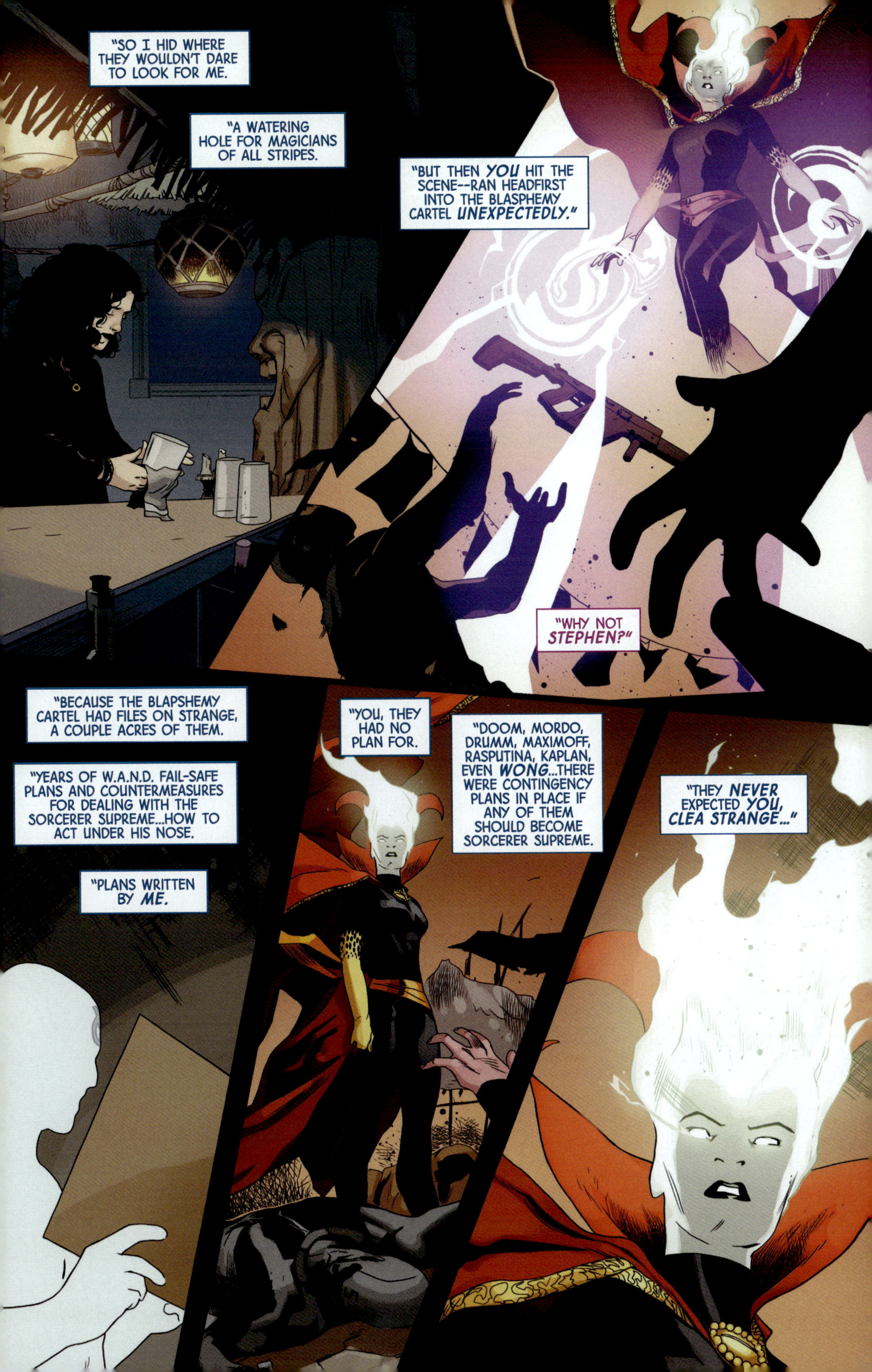
"SO I HID WHERE THEY WOULDN'T DARE TO LOOK FOR ME.
"A WATERING HOLE FOR MAGICIANS OF ALL STRIPES.
"BUT THEN YOU HIT THE SCENE--RAN HEADFIRST INTO THE BLASPHEMY CARTEL UNEXPECTEDLY."
"WHY NOT STEPHEN?"
"BECAUSE THE BLAPSHEMY CARTEL HAD FILES ON STRANGE, A COUPLE ACRES OF THEM.
"YEARS OF W.A.N.D. FAIL-SAFE PLANS AND COUNTERMEASURES FOR DEALING WITH THE SORCERER SUPREME...HOW TO ACT UNDER HIS NOSE.
"PLANS WRITTEN BY ME.
"YOU, THEY HAD NO PLAN FOR.
"DOOM, MORDO, DRUMM, MAXIMOFF, RASPUTINA, KAPLAN, EVEN WONG...THERE WERE CONTINGENCY PLANS IN PLACE IF ANY OF THEM SHOULD BECOME SORCERER SUPREME.
"THEY NEVER EXPECTED YOU, CLEA STRANGE..."

...THEY'RE CREATING THE REVENANTS THE SAME WAY THEY CREATED THEIR PROTOTYPES AT BIGBOX.
BUT I DON'T KNOW WHY.
BUT YOU DO KNOW SOMETHING, DON'T YOU, DIRECTOR PANDORA PETERS?
I DO.
I CAN SHOW YOU WHERE THEY'RE HEADQUARTERED.
I CAN GIVE YOU EMERALD CITY.

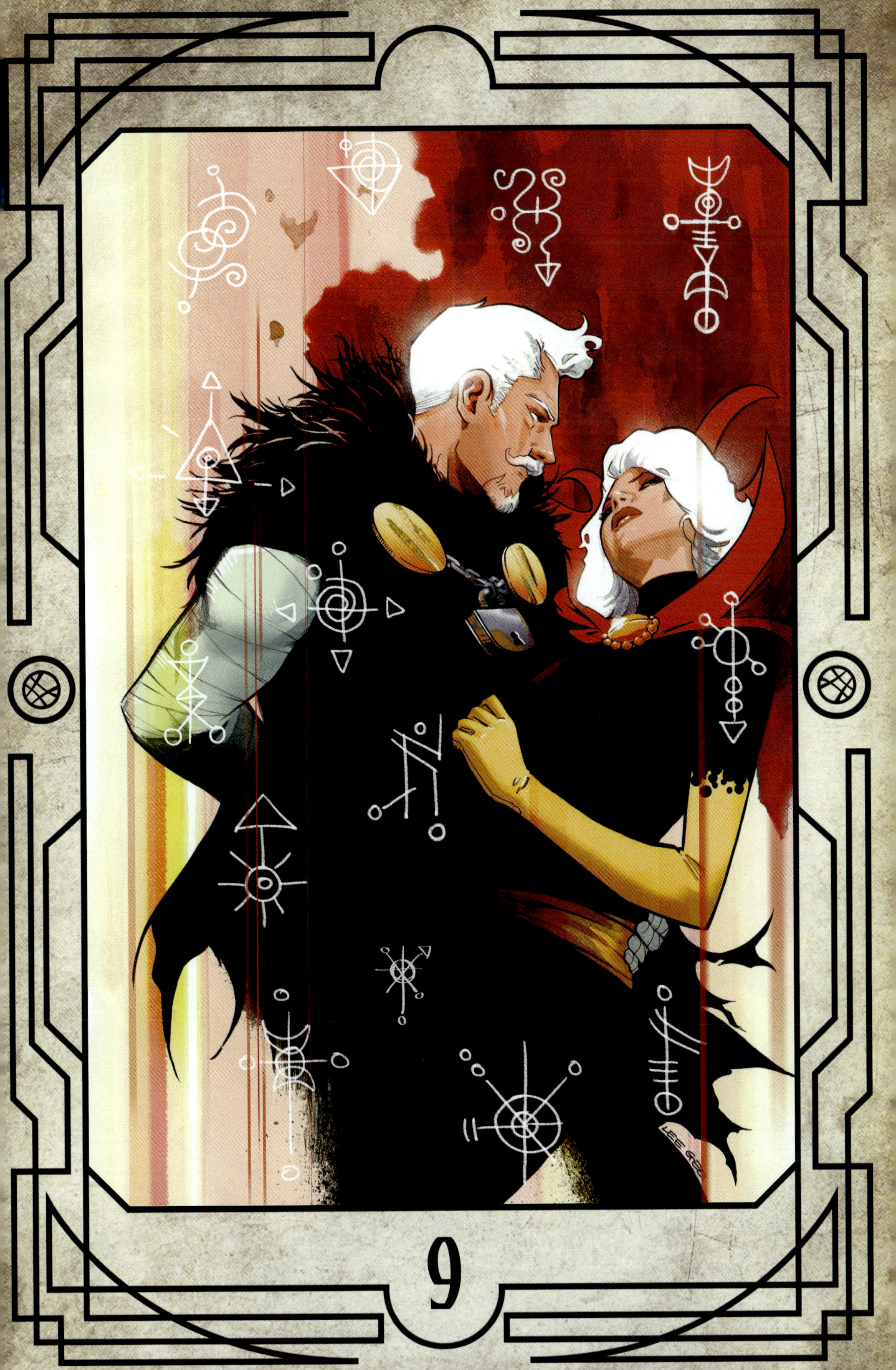
9

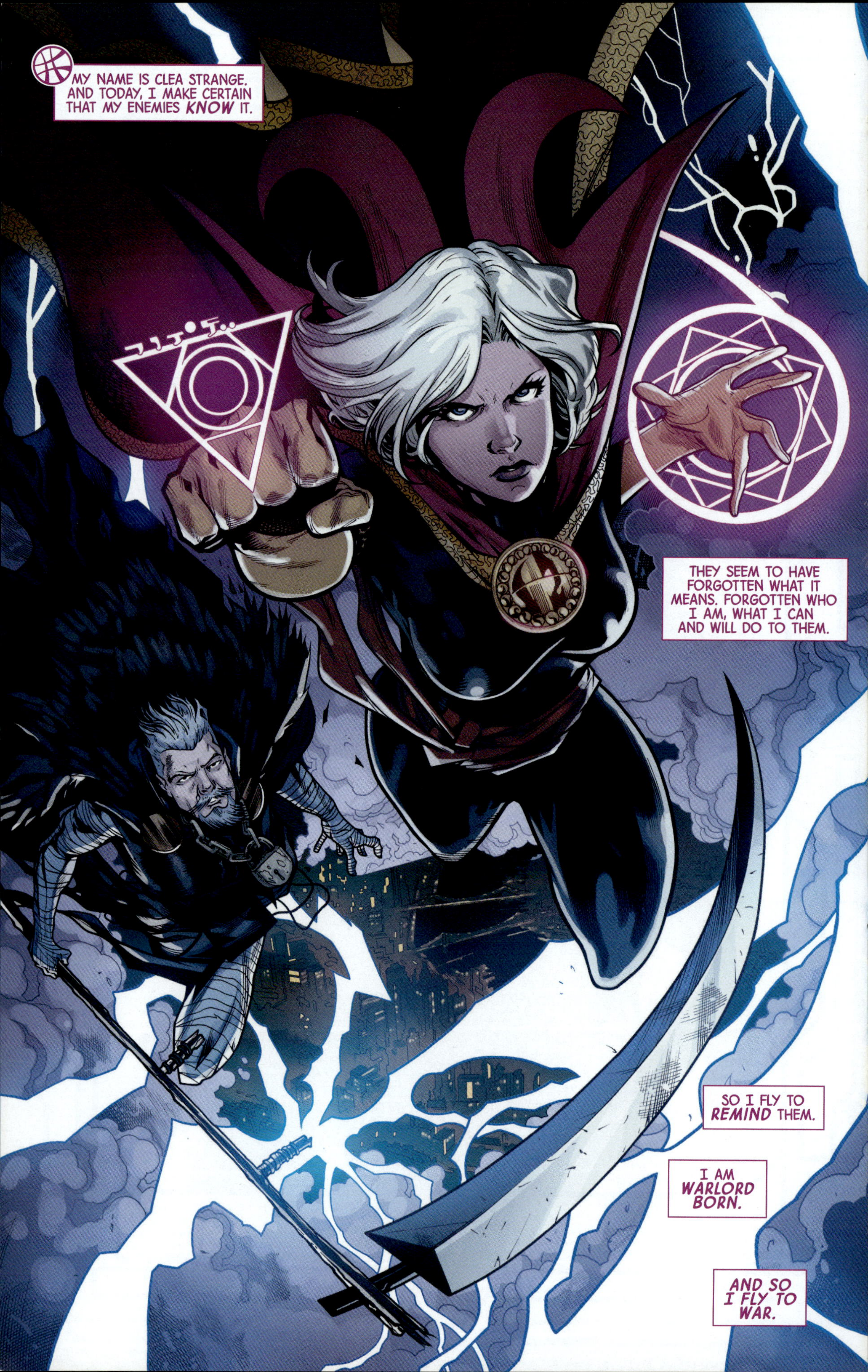
MY NAME IS CLEA STRANGE. AND TODAY, I MAKE CERTAIN THAT MY ENEMIES KNOW IT.
THEY SEEM TO HAVE FORGOTTEN WHAT IT MEANS. FORGOTTEN WHO I AM, WHAT I CAN AND WILL DO TO THEM.
SO I FLY TO REMIND THEM.
I AM WARLORD BORN.
AND SO I FLY TO WAR.

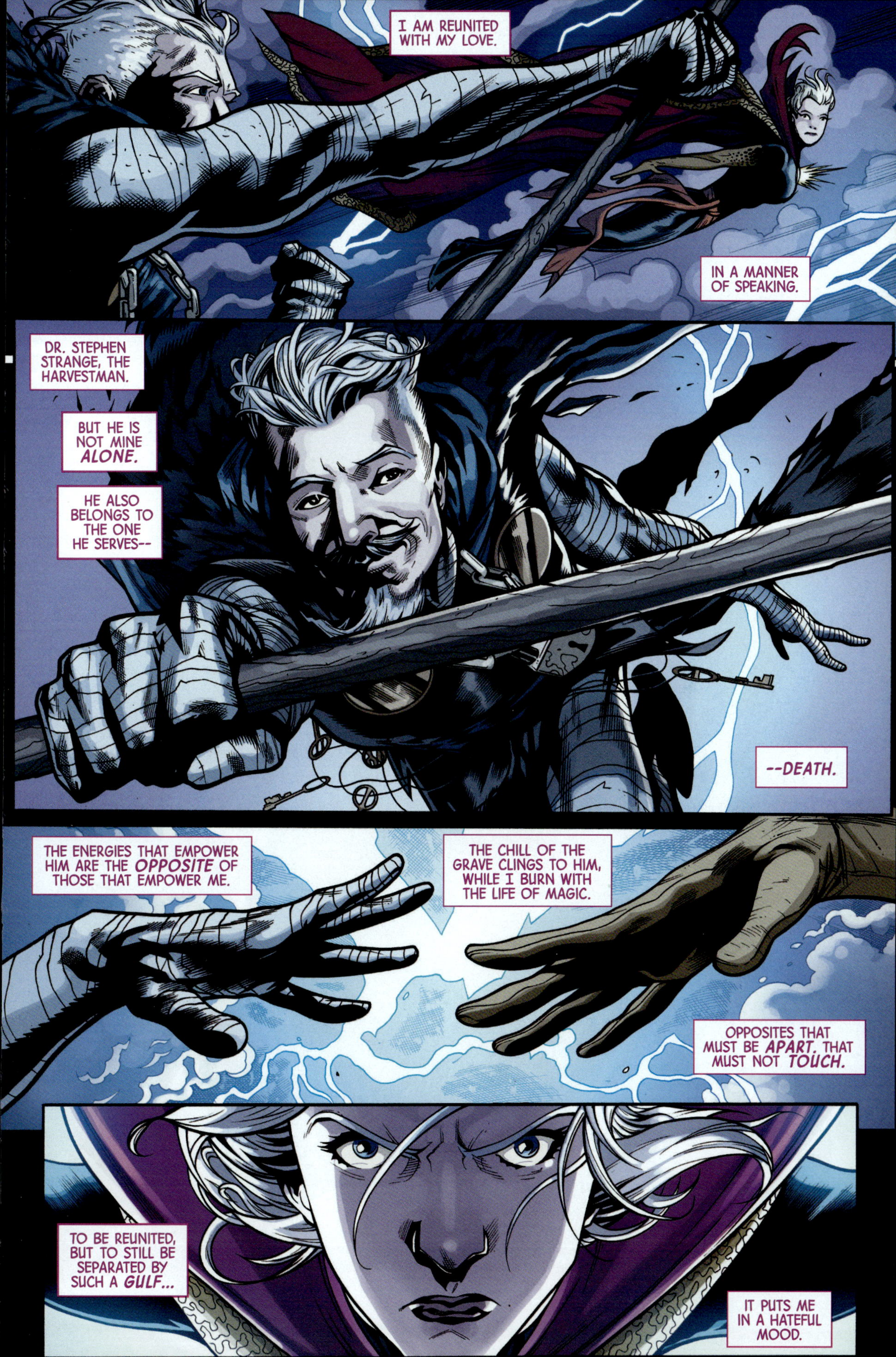
I AM REUNITED WITH MY LOVE.
IN A MANNER OF SPEAKING.
DR. STEPHEN STRANGE, THE HARVESTMAN.
BUT HE IS NOT MINE *ALONE.*
HE ALSO BELONGS TO THE ONE HE SERVES--
--DEATH.
THE ENERGIES THAT EMPOWER HIM ARE THE *OPPOSITE* OF THOSE THAT EMPOWER ME.
THE CHILL OF THE GRAVE CLINGS TO HIM, WHILE I BURN WITH THE LIFE OF MAGIC.
OPPOSITES THAT MUST BE *APART.* THAT MUST NOT *TOUCH.*
TO BE REUNITED, BUT TO STILL BE SEPARATED BY SUCH A *GULF*...
IT PUTS ME IN A HATEFUL MOOD.

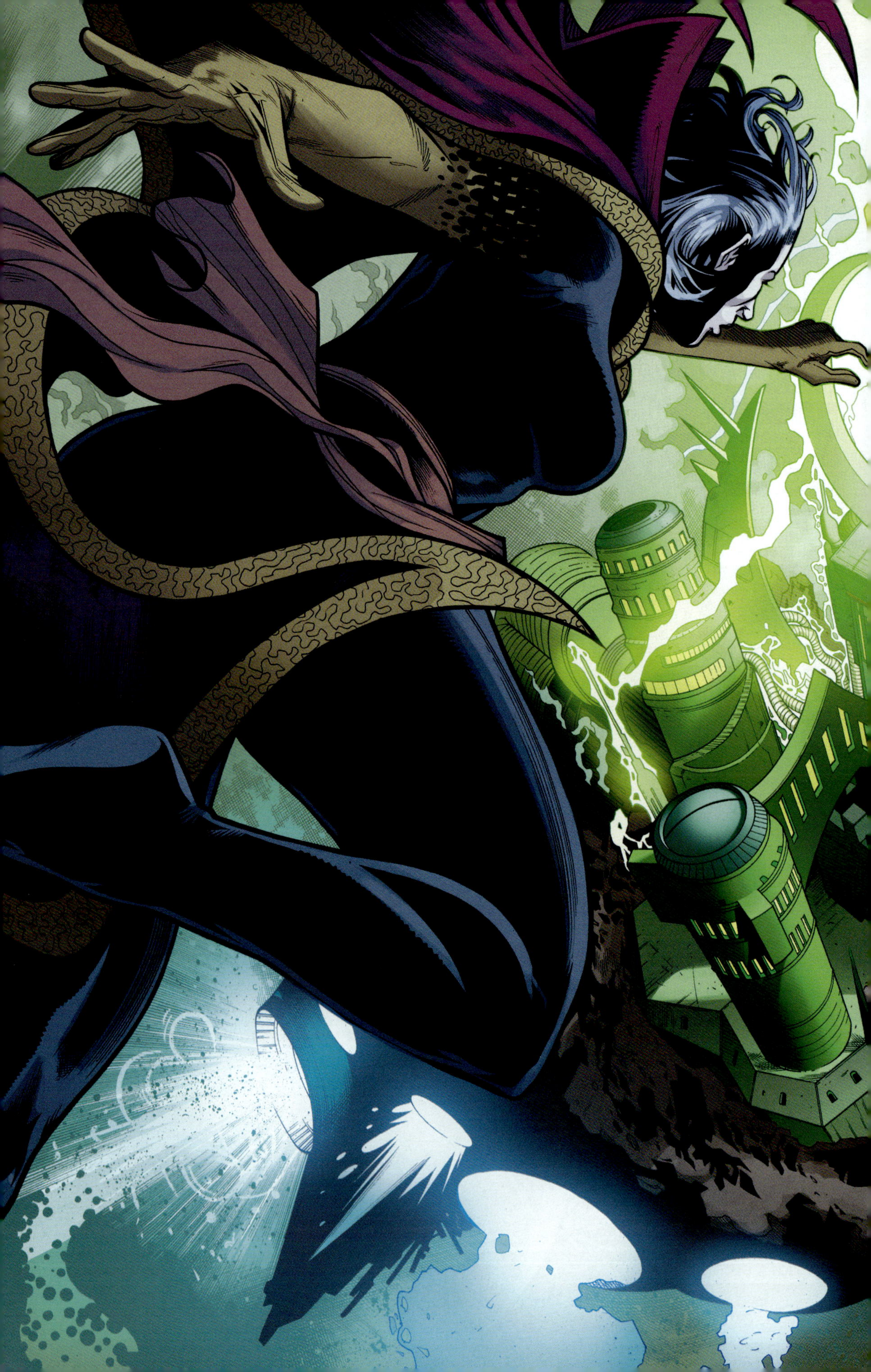

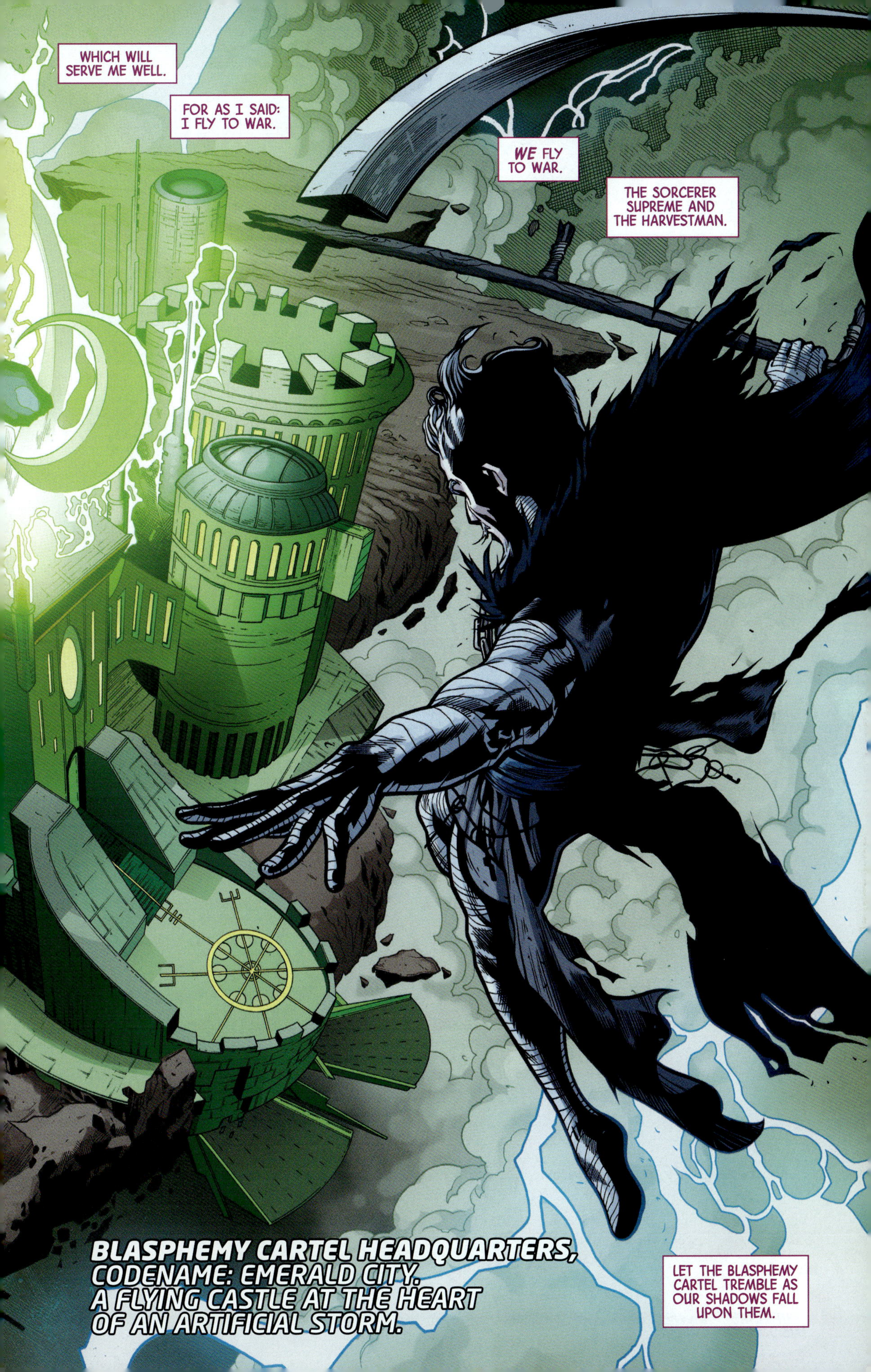
WHICH WILL SERVE ME WELL.
FOR AS I SAID: I FLY TO WAR.
WE FLY TO WAR.
THE SORCERER SUPREME AND THE HARVESTMAN.
BLASPHEMY CARTEL HEADQUARTERS, CODENAME: EMERALD CITY. A FLYING CASTLE AT THE HEART OF AN ARTIFICIAL STORM.
LET THE BLASPHEMY CARTEL TREMBLE AS OUR SHADOWS FALL UPON THEM.

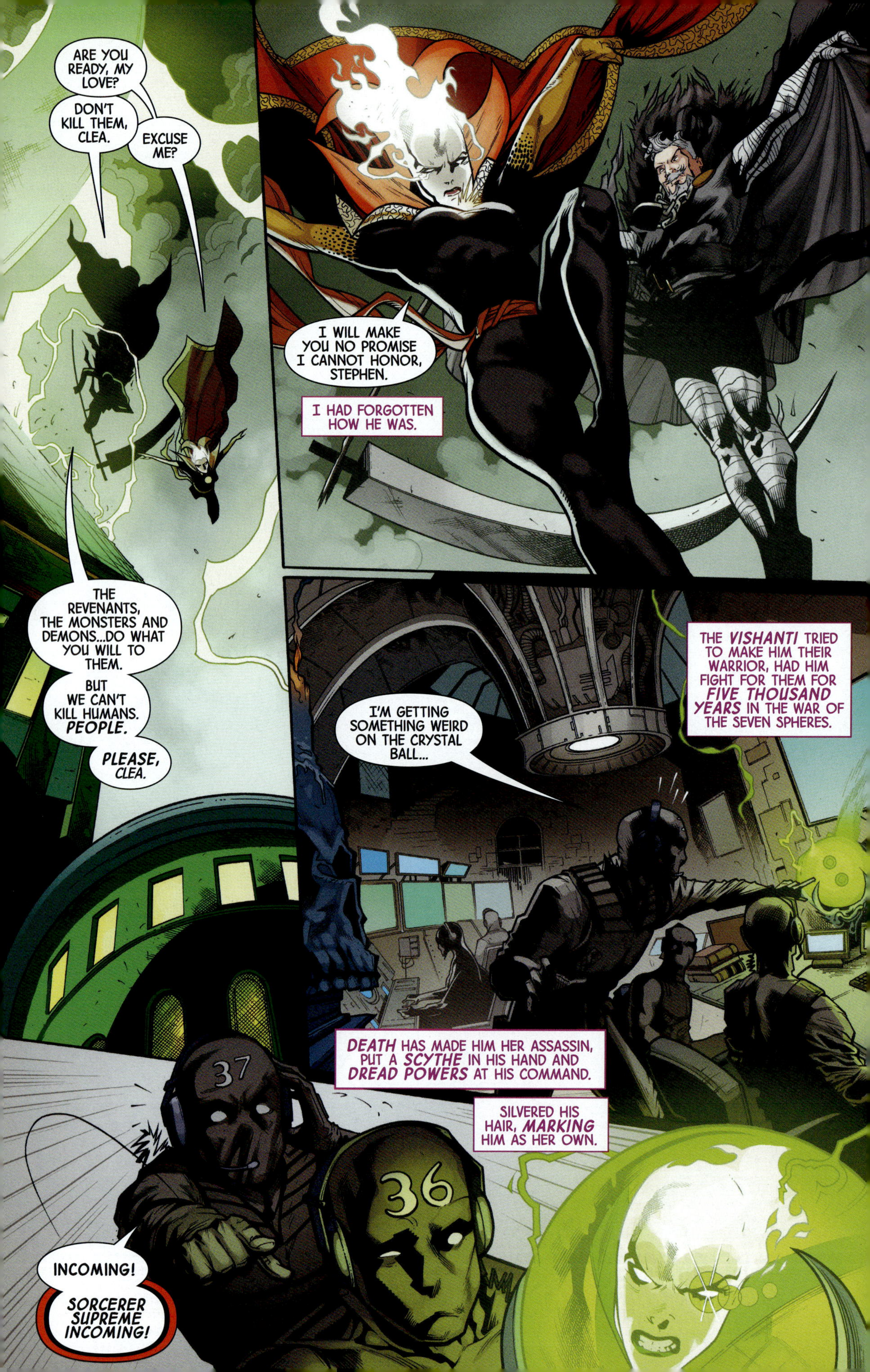

ARE YOU READY, MY LOVE?
DON'T KILL THEM, CLEA.
EXCUSE ME?
I WILL MAKE YOU NO PROMISE I CANNOT HONOR, STEPHEN.
I HAD FORGOTTEN HOW HE WAS.
THE REVENANTS, THE MONSTERS AND DEMONS...DO WHAT YOU WILL TO THEM.
BUT WE CAN'T KILL HUMANS. PEOPLE.
PLEASE, CLEA.
THE VISHANTI TRIED TO MAKE HIM THEIR WARRIOR, HAD HIM FIGHT FOR THEM FOR FIVE THOUSAND YEARS IN THE WAR OF THE SEVEN SPHERES.
I'M GETTING SOMETHING WEIRD ON THE CRYSTAL BALL...
DEATH HAS MADE HIM HER ASSASSIN, PUT A SCYTHE IN HIS HAND AND DREAD POWERS AT HIS COMMAND.
SILVERED HIS HAIR, MARKING HIM AS HER OWN.
37
36
INCOMING!
SORCERER SUPREME INCOMING!

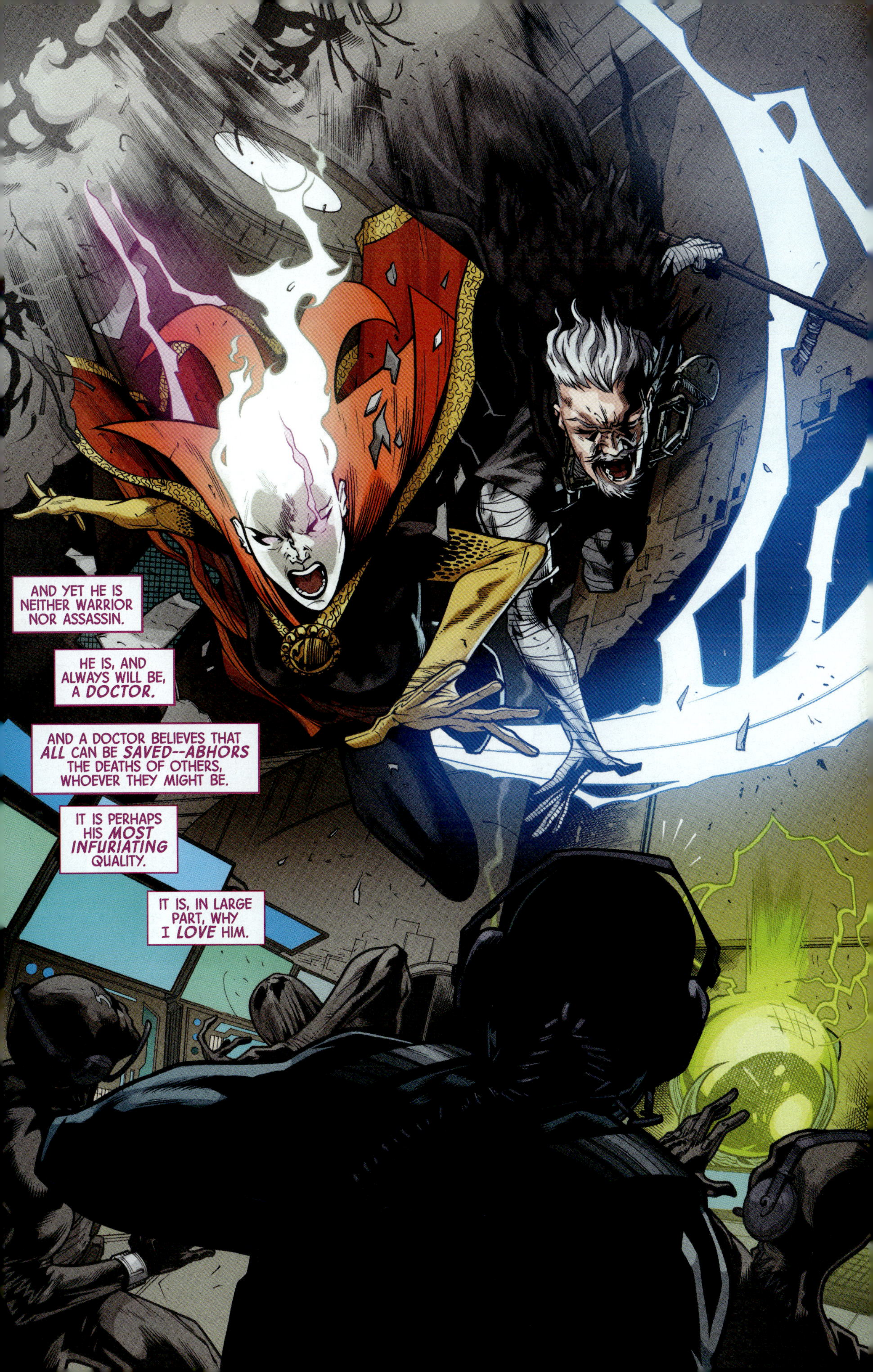
AND YET HE IS NEITHER WARRIOR NOR ASSASSIN.
HE IS, AND ALWAYS WILL BE, A DOCTOR.
AND A DOCTOR BELIEVES THAT ALL CAN BE SAVED--ABHORS THE DEATHS OF OTHERS, WHOEVER THEY MIGHT BE.
IT IS PERHAPS HIS MOST INFURIATING QUALITY.
IT IS, IN LARGE PART, WHY I LOVE HIM.

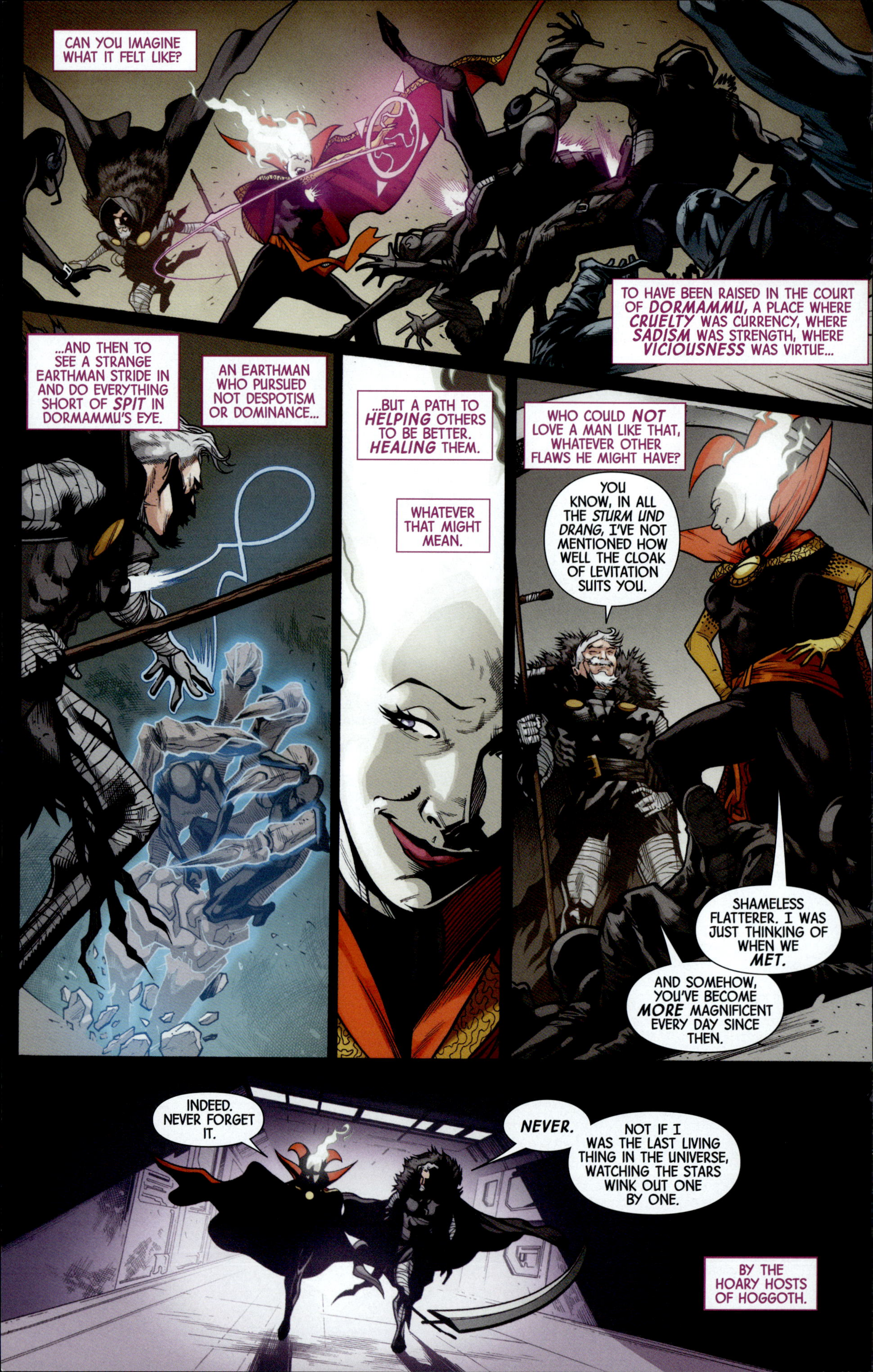
CAN YOU IMAGINE WHAT IT FELT LIKE?
TO HAVE BEEN RAISED IN THE COURT OF DORMAMMU, A PLACE WHERE CRUELTY WAS CURRENCY, WHERE SADISM WAS STRENGTH, WHERE VICIOUSNESS WAS VIRTUE...
...AND THEN TO SEE A STRANGE EARTHMAN STRIDE IN AND DO EVERYTHING SHORT OF SPIT IN DORMAMMU'S EYE.
AN EARTHMAN WHO PURSUED NOT DESPOTISM OR DOMINANCE...
...BUT A PATH TO HELPING OTHERS TO BE BETTER. HEALING THEM.
WHATEVER THAT MIGHT MEAN.
WHO COULD NOT LOVE A MAN LIKE THAT, WHATEVER OTHER FLAWS HE MIGHT HAVE?
YOU KNOW, IN ALL THE STURM UND DRANG, I'VE NOT MENTIONED HOW WELL THE CLOAK OF LEVITATION SUITS YOU.
SHAMELESS FLATTERER. I WAS JUST THINKING OF WHEN WE MET.
AND SOMEHOW, YOU'VE BECOME MORE MAGNIFICENT EVERY DAY SINCE THEN.
INDEED. NEVER FORGET IT.
NEVER.
NOT IF I WAS THE LAST LIVING THING IN THE UNIVERSE, WATCHING THE STARS WINK OUT ONE BY ONE.
BY THE HOARY HOSTS OF HOGGOTH.

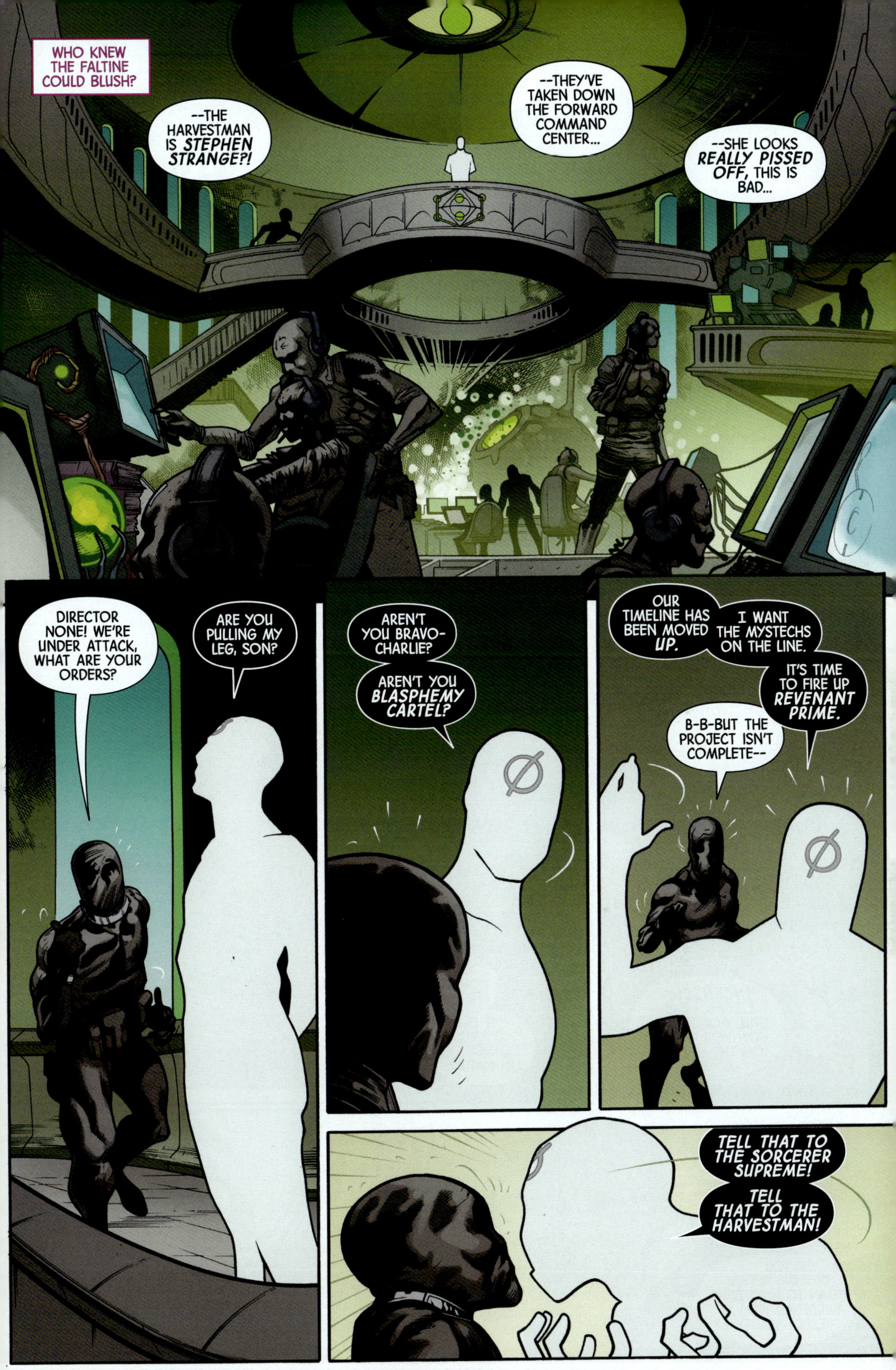
WHO KNEW THE FALTINE COULD BLUSH?
--THE HARVESTMAN IS STEPHEN STRANGE?!
--THEY'VE TAKEN DOWN THE FORWARD COMMAND CENTER...
--SHE LOOKS REALLY PISSED OFF, THIS IS BAD...
DIRECTOR NONE! WE'RE UNDER ATTACK, WHAT ARE YOUR ORDERS?
ARE YOU PULLING MY LEG, SON?
AREN'T YOU BRAVO-CHARLIE?
AREN'T YOU BLASPHEMY CARTEL?
OUR TIMELINE HAS BEEN MOVED UP.
I WANT THE MYSTECHS ON THE LINE.
IT'S TIME TO FIRE UP REVENANT PRIME.
B-B-BUT THE PROJECT ISN'T COMPLETE--
TELL THAT TO THE SORCERER SUPREME!
TELL THAT TO THE HARVESTMAN!

"THERE'S ONLY ONE THING THAT CAN STOP THEM!"
--AND HAS ANYONE GIVEN YOU ANY TROUBLE?
NO, EVERYONE HAS BEEN QUITE NICE. MOON KNIGHT WAS A DEAR.
WHO WAS A WHAT?!
DOOM WAS BY TO VISIT ON PRACTICALLY MY FIRST DAY AS SORCERER SUPREME, HOWEVER.
I'M NOT SURPRISED. WAS HE ANGRY?
INCENSED. I THINK HE IS STILL WONDERING HOW YOU PASSED ON THE MANTLE TO ME.
OF COURSE HE IS.
IT IS UTTERLY OUTSIDE OF HIS NATURE.
YES.
DOOM TAKES. HE COULD NEVER CONCEIVE OF GIVING SOMETHING OF HIMSELF, NO MATTER HOW SMALL, TO BETTER OTHERS.
I AM SORRY, MY LOVE.
YOU DESERVE BETTER THAN TO HAVE BEEN BURDENED WITH MY RESPONSIBILITIES.
I THOUGHT I'D LOST YOU. AGAIN.
WHATEVER YOUR LAST WISH WAS, I WOULD SEE IT THROUGH. WHATEVER IT TOOK TO KEEP SAFE THE WORLD YOU LOVE SO MUCH.

"EVEN IF IT MEANT GRAFTING A FRAGMENT OF YOUR SOUL TO MINE, TO ANCHOR THE OFFICE OF SORCERER SUPREME TO ME.*"
*SEE DEATH OF DOCTOR STRANGE #5! --DS
DEATH MAY OWN YOUR SOUL.
BUT A PART OF IT BELONGS TO ME.
NO.
WE CAN'T. REMEMBER?
DOCTOR STEPHEN STRANGE.

THE HARVESTMAN. DIDN'T SEE THAT COMING, THOUGH I PROBABLY SHOULD HAVE.
THE TWO OF YOU.
X-FACTORS... UNKNOWN VARIABLES.
AND I HATE VARIABLES THAT I CAN'T CONTROL.
IRONICALLY, YOU DYING WAS THE WORST THING THAT COULD HAVE HAPPENED TO US, STRANGE.
WE HAD PLANS FOR YOU. WE KNEW HOW TO KEEP OUT OF YOUR SIGHT LINE. BUT NOT HER.
DIRECTOR NONE.
BEFORE I FIND YOU AND KILL YOU--
--YES, I KNOW, STEPHEN--
--WHY? WHY HAVE YOU BEEN DOING ALL THIS? TO WHAT END HAVE YOU BEEN CREATING REVENANTS?
I'LL TELL YOU WHAT.
YOU MAKE IT THROUGH THE NEXT WAVE AND MEET UP WITH ME, I'LL TELL YOU.
DIRECTOR NONE OUT.
CLICK
RELEASE ALL THE LAZARUS AGENTS WE HAVE ON HAND.

I DON'T CARE WHAT YOU SAY, I AM GOING TO KILL HIM.
CLEA.
FINE. I'LL LEAVE HIM IN THE DARK DIMENSION, THEN-- LET THE MINDLESS ONES DO IT.
CLEA.
MOON KNIGHT WOULD LET ME.
THAT'S BECAUSE MOON KNIGHT IS A--BY THE HOARY HOSTS OF HOGGOTH.
WHAT--?
OH.
THEY'VE BEEN BUSY.

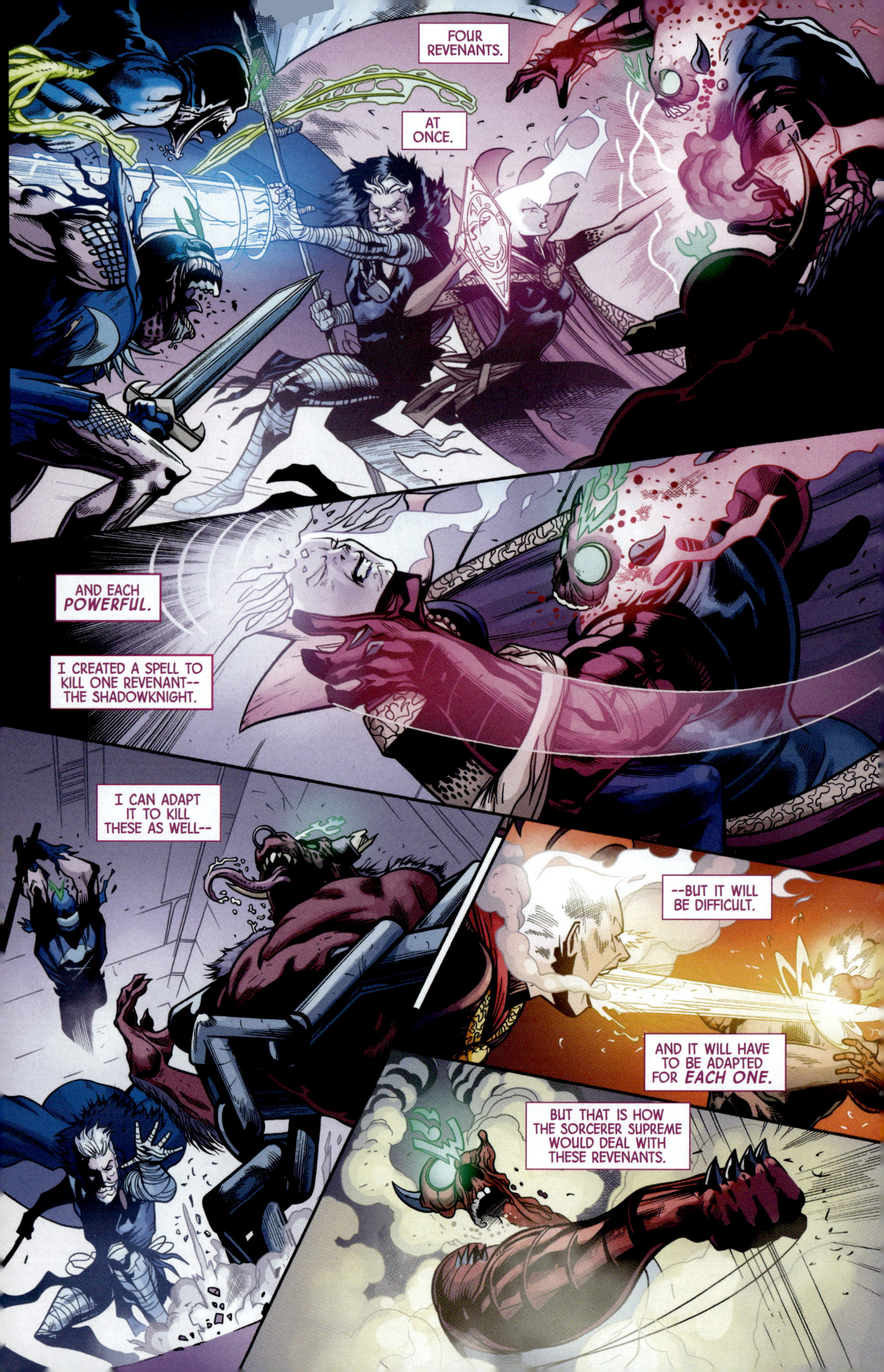
FOUR REVENANTS.
AT ONCE.
AND EACH *POWERFUL.*
I CREATED A SPELL TO KILL ONE REVENANT-- THE SHADOWKNIGHT.
I CAN ADAPT IT TO KILL THESE AS WELL--
--BUT IT WILL BE DIFFICULT.
AND IT WILL HAVE TO BE ADAPTED FOR *EACH ONE.*
BUT THAT IS HOW THE SORCERER SUPREME WOULD DEAL WITH THESE REVENANTS.

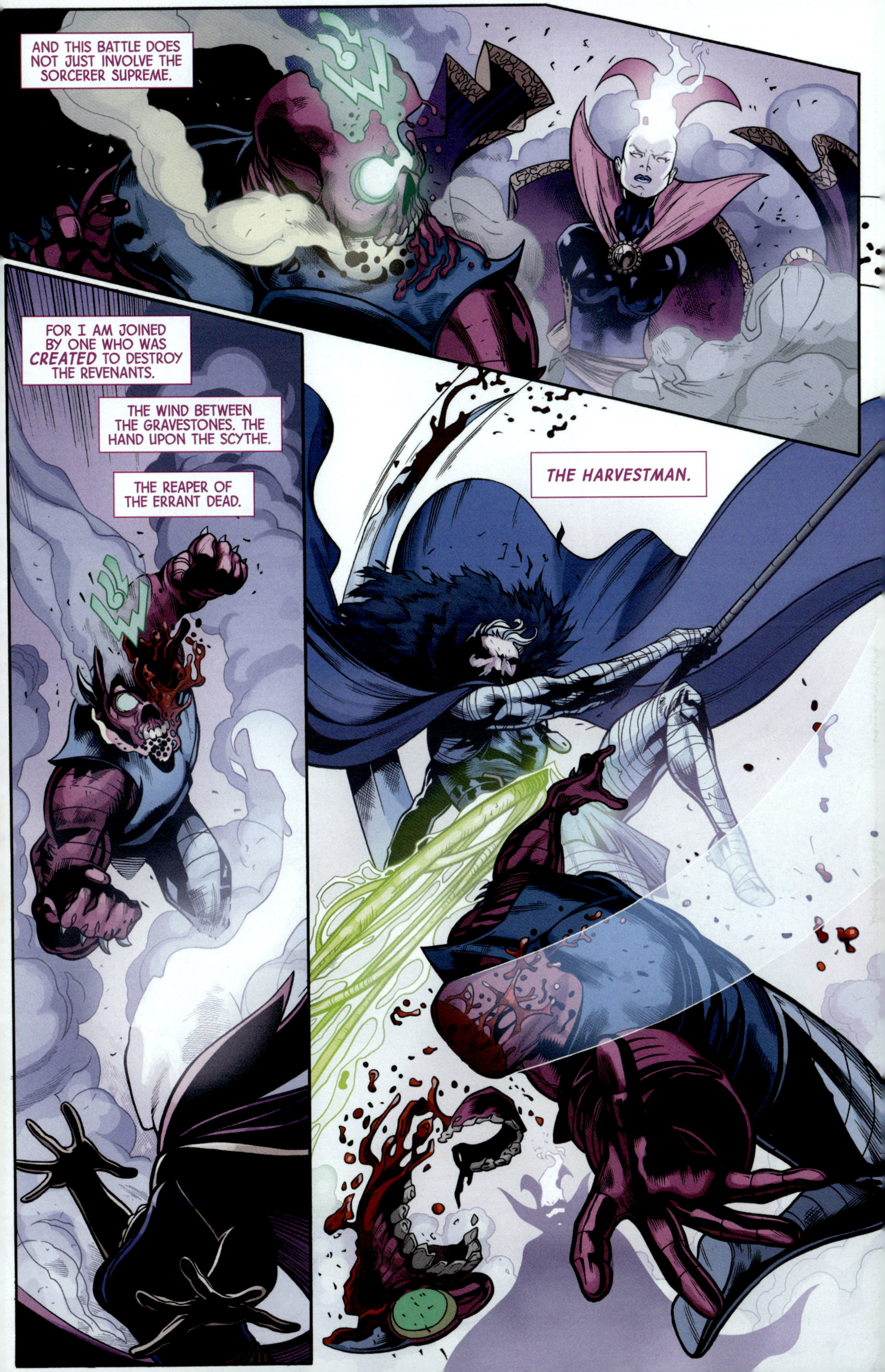
AND THIS BATTLE DOES NOT JUST INVOLVE THE SORCERER SUPREME.
FOR I AM JOINED BY ONE WHO WAS *CREATED* TO DESTROY THE REVENANTS.
THE WIND BETWEEN THE GRAVESTONES. THE HAND UPON THE SCYTHE.
THE REAPER OF THE ERRANT DEAD.
THE HARVESTMAN.

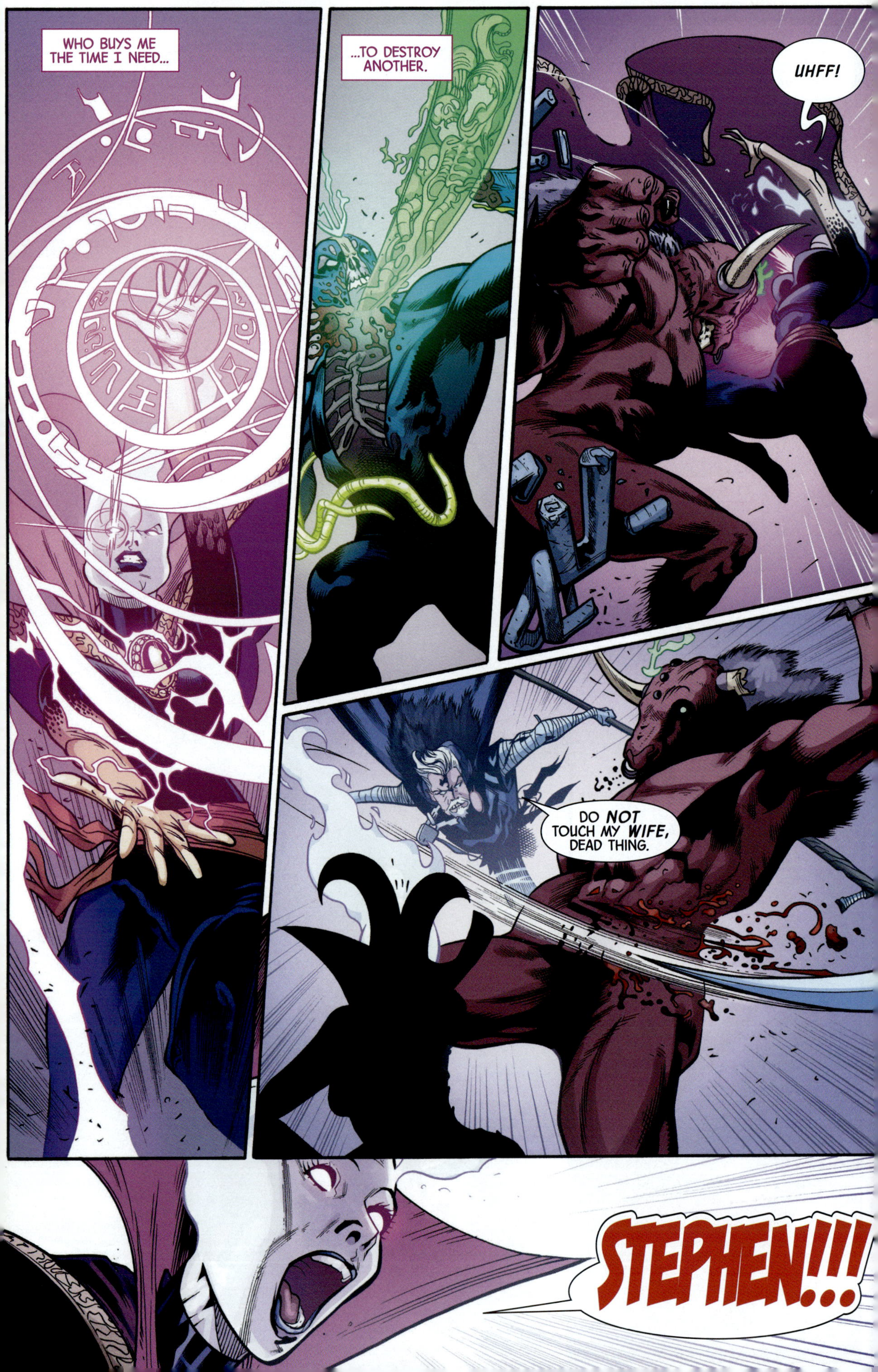
WHO BUYS ME THE TIME I NEED...
...TO DESTROY ANOTHER.
UHFF!
DO NOT TOUCH MY WIFE, DEAD THING.
STEPHEN!!!

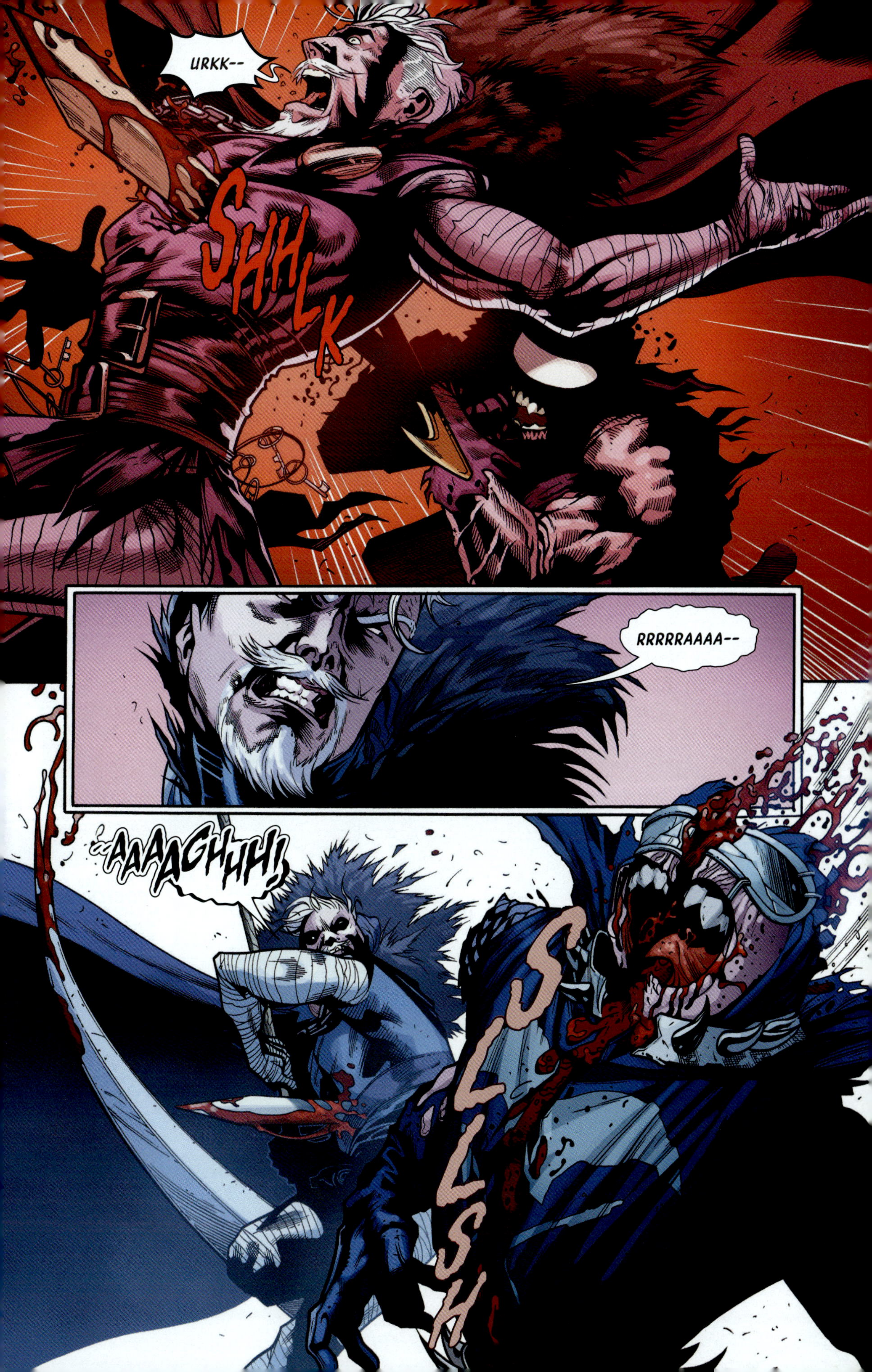
URKK--
SHHLK
RRRRRAAAA--
--AAAAGHHH!
SLLSH

ARE--
--ARE YOU ALL RIGHT?
NO.
I AM DEAD.
AND THIS WEAPON DRIVEN THROUGH MY CHEST SERVES TO REMIND ME OF THAT.
BUT THIS BODY I USE WAS CREATED BY DEATH HERSELF TO BE HER WEAPON.
I AM MADE OF STERN STUFF INDEED, IT WOULD SEEM.
IT IS SIMPLY ANOTHER PROBLEM-- ONE WE WILL SOLVE TOGETHER.
YOU ARE A DOCTOR, YOU ARE USED TO FIXING THINGS. AND I AM A WARLORD, I AM USED TO GETTING WHAT I WANT.
WHAT POWER CAN STAND AGAINST THE TWO OF US TOGETHER?
WHAT POWER INDEED?
LET ME TELL YOU.

I NEVER LIKED PANDORA PETERS. NOT ONE BIT, FROM DAY ONE. SHE WAS WEAK--LACKED VISION.
EVEN BEFORE W.A.N.D. FELL AND THE BLASPHEMY CARTEL PICKED UP THE PIECES, I KNEW THERE WERE *BIGGER, BETTER* BOSSES.
BOSSES WHO HISSED THINGS IN THE DARKNESS BETWEEN THE STARS. BOSSES WHO PROMISED SUCH *INTERESTING* THINGS.
THAT WAS WHEN I MADE CONTACT WITH *MANAGEMENT.*
NOT WHAT *YOU* KNOW THEM AS THOUGH, STRANGE.
THEY'RE OLD *FRIENDS* OF YOURS.
GRIEFSAVOR. YGMLOSVORRAICH. MOTHER-OF-PAIN.
THE TRINITY OF ASHES.
I'M TOLD YOU FOUGHT THEM IN THE WAR OF THE SEVEN SPHERES. FIVE THOUSAND YEARS OF WAR.
I KNOW YOU DON'T *REMEMBER* THE WAR YEARS. BECAUSE OF WHAT THE VISHANTI DID TO YOU--THE PRICE FOR PEACE WITH THE TRINITY.
YOU'RE RIGHT, I *DON'T* REMEMBER--
BUT THEY DIDN'T FORGET.
THEY *NEVER* FORGOT WHAT YOU DID TO THEM.
CREAAAAKK

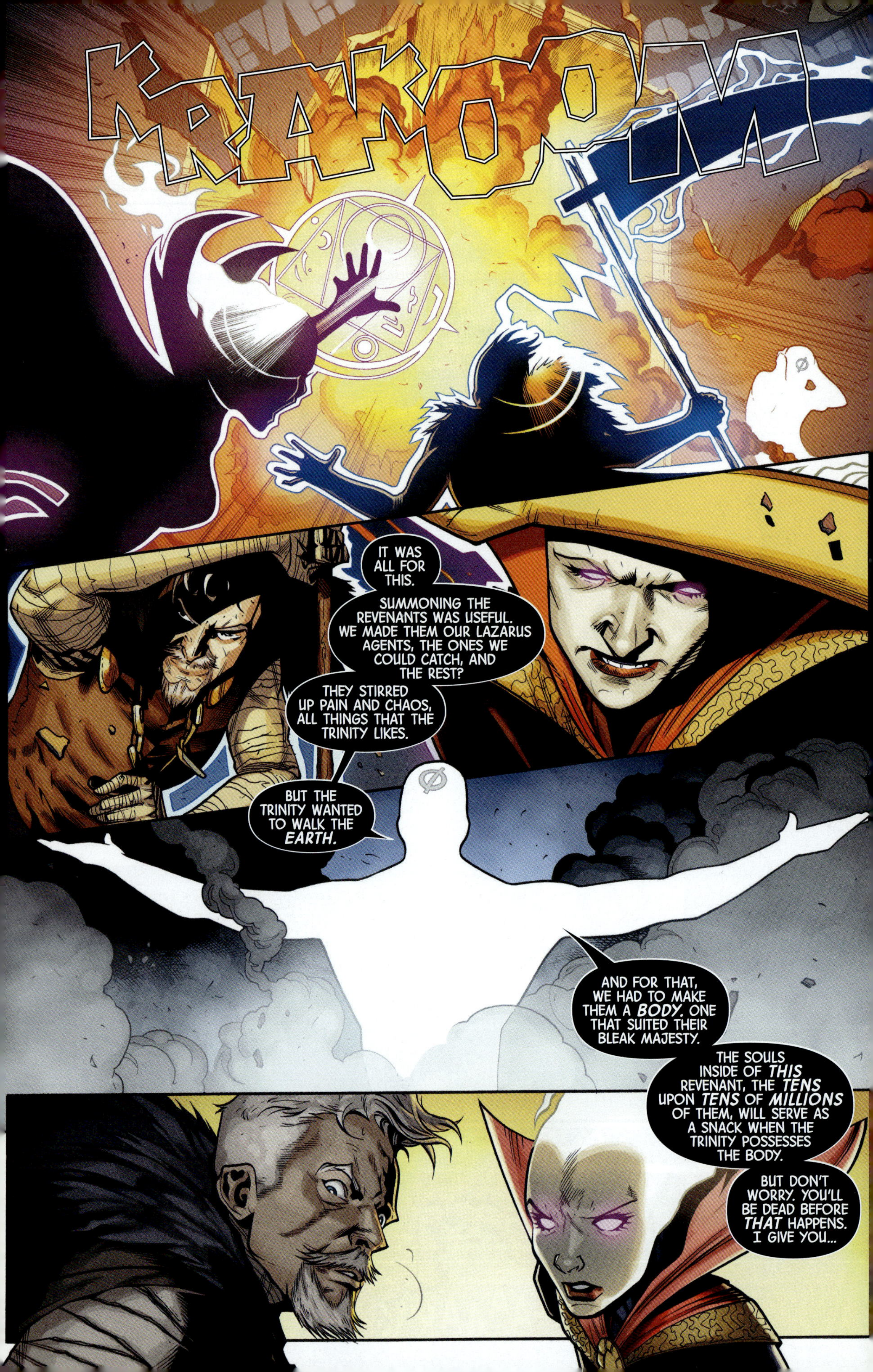
KRAKOOM
IT WAS ALL FOR THIS.
SUMMONING THE REVENANTS WAS USEFUL. WE MADE THEM OUR LAZARUS AGENTS, THE ONES WE COULD CATCH, AND THE REST?
THEY STIRRED UP PAIN AND CHAOS, ALL THINGS THAT THE TRINITY LIKES.
BUT THE TRINITY WANTED TO WALK THE *EARTH.*
AND FOR THAT, WE HAD TO MAKE THEM A *BODY.* ONE THAT SUITED THEIR BLEAK MAJESTY.
THE SOULS INSIDE OF *THIS* REVENANT, THE *TENS* UPON *TENS* OF *MILLIONS* OF THEM, WILL SERVE AS A SNACK WHEN THE TRINITY POSSESSES THE BODY.
BUT DON'T WORRY. YOU'LL BE DEAD BEFORE *THAT* HAPPENS. I GIVE YOU...

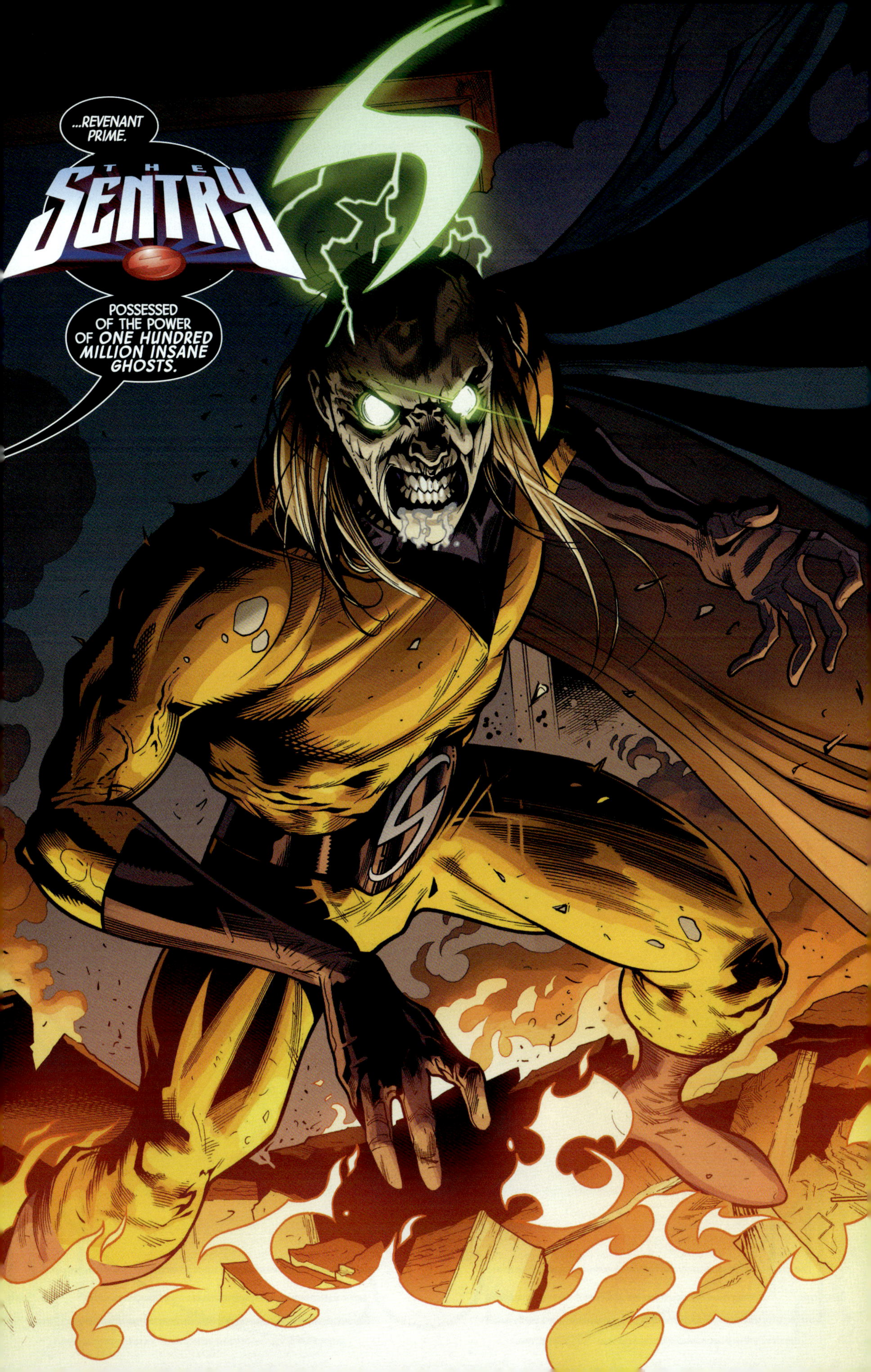
...REVENANT PRIME.
THE SENTRY
POSSESSED OF THE POWER OF ONE HUNDRED MILLION INSANE GHOSTS.

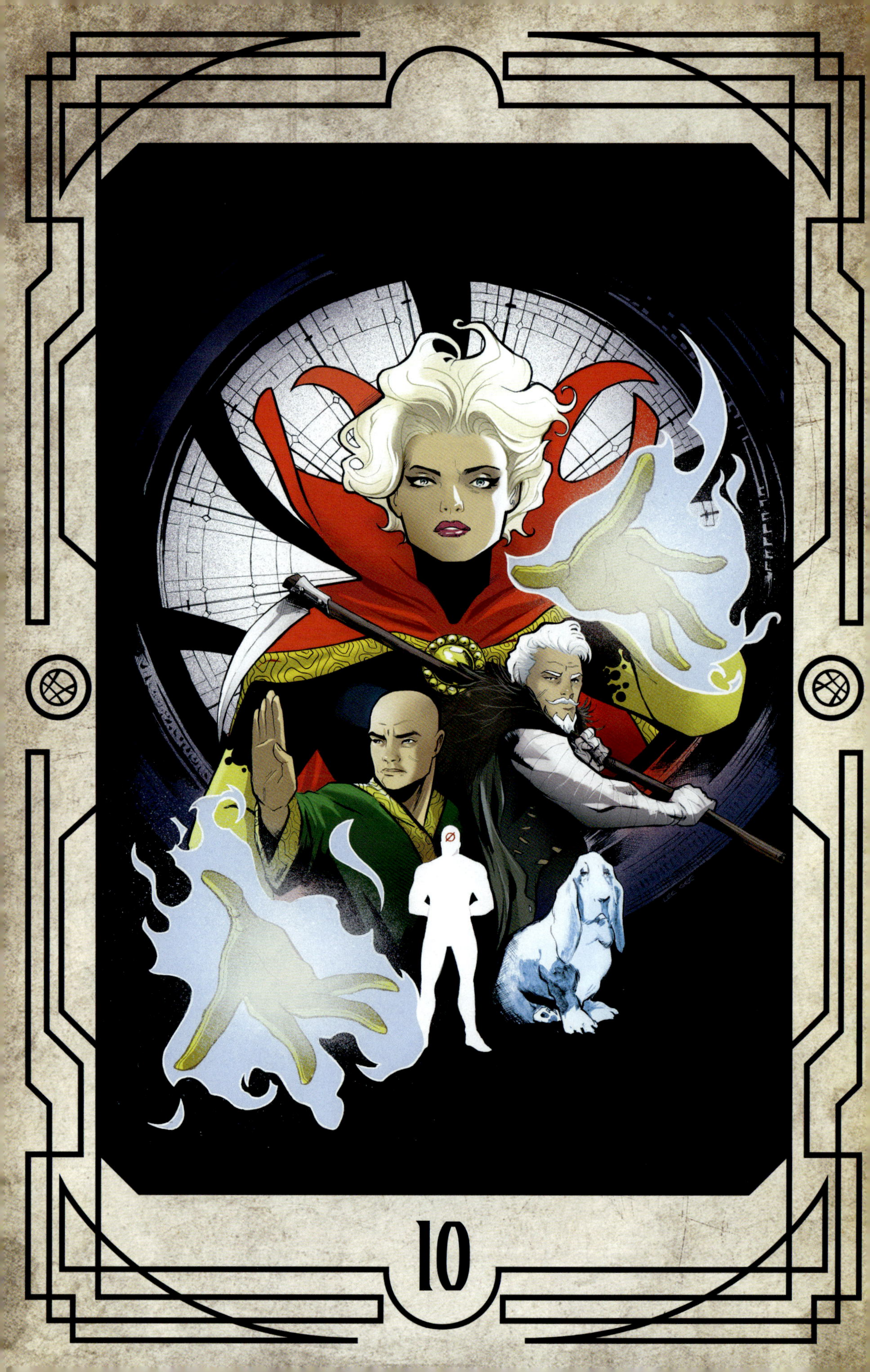
10

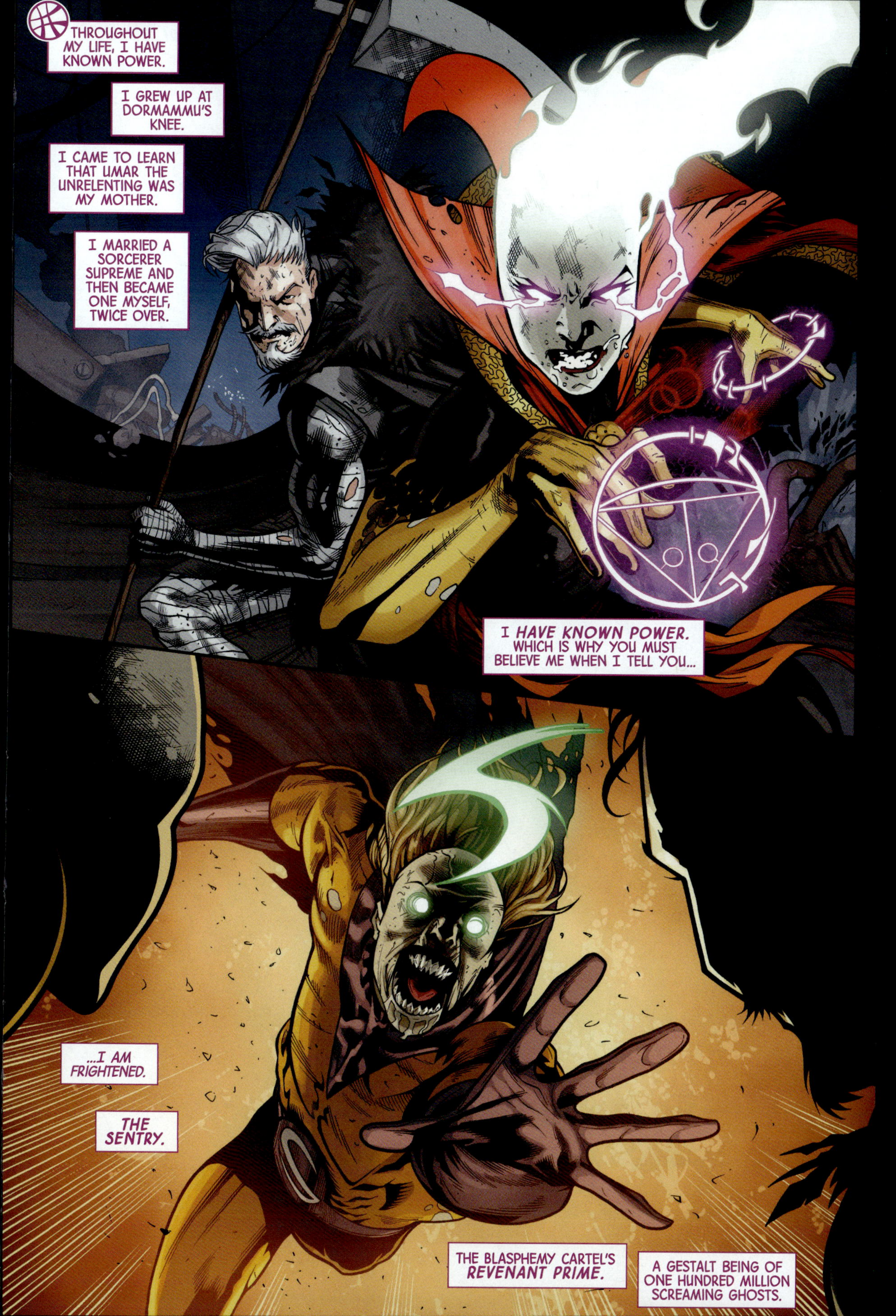
THROUGHOUT MY LIFE, I HAVE KNOWN POWER.
I GREW UP AT DORMAMMU'S KNEE.
I CAME TO LEARN THAT UMAR THE UNRELENTING WAS MY MOTHER.
I MARRIED A SORCERER SUPREME AND THEN BECAME ONE MYSELF, TWICE OVER.
I *HAVE KNOWN POWER.* WHICH IS WHY YOU MUST BELIEVE ME WHEN I TELL YOU...
...I AM FRIGHTENED.
THE SENTRY.
THE BLASPHEMY CARTEL'S *REVENANT PRIME.*
A GESTALT BEING OF ONE HUNDRED MILLION SCREAMING GHOSTS.

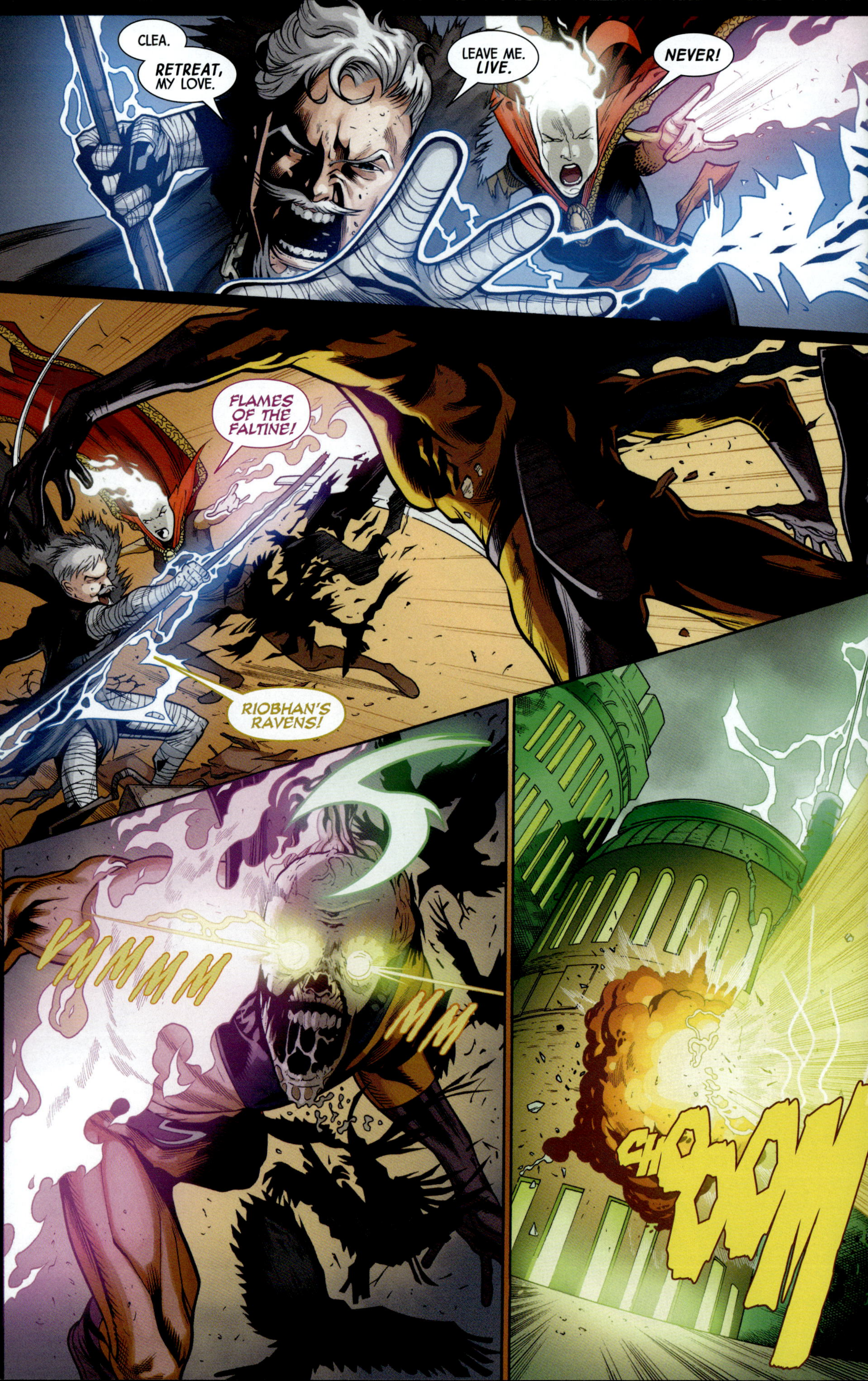
CLEA.
RETREAT, MY LOVE.
LEAVE ME. LIVE.
NEVER!
FLAMES OF THE FALTINE!
RIOBHAN'S RAVENS!
VMMMMMMM
SHOOOM

IN *LIFE,* THE SENTRY WAS A GOD WALKING THE EARTH.
EURGHH...
IN *DEATH*...
...HE IS A *GOD OF DEMONS.*
NO.
TALONS OF TARKHIZ!
I DO NOT ACCEPT THIS.
NOT AFTER ALL I HAVE DONE--
URK!

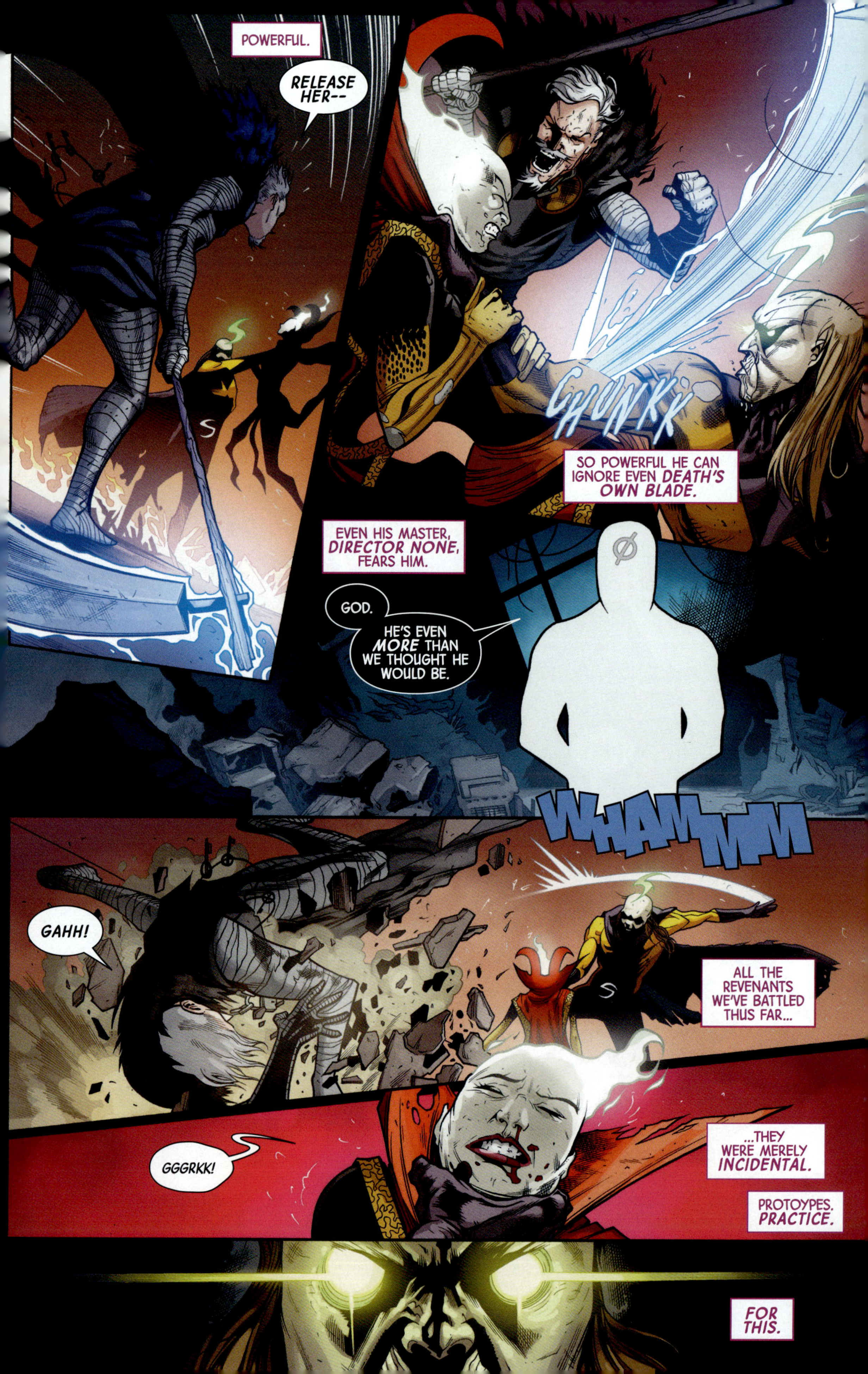

POWERFUL.
RELEASE HER--
CHUNKK
SO POWERFUL HE CAN IGNORE EVEN DEATH'S OWN BLADE.
EVEN HIS MASTER, DIRECTOR NONE, FEARS HIM.
GOD.
HE'S EVEN MORE THAN WE THOUGHT HE WOULD BE.
WHAMMM
GAHH!
ALL THE REVENANTS WE'VE BATTLED THUS FAR...
GGGRKK!
...THEY WERE MERELY INCIDENTAL.
PROTOYPES. PRACTICE.
FOR THIS.

CLEA, NO--
SHIELD OF THE SERAPHIM!
WHAM
GAAAHHH!
TO THE ARCHIPELAGO OF ANGUISH WITH YOU--
ENOUGH!
KRASSHH
THE PERFECT SPECIMEN.
NO MIND TO SUBORN.
YOUR QUICK CANTRIPS AND ROTES SLIDE RIGHT OFF OF HIM.
AND YOUR GREATER MAGICS?
"YOU'LL NEVER GET THE FEW MOMENTS YOU NEED TO CAST THEM."
WHAM WHAM WHAM

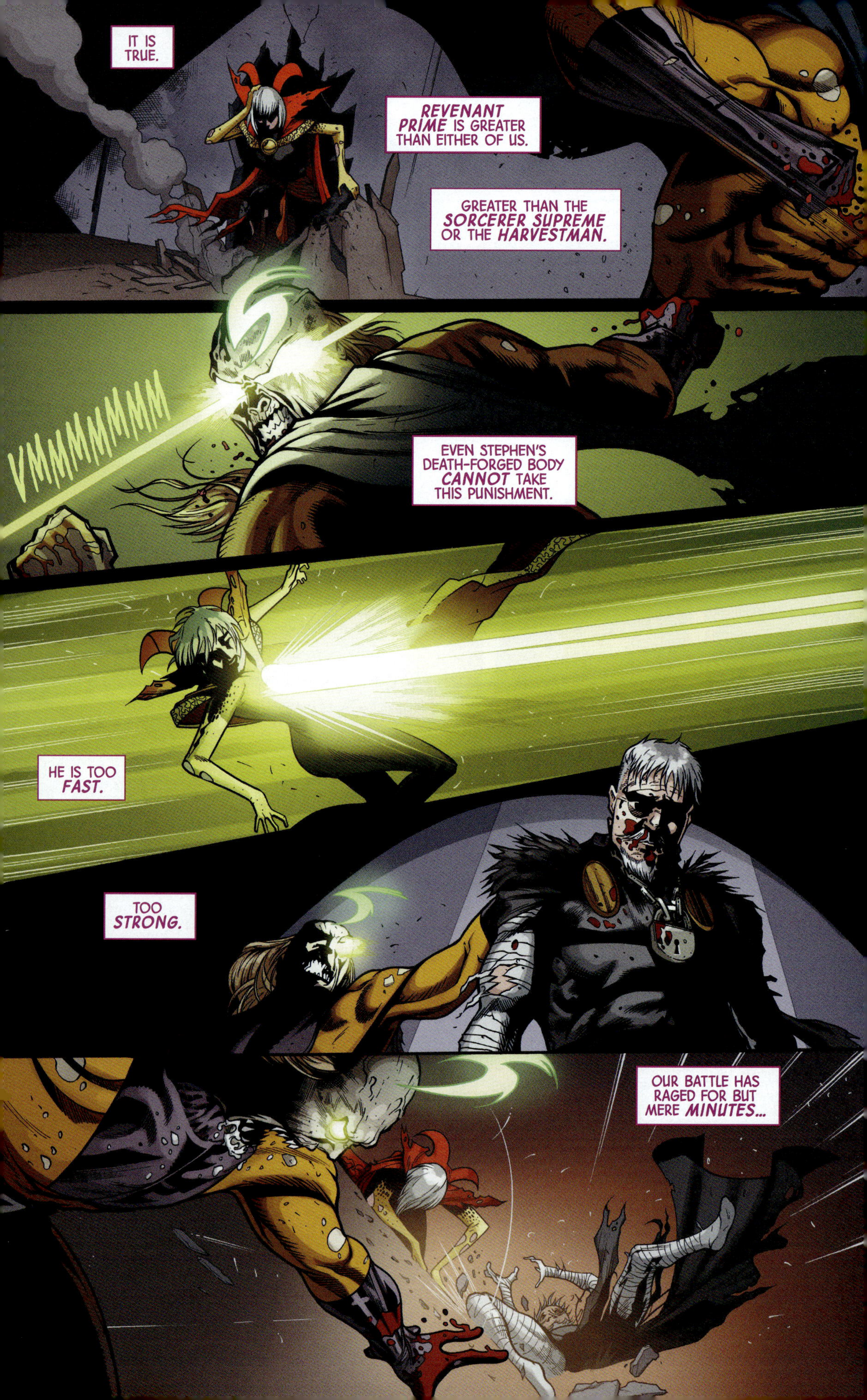
IT IS TRUE.
REVENANT PRIME IS GREATER THAN EITHER OF US.
GREATER THAN THE SORCERER SUPREME OR THE HARVESTMAN.
VMMMMMMM
EVEN STEPHEN'S DEATH-FORGED BODY CANNOT TAKE THIS PUNISHMENT.
HE IS TOO FAST.
TOO STRONG.
OUR BATTLE HAS RAGED FOR BUT MERE MINUTES...

...AND ALREADY, WE ARE UNDONE.
...STEPHEN...
...NO. IT CANNOT BE.
I CANNOT HAVE FOUND YOU ONLY TO LOSE YOU AGAIN SO QUICKLY.
...CLEA... FLEE...
YES, CLEA STRANGE.
YES, YOU HAVE.
THAT IS EXACTLY WHAT IS HAPPENING HERE.
I'M A LITTLE DISAPPOINTED, TO BE HONEST.
MANAGEMENT--THE TRINITY OF ASHES--WERE TERRIFIED OF YOU, STRANGE--STEPHEN, I MEAN. TERRIFIED OF WHAT YOU DID IN THE WAR OF THE SEVEN SPHERES. WHAT YOU BECAME.
BUT THIS SHOWING? PATHETIC.
I WILL NOT LEAVE YOU.
LIVE OR DIE, WE DO IT TOGETHER.

...NO, CLEA...
...TO TOUCH...
...CATASTROPHIC...
THEN IF THIS ACT IS TO BE OUR LAST...
...LET IT BE ONE OF LOVE.
OF DEFIANCE.
WAIT, NO!
OF CATASTROPHE!

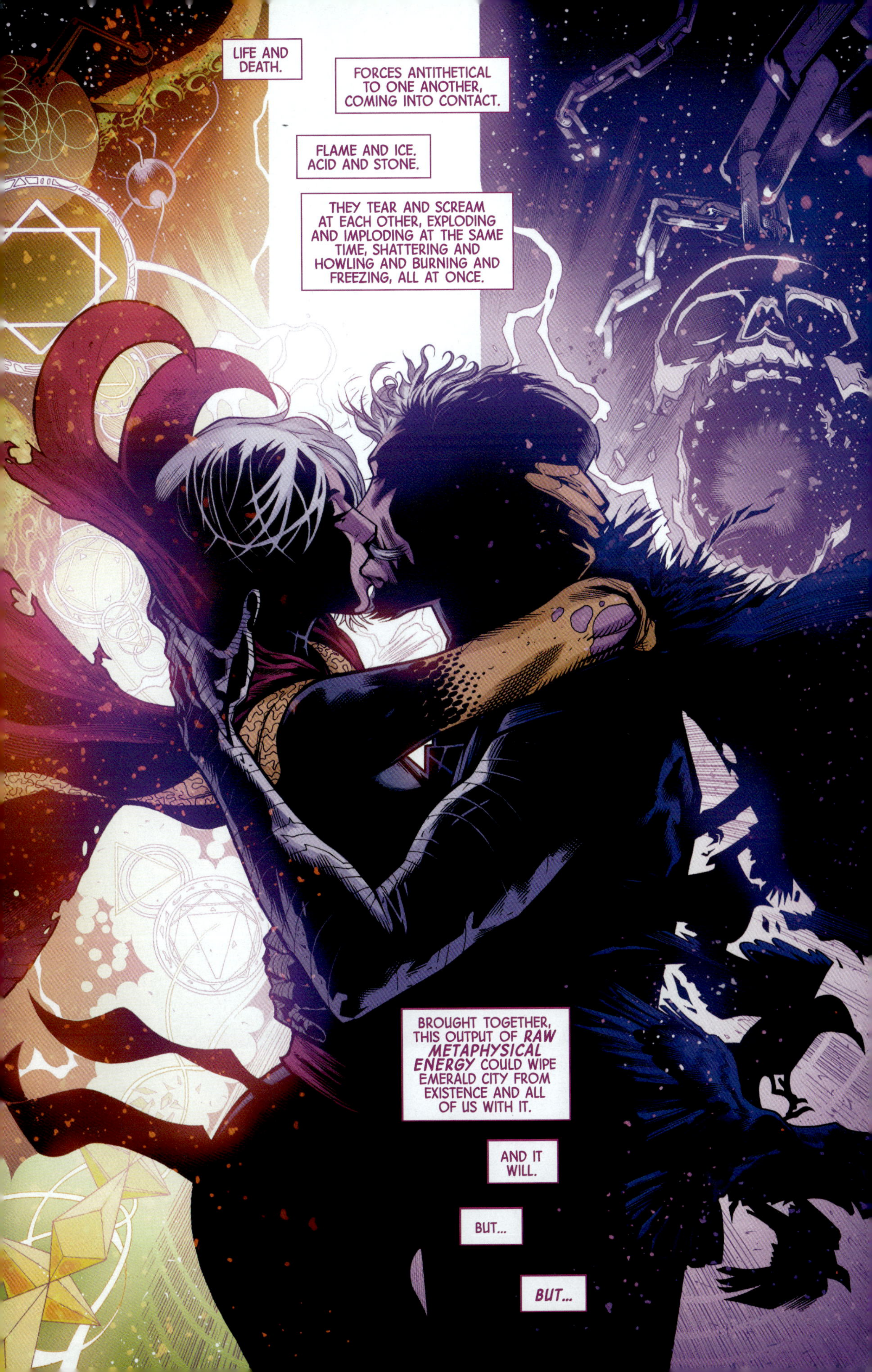
LIFE AND DEATH.
FORCES ANTITHETICAL TO ONE ANOTHER, COMING INTO CONTACT.
FLAME AND ICE. ACID AND STONE.
THEY TEAR AND SCREAM AT EACH OTHER, EXPLODING AND IMPLODING AT THE SAME TIME, SHATTERING AND HOWLING AND BURNING AND FREEZING, ALL AT ONCE.
BROUGHT TOGETHER, THIS OUTPUT OF *RAW METAPHYSICAL ENERGY* COULD WIPE EMERALD CITY FROM EXISTENCE AND ALL OF US WITH IT.
AND IT WILL.
BUT...
BUT...

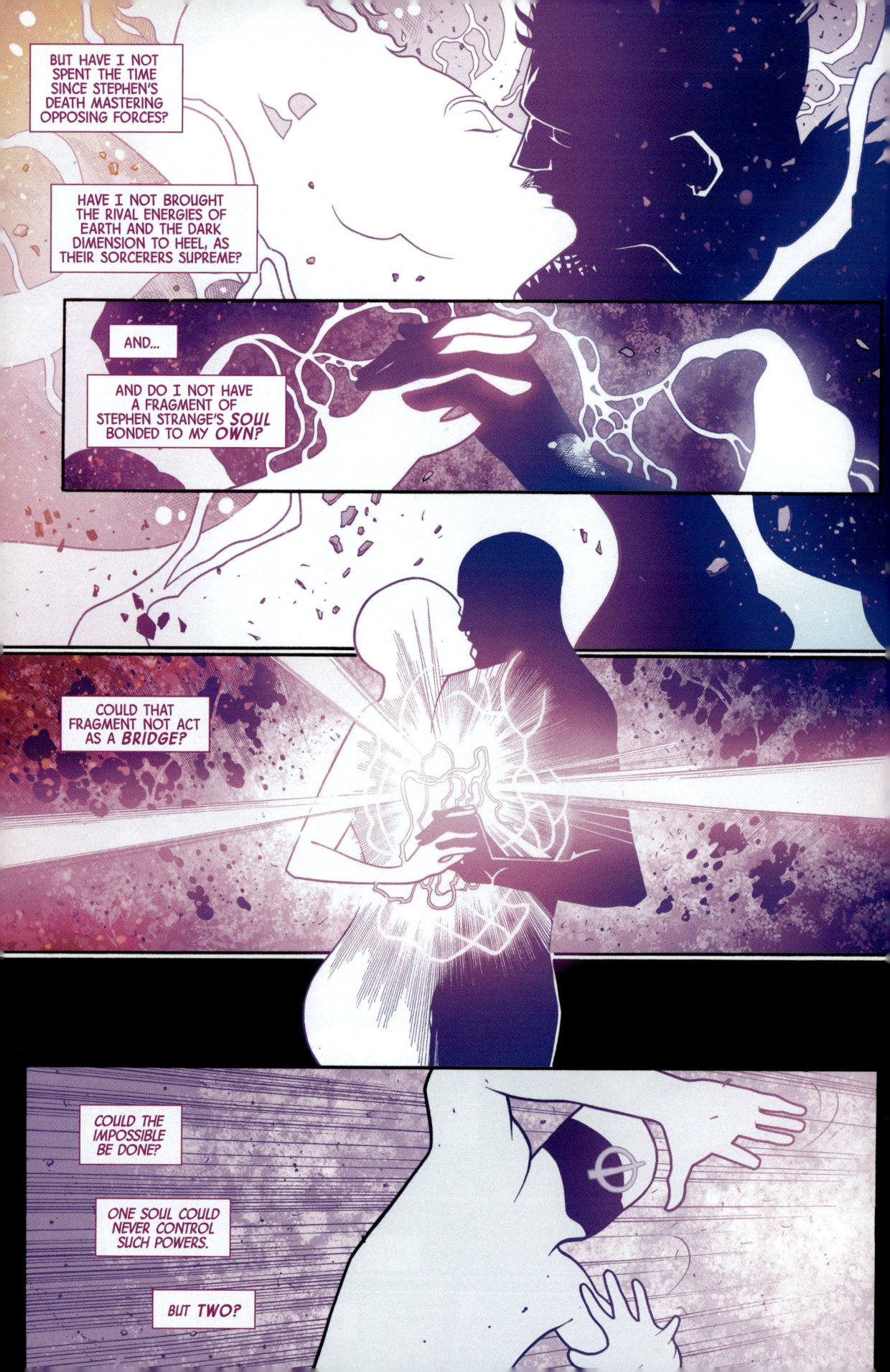

BUT HAVE I NOT SPENT THE TIME SINCE STEPHEN'S DEATH MASTERING OPPOSING FORCES?

HAVE I NOT BROUGHT THE RIVAL ENERGIES OF EARTH AND THE DARK DIMENSION TO HEEL, AS THEIR SORCERERS SUPREME?

AND...

AND DO I NOT HAVE A FRAGMENT OF STEPHEN STRANGE'S *SOUL* BONDED TO MY *OWN*?

COULD THAT FRAGMENT NOT ACT AS A *BRIDGE*?

COULD THE IMPOSSIBLE BE DONE?

ONE SOUL COULD NEVER CONTROL SUCH POWERS.

BUT *TWO*?

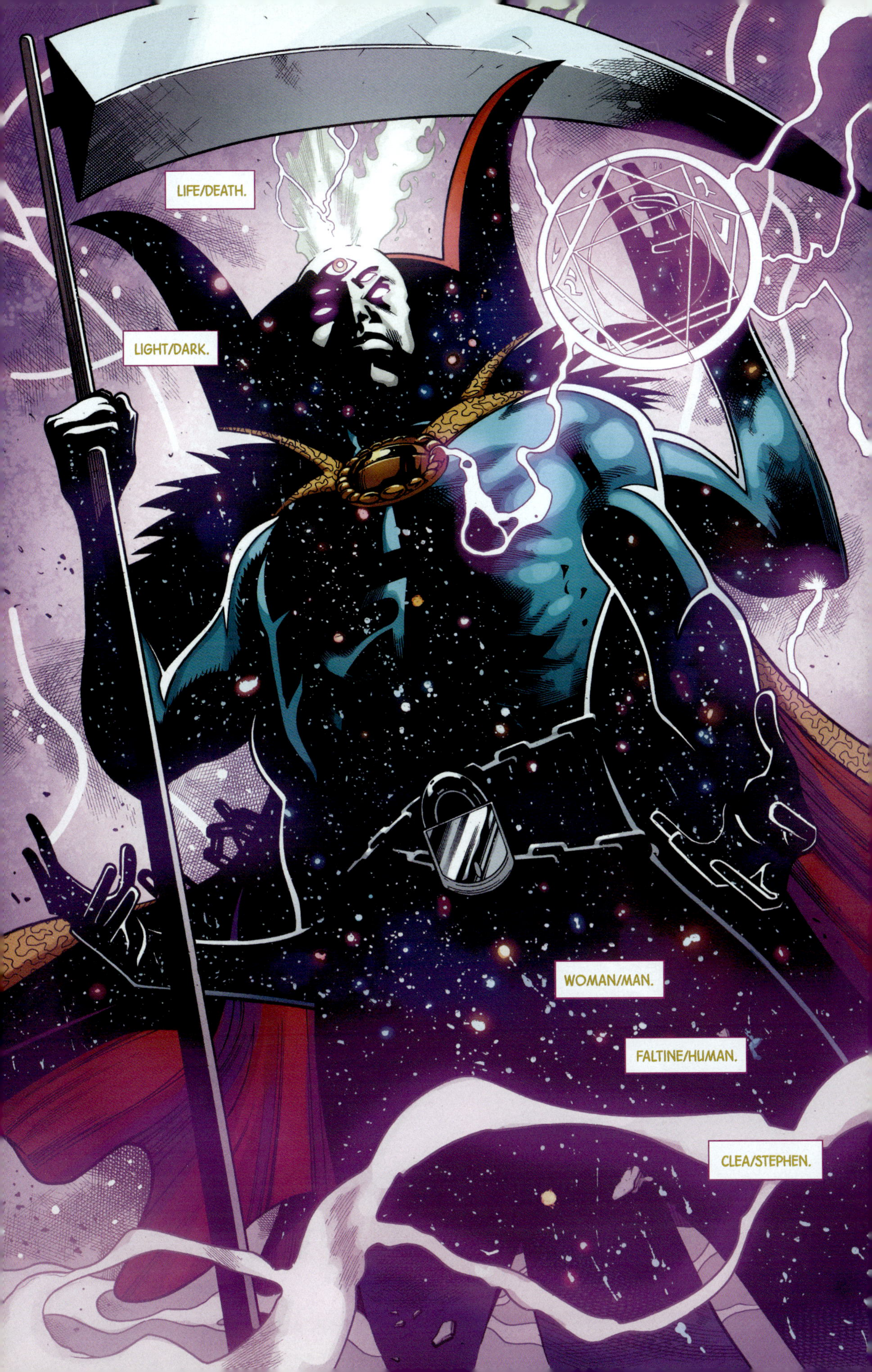
LIFE/DEATH.
LIGHT/DARK.
WOMAN/MAN.
FALTINE/HUMAN.
CLEA/STEPHEN.

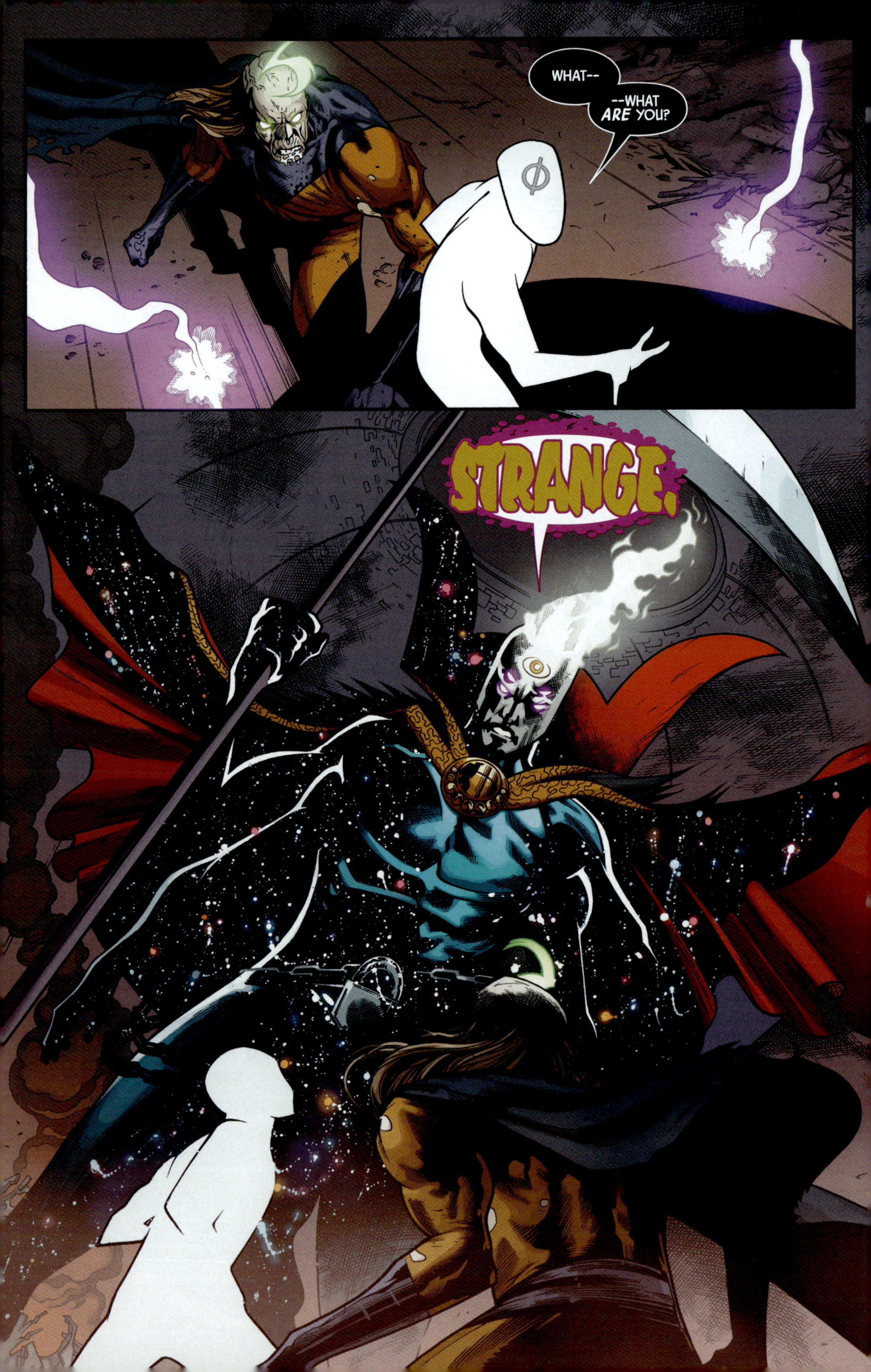
WHAT--
--WHAT ARE YOU?
STRANGE.

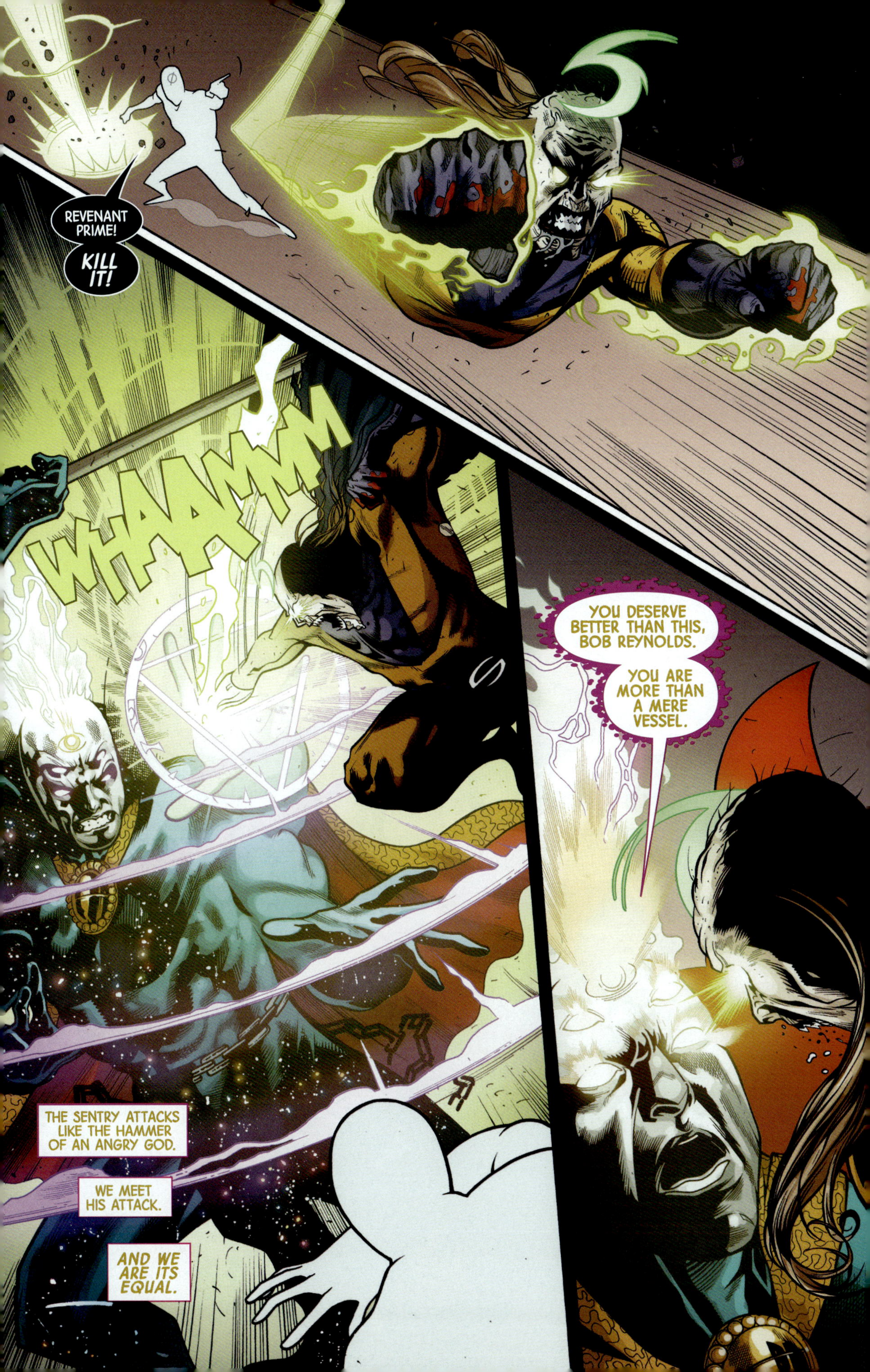
REVENANT PRIME!
KILL IT!
WHAAMMM
THE SENTRY ATTACKS LIKE THE HAMMER OF AN ANGRY GOD.
WE MEET HIS ATTACK.
AND WE ARE ITS EQUAL.
YOU DESERVE BETTER THAN THIS, BOB REYNOLDS.
YOU ARE MORE THAN A MERE VESSEL.

THE SHACKLES OF MAGIC THAT HOLD THE MILLIONS OF SOULS INSIDE OF YOU--
--BROKEN.
WHAT HAVE YOU DONE?!
THERE ARE ONE HUNDRED MILLION GHOSTS IN REVENANT PRIME!
THEIR EXODUS WILL ANNIHILATE EVERYTHING IN A MILE'S RADIUS!
THAT IS OF LITTLE CONCERN TO US.
CLEA!
THERE ARE HUNDREDS OF PEOPLE ON THIS BASE, MY LOVE. WE CANNOT ALLOW THEM ALL TO DIE!
THEY ARE OF NO IMPORT, STEPHEN!
FOR ALL THEY HAVE DONE TO US, LET THEM DIE!

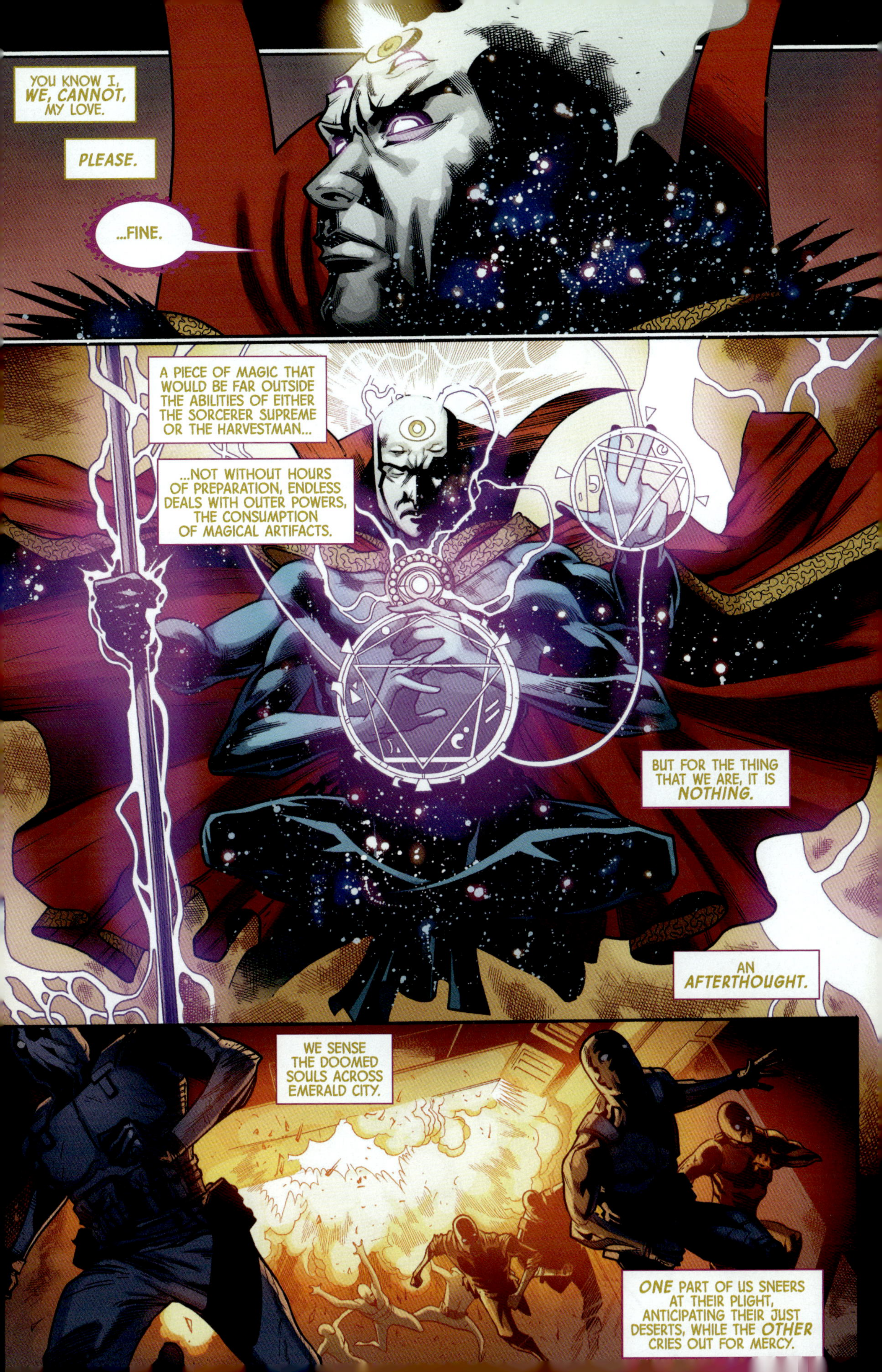

YOU KNOW I, WE, CANNOT, MY LOVE.
PLEASE.
...FINE.
A PIECE OF MAGIC THAT WOULD BE FAR OUTSIDE THE ABILITIES OF EITHER THE SORCERER SUPREME OR THE HARVESTMAN...
...NOT WITHOUT HOURS OF PREPARATION, ENDLESS DEALS WITH OUTER POWERS, THE CONSUMPTION OF MAGICAL ARTIFACTS.
BUT FOR THE THING THAT WE ARE, IT IS NOTHING.
AN AFTERTHOUGHT.
WE SENSE THE DOOMED SOULS ACROSS EMERALD CITY.
ONE PART OF US SNEERS AT THEIR PLIGHT, ANTICIPATING THEIR JUST DESERTS, WHILE THE OTHER CRIES OUT FOR MERCY.

OUR MAGICS SURROUND EACH ONE IN AN EMBRACE AS LOVING AS A MOTHER'S. AS INESCAPABLE AS SLEEP...
RUN! HURRY!
...AND WE PLACE THEM SAFELY ACROSS THE EARTH, ANNIHILATING FROM THEIR MIND EVERY MEMORY OF THEIR LIVES AS BLASPHEMY CARTEL AGENTS.
WE GIVE THEM WHAT THEY (DO/DO NOT) DESERVE: A SECOND CHANCE AT HUMANITY.
GOTTA HURRY, I'M GOING TO MISS MY BUS!
EXCEPT FOR ONE.
WE (ARE/ARE NOT) SORRY, DIRECTOR NONE.
YOU HAVE MADE YOURSELF A GHOST OF A SORT. WE CANNOT SAVE YOU AS WE DID YOUR MEN.
DO YOU THINK I WANT TO BE SAVED BY THE LIKES OF YOU?
DO YOU THINK YOU'VE BEATEN THE TRINITY OF ASHES WITH A PARLOR TRICK?!
DO YOU THINK THIS IS OVER?!

NO.
NOTHING IS EVER OVER.
GOODBYE.
GRIEFSAVOR!
MOTHER-OF-PAIN!
YGMLOSVORRAICH!
SAVE ME--
KA-KOOOOM

WE SEPARATE.
TO BE OF JUST A SINGLE MIND, EVEN FOR SUCH A SHORT TIME, AS A CONJOINED COSMIC BEING IS...JARRING.
IT IS DONE.
THE BLASPHEMY CARTEL IS DONE.
INDEED. BUT WHAT NEX--?
YAAAAAAH!!!
STEPHEN!
HANG ON, MY LOVE--
WHATEVER IT IS, I'LL--
NO, IT'S...

I--
--I LIVE AGAIN!
indeed.
i do not renege on my bargains, stephen strange.
the revenant threat is ended. your time as the harvestman is complete.
you have earned back your life...
...use it well.
until we meet again, doctor strange.

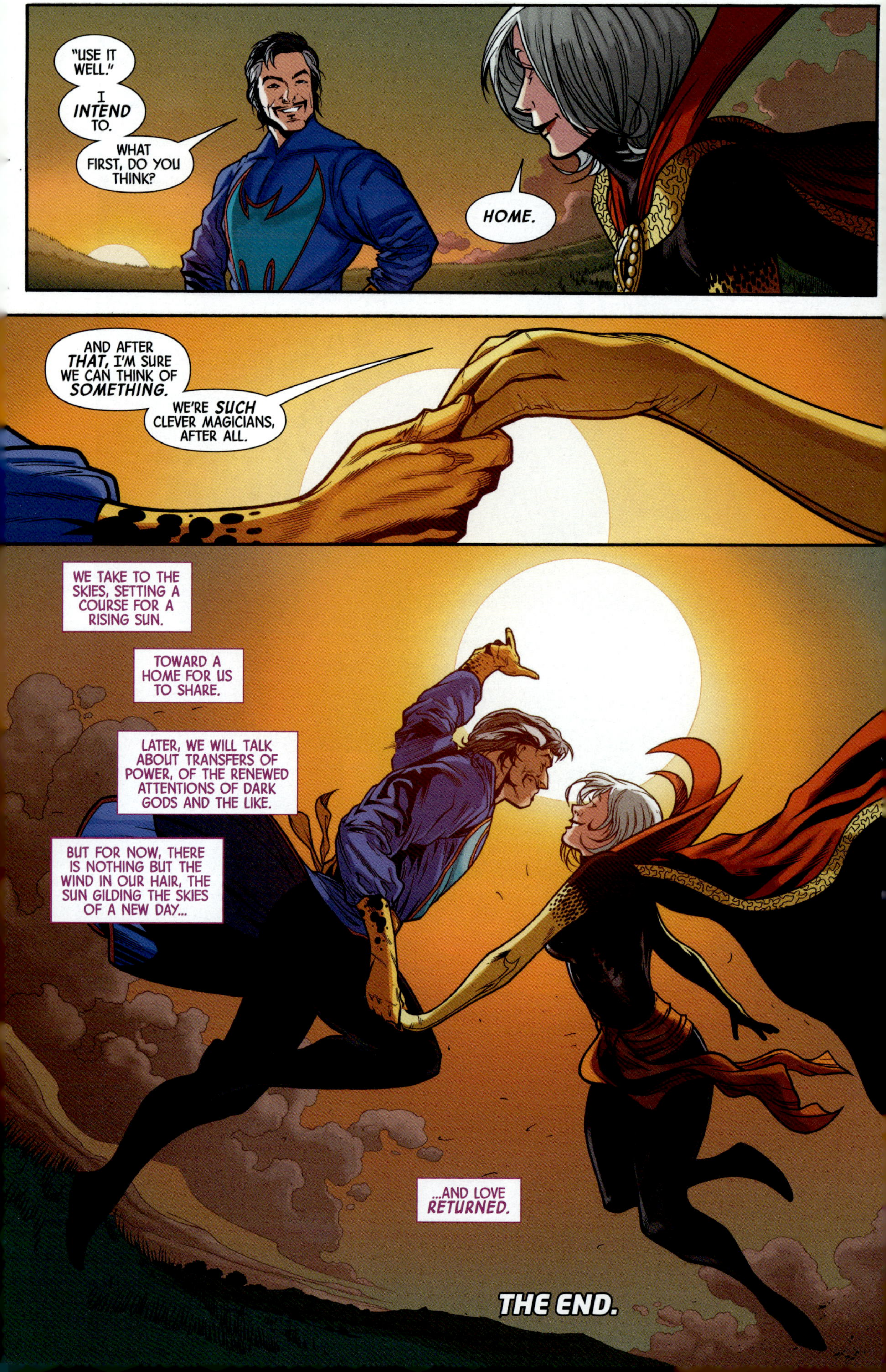
"USE IT WELL."
I *INTEND* TO.
WHAT FIRST, DO YOU THINK?
HOME.
AND AFTER *THAT,* I'M SURE WE CAN THINK OF *SOMETHING.*
WE'RE *SUCH* CLEVER MAGICIANS, AFTER ALL.
WE TAKE TO THE SKIES, SETTING A COURSE FOR A RISING SUN.
TOWARD A HOME FOR US TO SHARE.
LATER, WE WILL TALK ABOUT TRANSFERS OF POWER, OF THE RENEWED ATTENTIONS OF DARK GODS AND THE LIKE.
BUT FOR NOW, THERE IS NOTHING BUT THE WIND IN OUR HAIR, THE SUN GILDING THE SKIES OF A NEW DAY...
...AND LOVE *RETURNED.*
THE END.

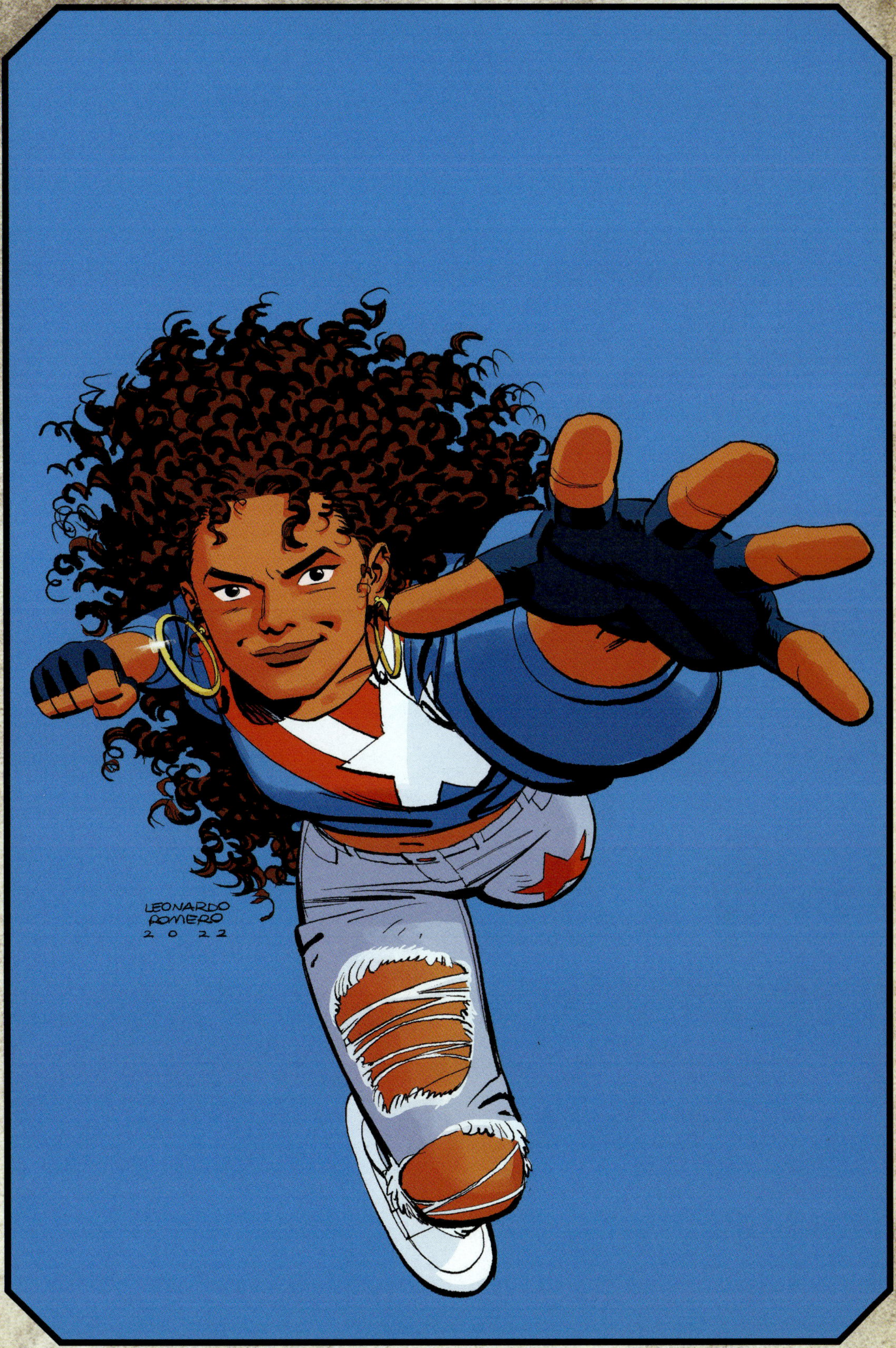
LEONARDO ROMERO 2022

Leonardo Romero

#6 COMMUNITY VARIANT

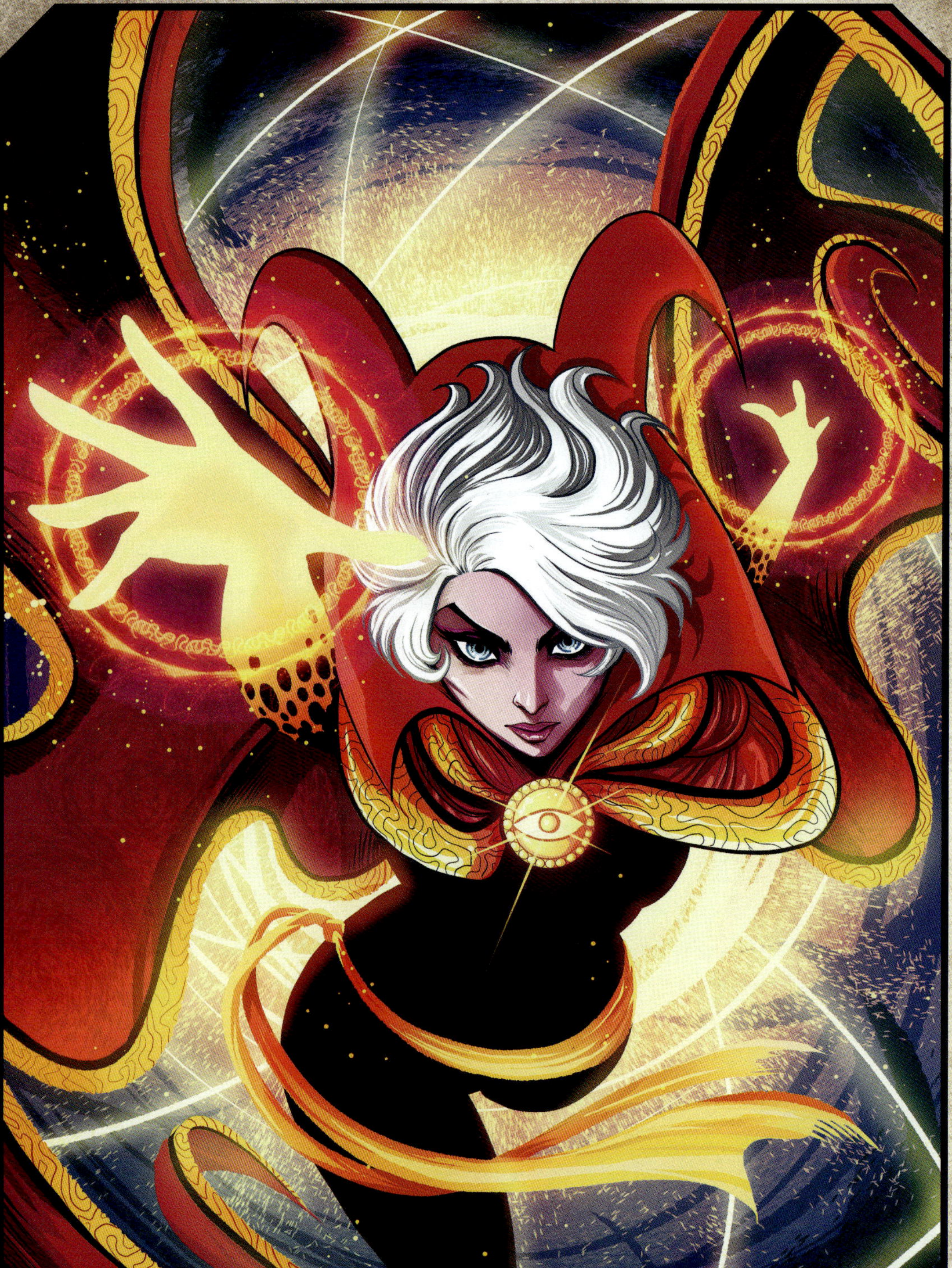

Luciano Vecchio

#7 VARIANT

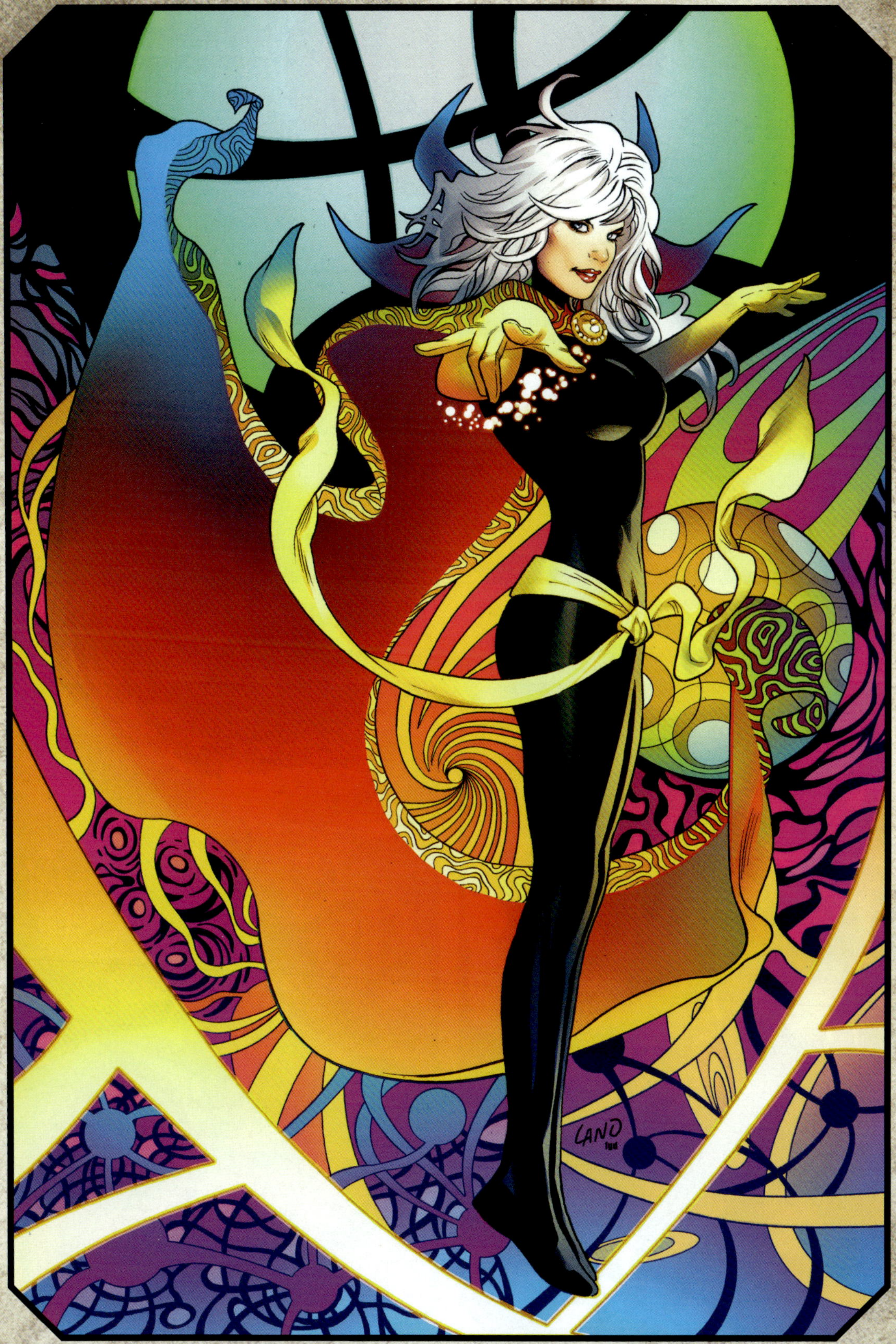
LAND

Greg Land & Frank D'Armata
#8 VARIANT

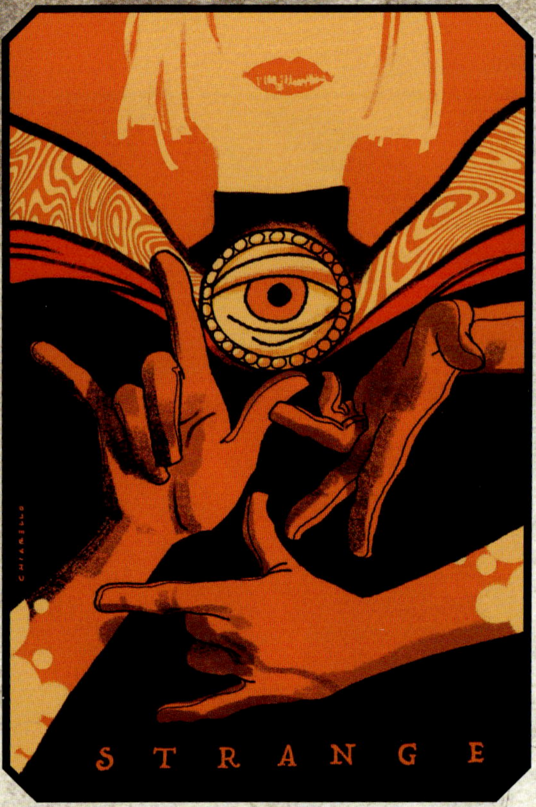
STRANGE

Mark Chiarello
#9 VARIANT

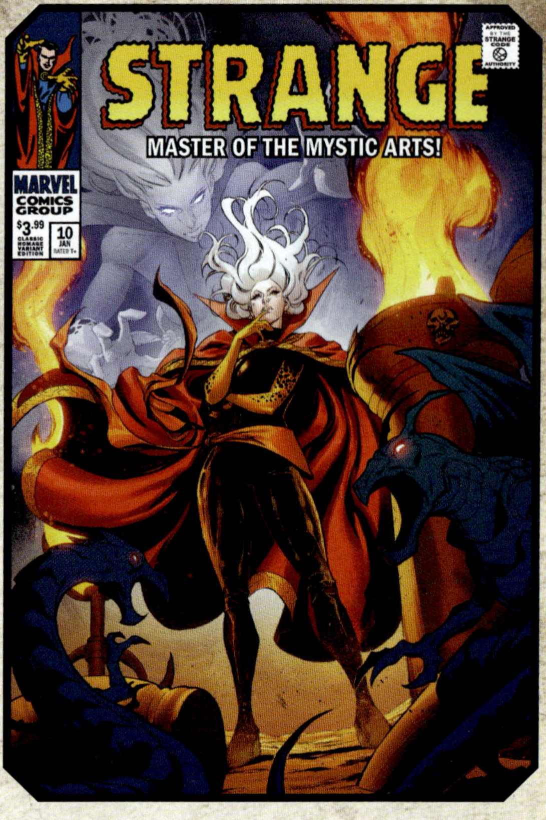
STRANGE
MASTER OF THE MYSTIC ARTS!
MARVEL COMICS GROUP
$3.99
10
JAN

Iban Coello & Alejandro Sánchez
#10 CLASSIC HOMAGE VARIANT

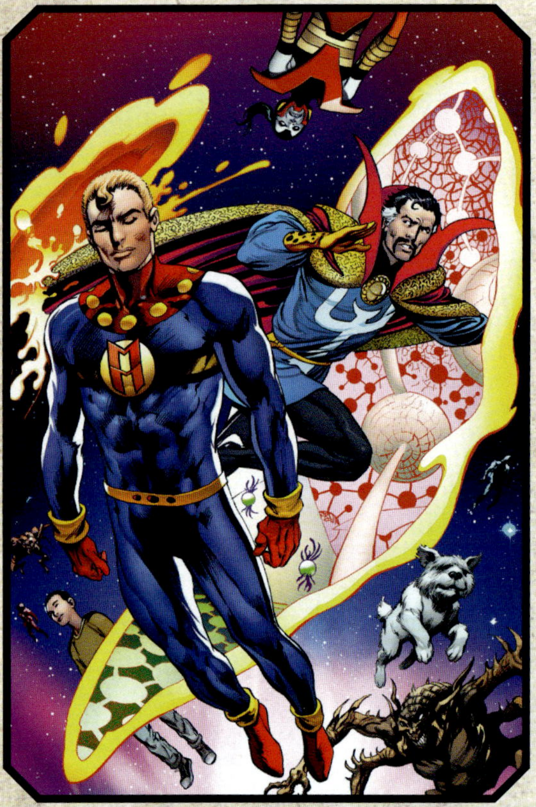

Alan Davis & David Curiel
#7 MIRACLEMAN VARIANT

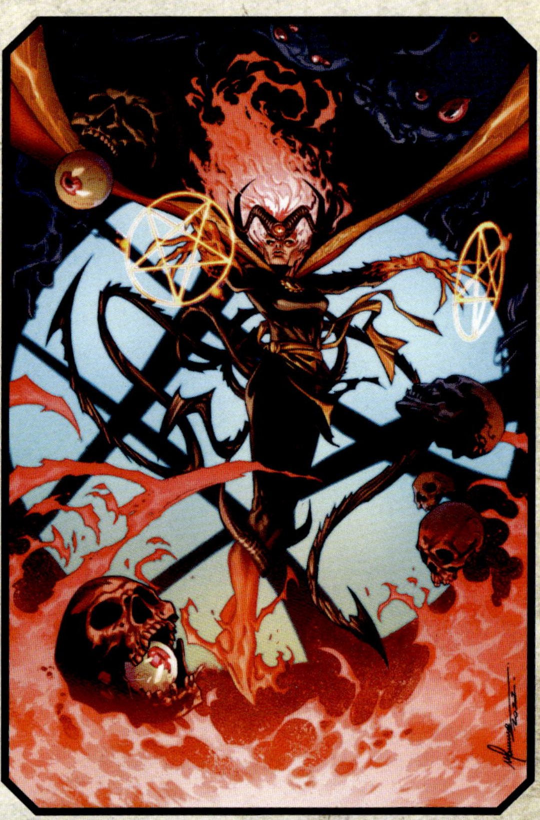

Francesco Manna & Flavio Dispenza
#10 DEMONIZED VARIANT